The

J.M. Barrie

Ladies'

Swimming

Society

The
J.M. Barrie
Ladies'
Swimming
Society

Barbara J. Zitwer

MARBLE ARCH
PRESS

MARBLE ARCH
PRESS

Marble Arch Press
1230 Avenue of the Americas
New York, NY 10020

First Marble Arch Press trade paperback edition December 2012

Marble Arch Press is a publishing collaboration between Short
Books, UK, and Atria Books, US.

Marble Arch Press and colophon are trademarks of Short Books.

For information about special discounts for bulk purchases, please
contact Simon & Schuster Special Sales at 1-866-506-1949 or
business@simonandschuster.com

The Simon & Schuster Speakers Bureau can bring authors to your
live event. For more information or to book an event, contact the
Simon & Schuster Speakers Bureau at 1-866-248-3049 or visit our
website at www.simonspeakers.com.

Manufactured in the United States of America

10 9 8 7 6 5 4 3 2

Library of Congress Cataloging-in-Publication Data

ISBN 978-1-4767-1873-6
ISBN 978-1-4767-1874-3 (ebook)

Disclaimer

Although this book refers to some real events and places, it is entirely fictionalised, and any resemblance to living persons is purely coincidental.

Dedicated to my mother, Edith, who inspired
this story

———————————————

"To love would be an awfully big adventure."
J.M. Barrie, *Peter Pan*

The J.M. Barrie
Ladies' Swimming Society
Manifesto

We hereby declare the intent of our all female society devoted
to the pursuit of aquatic exercise and good health, liberty,
free speech and ever-lasting friendship, following in the
footsteps of our spiritual guide, James Matthew Barrie, and his
most famous of creations, the boy who never grew up: Peter Pan.

Meetings shall take place as often as circumstances allow,
and shall be cancelled only in the event of attacks by:
pirates, lost boys, Indians, crocodiles.

Members may swim clothed or unclothed

Each member, when on land, each and every day, shall hold
their breath for as long as they can, and then for five minutes
more, thereby increasing their stamina and ability to lifetime
membership.

Each member is free to laugh as loudly as she wants, whenever
she wants, and with no threat of admonishment by grown-ups.

Each member is free to sing whatever and whenever she so
desires, whether she sounds like a frog or Maria Callas.

Each member, whether an animal lover or not, shall be kind to
the ducks, and never disrupt them nor capture them nor cook
them for dinner.

No member shall be criticized for alcoholic drinking in excess
or not drinking at all.

Expulsion from this society shall be immediate if any member
shall allow a man of any age, height, weight, whether he be
the Prince of Wales or a troll, to accompany her or to visit,
without the prior written permission of each member.

Above all, members shall listen to each other with compassion,
help each other to see sunshine in their darkest hour,
and to feel new adventure in their hearts.

Chapter 1

Joey Rubin paused and looked up from her drafting table. As she wandered to the windows at the back of her apartment, Tink raised her head from her basket, then flopped back down and closed her eyes. Joey couldn't see the moon from the rear windows, but its dappled blue-grey light shone on all the neighbouring buildings, casting deep, dramatic shadows.

It was three am and she suddenly felt bone-tired. She also realised that any more work on tomorrow's presentation was likely to be counter-productive. Her professor in architecture school had stressed the importance of recognising this moment, when *more* work on a project, *more* thought, *more* ideas might actually damage a concept that was already fully realised. She crossed the space and looked at her illustration – a large watercolour of Stanway House, the historic English building that her firm was developing – and then, reluctantly, turned out the light.

✻ ✻ ✻

Street sounds had woken her, a sure sign that she'd been sleeping very lightly. She glanced at the clock on her bedside table – not yet six – then turned her pillow over, and snuggled back down.

Joey had lived on the top floor of her building on Lexington Avenue, on the Upper East Side of Manhattan, for thirty-three of her thirty-seven years, and only rarely did street sounds other than passing sirens reach her ears. From July to August, when the apartment heated up like a furnace, she'd have the air conditioners in the windows going full blast. But on warm spring evenings, or when the cool autumn winds blew new life into a tired and wilting city, she loved to throw open her windows and climb out onto the fire escape that zigzagged up the front of her building.

She had always dreamed of doing this, growing up in the apartment with her parents. She had pleaded to be allowed to sleep out there with her best friend Sarah, who lived on the third floor. She imagined them dragging pillows and blankets out of the Rubins' front room window and settling in under the invisible stars. They would *not* fall off! They could put a *chair* across the opening at the top of the stairs so they wouldn't roll down in their sleep. But Joey's parents wouldn't hear of it, no matter how old she and Sarah got, and no matter how hard they begged.

Fifteen years ago, when Joey's father had left for Florida with his new wife, Joey had crawled out onto the fire escape with a bottle of champagne left over from the wedding. She wasn't quite sure what she was celebrating. Her father had given her the deeds and the extra sets of keys as though it were no big deal. That's when she knew that he and Amy wouldn't be coming back, and if they ever did, they wouldn't be coming here. For the first few days, she had felt she was rattling around in the apartment. Much of its furniture was already on its way to Myrtle Beach, and most of what was left she couldn't wait to replace. But at least the place was officially hers.

※ ※ ※

Joey could usually talk herself out of pre-meeting nerves, especially when the real responsibility for a presentation's success or failure rested with someone else, as it did today. But, as she fixed her coffee and breakfast, she could feel anxiety beginning to build.

Anxiety, and something else too... Truth be told, Joey was envious that Dave Wilson, her boss, and not she herself, would be going to England to live in the house and supervise its conversion. Stanway was a place dear to her heart; the house where her favourite author, J.M. Barrie, had spent his holidays – and where he had reputedly written *Peter Pan*. Joey had invested a lot of herself into this project, months of design and renderings, for which – as she knew all too well – Dave was ultimately likely to get the credit.

Joey had been with the Apex Group for seven years now, and her overall professional strategy – just be better than everyone else, and eventually people will notice – was starting to seem flawed. Anyone who knew her work knew that she could talk materials, calculate load-bearing capacities and draw irreproachable specs with the best of them. Her colleagues competed to have her on their teams, because it was widely appreciated – if never openly acknowledged – that Joey worked harder, later and longer than anyone else. And yet, rather than being singled out for promotions and raises, she found herself the perpetual bridesmaid, always in demand to support the beaming brides. Or in the case of her firm, the grinning grooms.

To make matters worse, Alex Wilder was going to be sitting in on today's meeting. She'd run into him just as she was leaving the office on Friday night, and over the weekend she'd spent more time than she cared to think about pressing on the bruise of this annoying development. What was *he* coming for? He had nothing to do with the Stanway restoration. Didn't he have enough to do, with that neighbourhood association raising issues about the development of the Canal Street settlement? Why was he poking his nose into International, when they had sixteen projects in various stages of completion in New York City alone, on seven of which he was the principal architect?

Six months ago, Alex wouldn't have come near the conference room when Joey was giving a presentation, for fear of fanning the flames of the rumours that were beginning to circulate. After a year of managing to keep their relationship secret, they'd been seen by one of the secretaries, a notorious busybody, having dinner together in a restaurant in the Meatpacking District. For a month before he broke things off, abruptly and with the lamest of excuses, Joey could see curiosity and suspicion in the eyes of her colleagues. At least she didn't have to deal with that any more.

Joey glanced over at Tink, who was just finishing up her own breakfast, and wondered for the thousandth time which breeds of dog had contributed the DNA that defined her pet: Tink's sweet, impatient temper; her love of digging; the ears that flopped over at the halfway point; the legs that seemed too short for her torso; the tail that curled up grandly like an acanthus leaf.

Tink looked up and gave a little yip.

"In a minute."

Joey poured her coffee into a travel mug, returned to her bedroom and pulled on yoga pants and a jacket. In the hall, she slipped Tink's leash off the hook beside the door.

It was freezing when she stepped outside, much colder than it had been for the past few days. Tink grandly led the way, pulling Joey toward the corner of Fifth Avenue, where vans were idling near the entrance of Neue Galerie. Joey had gone there three times to see the exhibition on turn-of-the-century Viennese art and style, lingering before the portraits by Klimt and Kokoschka, but ending up every time on the third floor, to worship at the altar of one of her idols, the Austrian architect Otto Wagner. Studying the photographs of his buildings, she'd found herself hoping that at least once in her life she would get the chance to design something as structurally austere and yet visually playful as Wagner's Majolica Haus.

Tink resisted Joey's turning onto East 84th. She wanted to go to Central Park and she put every ounce of her twenty-pound frame into the effort to pull her mistress in that direction. But Joey didn't have time for a leisurely ramble this morning.

As they passed the gracious brownstones that lined the block on both sides, Joey thought of the people she knew who lived or had lived within their walls: Mrs. Phelps, her mother's friend, who smelled of cigarettes and expensive perfume and never missed a weekly visit when her mother was sick. She always brought pastry or flowers and hugged Joey too tight when she left.

A little further along the block was the apartment where for three long years Joey had taken piano lessons from a Hungarian émigré named Frída Szabó – *Madame* Szabó, as she insisted on being called, who had reminded her each and every week that she had once performed a Mozart piano concerto with the world-famous conductor, János Sándor. The woman spent most of each half hour scolding Joey for not practising more, and when this had no discernible effect, finally told Joey's parents that they were simply wasting their money. Joey couldn't have been happier.

Back at home an hour later, she made her final

inspection in the full-length mirror. She looked … fine. No, she looked — good! A little tired, maybe, and pale. But the suit fitted her perfectly, and the Fendi boots always gave her a confidence boost. She took them off for now and folded them into her shoulder bag, to be slipped back on when she'd cleared the muck and puddles of the cross-town trek.

Tink gave her a pitiful look, as she always did when her mistress was about to leave her alone, but Joey couldn't think about that right now. She had exactly one hour before she would be standing with Dave in the conference room.

Chapter 2

Much later than she would have liked, the cab pulled up in front of an eighty-storey glass skyscraper, its uppermost floors obscured by a layer of cloud. The driver took his time counting out the change. Joey raced to the revolving glass doors, only to have to wait in a line of a dozen people trying to thread their way inside. It struck her yet again that whoever had designed this entranceway was a truly lousy architect, almost as lousy as the genius who decided that only four elevators were needed to transport eighty storeys' worth of workers.

Four elevator cars came and went before she was able to squeeze in. Her good mood and her composure had vanished. By the time she stepped out of the elevator car and into the hallway of the fifty-fourth floor, she was frazzled, rumpled, exasperated, sweaty and late.

Alex Wilder was standing in the entryway as she hurried by.

"Morning, Joey."

"Morning."

"I don't envy you."

She stopped in her tracks and turned. "What does that mean?"

Alex gave her a wry grin. She tried hard not to notice the charming, crinkly lines by his eyes, or his healthy, windswept complexion, a glow no doubt acquired over the weekend on the slopes of Cannon Mountain.

"You haven't talked to Antoine?" he went on.

"No. Why?" Her stomach gave a little swoop. Something was wrong. Something was definitely wrong.

"You'd better talk to him, ASAP."

"What's going on?"

"I'll let him fill you in."

Joey sighed and glared at Alex. It was just like him, to dangle something like this in front of her and then refuse to explain. What did she ever see in him? Had he always been like this, or had he just become more evasive and manipulative in the past few months?

"Thanks," she said sharply then turned and hurried down the hall to the office of Antoine Weeks, the administrative assistant assigned to the Stanway hotel project. Antoine was standing at his desk, collating what were presumably handouts for the meeting.

"What's going on?" Joey asked.

Antoine looked up and shook his head.

"Dave had a accident in New Hampshire. He's in the hospital."

"What?"

Joey walked slowly to the chair beside Antoine's desk and lowered herself into it.

"He was rock climbing in the White Mountains, at Huntington's Ravine. His harness failed and he fell – a hundred and fifty feet or something – into a crevasse. Shattered a kneecap and the opposite leg and dislocated his shoulder. It took them eight hours to get him out."

"Oh my God!... Is he going to be okay?"

"He's having surgery right now. But yes, okay, I think, eventually."

Joey glanced at her watch: it was almost ten. "So who's running the meeting?"

Antoine pursed his lips and opened his eyes wide. He blinked a few times.

"No way," Joey said.

"You have to," Antoine replied. "No one else knows the material."

"I can't," she whispered. "I really can't. No way. No. I can do my little bit, but not the *whole thing*."

"Of course you can," Antoine sniffed. "You've done ninety per cent of the work and we both know it!"

"But I don't have the files!" Joey said.

"Everything's in there, all ready to go. I downloaded the specs and j-pegs and cabled a Mac to the projection system."

"Antoine, I'm not prepared! Is Richardson in there – the guy from England? I can't possibly stand up and do it in front of him! Why didn't you call me?"

"I just found out an hour ago!" Antoine said, looking a little hurt. "I figured you were already on your way. I've been racing around trying to get everything set up."

"I know, I know, I'm sorry. Thank you!"

Joey felt her heart beginning to race. She concentrated on taking deep breaths then stood up, cleared her throat and walked out into the hallway. Antoine was right: there was no one else who was familiar with the material. She was simply going to have to do it. People would understand if she made mistakes, they wouldn't expect every detail to be perfect.

She glanced through the floor-to-ceiling windows of the conference room. There was Alex, installed in the position of power at the end of the massive oval table. He chose just that moment to glance out into the hall and, seeing Joey, to turn on his megawatt smile.

"Louse!" Joey said, under her breath, returning his smile.

She wheeled around and walked back to Antoine's office. He must have seen signs of the panic she was suddenly feeling because he closed the door and steered her back to the chair beside his desk. He sat down opposite her.

"This is your big chance, Joey."

"But I'm not ready."

"You were ready ages ago. You and I both know that and so do half the people in that room."

"No. You're wrong."

"Look, sometimes careers are made when the soprano comes down with a sore throat and the understudy gets her chance."

"That's not going to happen."

"Well, it should."

"Thanks," Joey said.

"Now go in there and give it your all."

"I guess that's all I can do,' she conceded glumly.

"It's all anybody can do."

Joey nodded. In her own office, moments later, she slipped off her overcoat, slid into her boots and applied a fresh coat of lipstick. She wasn't ready, by any means, but she was as ready as she was ever going to be. She took a deep breath, walked down to the conference room and closed the door behind her.

❈   ❈   ❈

Forty-five minutes later, she was opening the floor up for questions and beginning to breathe easily again. She honestly had no idea how she'd made it through all the material, but somehow, she had. Whether or not it had been enough to convince the English management company was another matter. Michael Richardson, sitting right in front of her, had given nothing away.

"I'm curious about the East Tower," said Preston Kay, one of the founding partners of Apex, who was now holding up a finger. "Remember, this building has ultimately got to work commercially, which means using all the available space."

"Of the monks' dormitory?" Joey asked, locating the image and bringing it up on the screen.

Kay nodded. "What do you plan to do about that?"

Joey took a deep breath. "There are no original foundations under its walls, so there's a real possibility of collapse."

"But you're going to attempt to rebuild it?"

"We are — *attempt* being the operative word. We may have to let it go, but we won't without a fight. It was a beautiful structure, but over the centuries, many of the original stones were stripped, so they could be used in the other outbuildings and the gardens."

Joey pointed to the areas she was discussing, blown up on the projector screen. "Ivy growth has pushed out whole areas of the walls, and wild plants that have taken root in the holes have dislodged the crenelation. The weather's obviously a factor, too." She smiled and paused. Kay obviously wanted her to go on.

"We could let the tower collapse if we wanted to, no permits required for that. If we want to rebuild it — which we'd like to at least try to do — there will be a long planning process. But remember the planners are on our side, in a way. They, too, want these old buildings to be useable, not just empty shells that look pretty."

"So what do you plan to do?" Kay pressed.

"Our hope," Joey went on, "is to use as many of the original stones as we can locate on the property. To stabilise the structure, we'll be installing stainless steel rods and, of course, working with modern grouts and resins. Once the walls have been repaired, we'll stage the whole tower, pin it with steel beams, pour a new concrete foundation and seal everything up tight. We plan to install three floors, and of course a new roof. The rooms will be furnished as a couple of bedrooms and a bathroom, with a small reception room – to be available for rent separately from the main part of the hotel."

Kay sat back, looking pensive. Joey's gaze drifted to Alex Wilder, who was sitting forward in his chair, looking – well, actually rather interested. She didn't have time to savour this, though, because another hand went up, that of Philip Carlton, the representative from the English clients.

"What's the plan for the Barrie connection?" he asked.

Joey smiled. "We're not sure yet," she answered honestly. "We're definitely going to do something with it – J.M. Barrie being one of England's most beloved authors – but until we can get in and actually evaluate the space, see what feels right ... it's all just ideas."

"What kind of ideas?" Alex interrupted, abruptly.

Joey fixed him with her eyes. Was he trying to trip her up or throw her a question she could easily answer? With Alex, you could never be sure. Of course, there was also the possibility that he was not trying to do either of those things but was simply curious. Joey doubted that, though.

"We're entertaining a few possibilities," she shot back confidently. "We could go the route of the Hotel Monteleone in New Orleans – you know, with rooms honouring the likes of Faulkner, Capote, and Hemingway. Or, at the other extreme, a place like Bemelmans Bar at the Carlyle, which has Madeline murals painted by Ludwig Bemelmans himself...

"Remember, Barrie didn't own this house, he just stayed there. But it was where he wrote *Peter Pan*, so I propose we find a point somewhere between the two: if the research suggests that it could be successfully marketed as a destination, and if we can identify the right rooms for this, the idea would be to create a family suite and furnish it like the Darlings' home, with a comfortable Victorian room for the grown-ups and a highly fanciful suite for children – stars, canopies, hand-painted murals relating to the story. We could do Peter Pan-themed birthday parties, for children. Or for adults, I suppose!"

Joey paused. "The suite would be dog-friendly, of course," she added, with a smile.

Alex frowned. He looked genuinely baffled.

"Well, there wouldn't have been a story without Nana, would there?" Joey answered sweetly.

Alex glanced around to see if everyone else understood. "Nana?" he queried sheepishly.

"Nana was the dog," explained Preston Kay, smiling. "She was left in charge of the children."

"Ah," said Alex, slumping down a little in his seat.

Joey had a sinking sense that she hadn't quite satisfied the partners with these generalised responses. Suddenly she had a thought. "Will you excuse me for a moment?" she asked.

There were puzzled nods all around. Joey dashed down to her office and retrieved from her briefcase something she had tucked into it at the last minute, for good luck: a first edition *Peter Pan*, with illustrations by Francis Donkin Bedford, that her mother had given her. She hurried back to the conference room.

"This – is what I, personally, would like to honour," she said quietly. "The spirit of this particular edition. I should say, though, Dave and I haven't yet discussed this in detail."

"Go on," Preston said.

Joey held up the book. "I've loved J.M. Barrie, and especially *Peter Pan*, my whole life. My mother bought me this for my thirteenth birthday." Joey handed the book to Preston.

He opened it and began to examine the illustrations.

"Lots of people have illustrated it over the years, Arthur Rackham, Al Dempster – he did the Disney characters – Michael Hague, Scott McKowen and many others. But there's a beautiful, stark purity to Bedford's illustrations. More than any others, they feel mystical and other-worldly to me – as though they've tapped into the very essence of what it feels like to be a child – the wonder, the hope, the sense of mystery and awe. Just look at this one… "

Porter handed her back the book and she turned to an illustration of Mr. and Mrs. Darling prostrated in grief, having discovered their children missing from the bedroom. Nana, slumped on the bed with them, staring out the window at a sky full of streaking stars. The illustration was captioned, "The Birds Were Flown". Joey handed the book around the table.

"I love the messiness of the room," she said. "I love the drawers hanging open and the clothes strewn around, and that sense he captures of hasty departure. And of the majesty and terror of that deep black sky over London. How immense and beautiful and terrifying it is, just outside the window. But inside, there's Nana standing guard and it's bright and homey – and entirely empty of what really gave it life – the children."

Joey paused, fighting back a sudden fit of nerves. She really had no idea where she was going with these thoughts. But the partners were nodding seriously, evidently interested in the illustration. She had to bring this around somehow.

"I don't know why I'm telling you this," she admitted.

Alex looked up, smugly. He was just waiting for her to fail. Joey could see it.

"It's just that when I think of Stanway House, and all it's seen and been through in all these centuries, the monks chanting, hundred of years of the rhythms of the seasons, babies being born into that house, people marrying in the great room, people getting old and dying right there, to be buried practically within sight of the house, well, it all seems so mysterious, the way the house holds and contains all that life and yet outlives it, so to speak. It's bigger and older than any of us and it will endure long after we're gone. That's the spirit we have to hold on to, that spirit of Stanway being a kind of Neverland. A place apart, other-worldly, casting a spell of feeling and memory and a kind of happiness that so often disappears with childhood."

Joey let out a sigh. She was gushing, she knew. Why did she always have to ruin big moments like this? She sat down resignedly as the book was handed around the table and back to her.

Richardson, the English agent, coughed and sat up. Everyone looked at him, expectant. "Thank you, Joey," he said. "That was one of the most interesting presentations I have ever sat through. What you said about Barrie was very thoughtful."

Joey glanced around the table — everyone nodding, smiling. She couldn't believe it. "Thank you," she stammered.

The meeting was over.

❋　❋　❋

In the hallway, Alex patted Joey on the back. "Well done, seriously well done."

"What were you doing in there? You're not on the project, are you?" asked Joey. She felt a rush of anxiety. It was difficult to be in such close proximity to her ex.

"No. Just curious."

"About what? How I'd do?"

Alex flashed his best movie star smile and Joey tried to

ignore the twinkling blue eyes that had once so irrevocably hooked her in. "Can I take you to lunch? Bemelmans Bar? For old time's sake?"

"No, thanks," Joey said, then turned and headed back to her office.

She locked the door behind her and lay down on the leather sofa that lined the back wall. The encounter with Alex had punctured her euphoria like a needle in a balloon, left her feeling anxious, confused and... embarrassed. That was the worst of it. Joey was so ashamed of where her relationship with Alex had taken her. With his expert assistance, she had turned herself into a walking cliché, a girl married to her job who had slept with her boss.

Even now, months after they had split up, she hated running into him, working just down the hall from him. Somehow, though, she knew, she was going to have to get over it. She wasn't leaving the Apex Group and neither was he.

❋   ❋   ❋

Two hours later, Joey was jolted awake by a loud knock. She glanced at her watch — had she really been asleep for that long? Running her fingers through her hair, she opened the door. Antoine stood before her, brandishing an envelope.

"Jesus Joey, sleeping on the job?"

"Very funny," she responded. "What do you want?"

"I've just had Preston on the phone, and I'm afraid to say, you've got your work cut out for you."

"P-lease," said Joey, "not more!"

"Well, if you've had enough..." Antoine turned on his heel: "I'll get onto the airline and cancel the flight."

"Give me a break, Antoine — what are you going on about?"

"You, sweetie, are going to England!" he practically sang.

He marched her over to her chair, and sat her down.

"Don't tease me, Antoine... I can't take it."

"Joey, you were brilliant! I was so proud of you. The English agent loved you. The Tower – the monks – Nana, Neverland – it was all just great. Dave's off work indefinitely and Alex is planning his wedding. Oh, sorry. Sore subject. The partners were unanimous – there's no one more passionate and qualified than you. And they're right. Congratulations! You knocked 'em dead!"

Joey felt tears rising to her eyes. "Really?"

"Really!"

"I'm actually going to run the project?"

"Yes, and you deserve it! You're leaving on New Year's Eve."

Chapter 3

She would have to call Sarah. But not quite yet. First, she had to figure out why the thought of seeing her oldest friend in the world aroused such mixed feelings. Joey padded over to the stack of mail on her kitchen table and opened the envelope that had arrived from London ten days ago.

Glitter fell all over the floor. Joey sighed in annoyance, remembering that she had already cleaned up one shower of glitter when she had opened the envelope first time round. Kids could make a mess from three thousand miles away.

The handmade card was inscribed "To Auntie Joey" and signed by Sarah's children, with varying degrees of wobbliness, Matilda, Zoë, Timmy and Christopher. Joey had never met these children, which she felt a little guilty about, and she found it more than a little strange that they would refer to her as "Auntie". She wouldn't know them if she passed them on the street!

She opened the card and reread the yearly letter, this one about Matilda's award for riding, Timmy's tadpoles that had turned into frogs in the bowl on the dining room table... Joey tried to concentrate, she really did, tried to imagine the mini-Sarahs and mini-Henrys in their Liberty prints and riding jackets, but she couldn't. And she couldn't help feeling irritated. Did Joey send Sarah holiday letters filled with news of people she and Henry had never met?

She stood up abruptly, walked over to the fridge and poured herself some wine. Flopping down into the chair by the front window, she realised she had two choices.

She could go to England and not even tell Sarah she was coming. That would probably be easiest, because if they saw each other, they were going to have to talk about what had happened in the past ten or twelve years, how Joey had missed their wedding, how Sarah had promised, year after year, to spend some real time in New York and had never managed to cross the Atlantic, not even when Joey's mother died.

On the other hand, they had grown up like sisters, she and Sarah, lived together both in college and afterward. At one time, Joey could not have imagined that they wouldn't always be close. No, you could share your present and future with any number of friends, Joey thought, sipping her wine. But in her life, there was only one friend who truly and deeply shared her past.

Joey picked up the phone. At the sound of Sarah's familiar warm voice, years of strain seemed to fade away.

"I can't think of a better Christmas present," Sarah enthused. Joey could detect a hint of English in her old friend's accent. "You must come and stay with us en route. The children will be so excited – they've begun to wonder whether Auntie Joey actually exists!"

Ten minutes later, the plan had been made. Joey would spend a day or two in London with Henry, Sarah and the children before heading out to the Cotswolds.

❋　❋　❋

The Christmas season had always been quiet for Joey, even when she was little. She had plenty of good holiday memories – going with her parents down to Coney Island every New Year's Day to watch the members of the Polar Bear Club make their annual plunge into the icy Atlantic, ice-skating with Sarah at Rockefeller Center during school vacation. But these days she tended to see Christmas as a period to be got through. For four or five years after her father's wedding, she had gone to Florida to spend ten days at the end of the year with him and Amy – until they had all come to the conclusion that it would be better if Joey waited and came in March. It made little sense to travel when rates were at their highest and half of America was trying to get somewhere in a hurry. And March was a great time to escape New York for a week.

This year, Joey was going to be far too busy preparing for her trip to feel the weight of the days. One thing she wasn't going to miss, though, was her own private tradition – a long run in Central Park on Christmas morning.

The day dawned crisp and clear, and as soon as she finished her coffee, she got into her running clothes and prepared to make the trip to the Jackie Onassis Reservoir, just a few blocks from her apartment. This run was her present to herself. She loved how deserted it always was on Christmas morning, loved having it virtually to herself as all over the neighbourhood, kids were opening presents. She especially loved running here at dawn, looking into the water and seeing the New York skyline glistening in the rising sun.

Joey let Tink off her leash and they both bounded up the small hill to the path round the reservoir. It had been four years ago this Christmas that Joey had found Tink at the reservoir. It had started out as a usual run, the Park virtually empty. It seemed that no one but Joey had the discipline to run on Christmas morning. So, she had rounded the 1.4 mile track five times before she spotted something strange, something she knew didn't belong lying dangerously close to the water: an abandoned red backpack. She stooped. Something in it moved! Adrenaline shot through her veins as she thought she heard a little whimper coming from the bag.

Without a second thought, Joey clambered over the fence. Someone had abandoned a baby. It was wriggling as Joey knelt down.

"What the heck?"

A cry emanated from the bag and goosebumps ran up Joey's arm. She grappled with the zipper and rope that bound it and, with a final tug, ripped the bag apart and freed its prisoner.

It was not a baby. It was Tink, tiny, wet and altogether alone in the world. Worse than alone! Someone had tried to drown her! She was only a couple of days old, Joey later learned, but she was alive and healthy and quite possibly the sweetest creature Joey had ever seen. She took her home that day, gave her a bath, wrapped her in warm towels and for the next week fed her with an eye-dropper, then later a bottle. It wasn't easy. Joey had never had a dog before and didn't know the first thing about the care and training of a puppy. None of that mattered, however. They were devoted to each other from that day on.

❅ ❅ ❅

Mr. Singh, Tink's vet, squeezed them in on the 27th.

"She's up-to-date on her all vaccinations," he said. "I'll just give you some sedatives to help keep her calm on the flight."

"She'll be OK, won't she?" Joey asked.

"Of course she will," Mr. Singh replied in his calm, velvety voice. "She may be a little drowsy for a while, but that'll soon wear off."

"Okaaaay. But won't it be cold back there in the hold? It sounds like torture to me."

"No no, don't worry — it's pressurised, just like the cabin. It can be a little lonely, and the noise can be stressful.

I wouldn't recommend it for old or sick animals, but Tink's young and healthy. She'll be fine."

"Fine?"

He nodded.

"And she won't have to be quarantined? You're sure about that."

"I'm sure," he replied. "Now stop fussing, and go and enjoy it."

❋   ❋   ❋

As the days wore on, Joey debated trying to see some of the people she hadn't seen in a while, though she suspected that most people would be out of town or booked solid with holiday commitments. A call from her would come out of the blue, and though friends might be glad to try to squeeze in a drink with her or invite her along to liven up a dreaded family or work party, Joey felt herself holding back. Thinking about this as she tried to fall asleep one night, she realised that two things lay behind her reluctance to pick up the phone.

The first was Alex Wilder. He had been obsessed with keeping their relationship quiet, which meant that they never went out with other couples, never met any of Joey's friends for a drink, never had people over for dinner or went to friends' apartments or country houses. Now that he wasn't in her life any more, Joey realised that she'd let a lot of her friendships go. She could think of five or six women she'd either grown up with or known since NYU from whom she had just drifted away.

What had she been thinking? How could she have let this happen? It really wasn't like her, and yet she had done it, weekend after weekend, so she could give all her time and attention to that heel! She had played by his rules from

Day One until the bitter end. She would never make that mistake again.

Secondly there was work. Joey knew she was capable of making the most of the opportunity she had been given, but she still had to be prepared. It was going to take all her focus and concentration to pull off what she was expected to do in the next few weeks. She had to keep things simple for now and knock herself out doing the best job she could on Stanway House. But when she came back to New York, she would have to make some changes.

Chapter 4

What looked like two hundred people were waiting to clear security at the airport. Another great New Year's Eve, Joey thought ruefully, scanning the sea of travellers: screaming babies, kissing lovers, elderly tourists and family groups of more nationalities than she could count.

It had been a while since she'd travelled internationally and the extent of the security measures came as a surprise. She wanted to be safe, for goodness sake, but was all this really necessary: all the unpacking and disrobing and scanning and X-raying? And what would they do about Tink? Would she have to take her out of her crate and let them search that? Joey didn't have enough hands to manage everything she was going to be required to do.

A guard challenged her gruffly as she kicked off her shoes. "You got a boarding pass for the dog?"

Joey fished it out of her bag and handed it to him.

"Gimme the crate," he ordered.

"Already? Can't I stay with her till boarding?"

"*Gimme the crate*," he said more sternly and Joey handed it over. She was afraid that if she protested, they would either assume she had something to hide or would delay or prevent her from getting on the plane. By the time she had redressed, repacked, filled out more forms and made her way to the waiting lounge, she was ready for a good, stiff drink. And then, looking up at the departures board, she saw, thankfully, that her flight was ready for boarding.

The plane filled up quickly. Joey folded her coat and placed it in the overhead bin along with her laptop and carry-on bag. She sat back down and sighed with relief. She hoped Tink was all right, knocked out by the sedative she'd gobbled up in a clump of cream cheese.

The cabin crew dimmed the lights and the general chatter faded as the plane taxied and lifted off. When the seat belt light was turned off, though, the party began. The flight attendants were passing out champagne and most of the travellers seemed positively jovial, chatting across the aisles and violating all the rules that normally governed the crossing of oceans and continents in a space that forced intimacy on strangers.

"Champagne?" asked a steward.

"Gin and tonic," Joey replied.

For a while she tried to watch the old black-and-white classic *Holiday*, with Katharine Hepburn and Cary Grant. The in-flight magazine had called it a "delicious seasonal romp" but the antics onscreen just added to her sense of being on the outside looking in. Cary Grant reminded her of Alex and that got her thinking of last New Year's Eve, when Alex had taken her to a luxurious B&B in the Hamptons. They'd eaten chateaubriand and drunk Dom Perignon and an old-vine Zinfandel that called up sensations of rich, dark earth. As midnight approached, they'd bundled up and walked down to the beach. They heard fireworks going off somewhere, but when the year passed into the next, they were hand-in hand by the water's edge, pointing out constellations in the moonlit sky.

Joey took off her headphones and glanced around. Everywhere she looked were families, lovers, married couples. Was she the only person on the entire plane who was travelling alone? It sure looked that way. A woman across the aisle, seated beside her dozing husband, shot Joey a curious glance, and Joey wondered what she was thinking. That Joey was on her way to meet a lover in London? Or that she was the kind of hard-driving career woman who wanted to get a jump on the new year by turning up for work at the first possible moment?

She slid open the window shield. Tiny pinpricks of light glittered above an expanse of cloud that looked like the frozen tundra. It was hard to believe that they were actually up above the cloud cover, and not just flying, in the darkness, over a landscape of eternal snow.

They would be arriving in London in just over three hours, and there, it was already day. The gin had made her sleepy, and she decided to try to get some rest. She awoke some time later, not quite sure why. The cabin was dark, except for a couple of reading lights. She threw off the skimpy fleece blanket and sat up. Sitting in the seat beside her was a little girl of about five. She was staring at Joey through little pink glasses. Her hair was jet black, cut into a short pageboy. She wore an indescribably adorable pinafore beneath which, Joey noticed, her small legs were encased in two painful-looking braces.

"Hi," Joey said.

"Hello!" she responded quietly.

Joey couldn't remember the last time she had actually spoken to a child. Most kids she came across seemed either to be bursting with unwarranted self-esteem, bratty, or completely uninterested in communicating with grown-ups. Joey had been on the shy side as a girl, easily intimidated by the older kids at school. Being an only child, she was used to the company of her parents and had never experienced the gentle teasing and joshing that toughened up kids in larger families. Even now, she felt perplexed and nervous in the presence of loud, boisterous children.

"What's your name?" Joey asked.

"Daisy. Where's your dog?"

"She's sleeping."

"But where did you put her? I saw you in the airport and I wanted to meet her."

"Well, she's not allowed on the plane, honey. Pets have to travel in their own special cabin. Imagine what it would be like if there were dogs barking at each other!"

"Isn't she lonely?" The child's British accent made Joey smile.

"I gave her some medicine to help her sleep. She's never been on a plane before, and I was afraid she might get scared."

Daisy took this in. "There's nothing to be afraid of. I fly all the time."

"Do you? Where do you go?"

"New York. To see Dr. Dan. He's the doctor for my legs."

Daisy stretched out one brace-clad limb. Joey wasn't sure what she was supposed to be seeing, but she smiled brightly.

"Yes, I see. Wow!"

Daisy smiled widely for the first time. Her two front teeth were missing. And then, as abruptly as she had appeared, she scrambled to her feet and reclaimed her seat next to a dozing woman across the aisle. What a sweet, funny girl, Joey thought. Maybe she liked kids, after all.

The plane began its final descent. Joey peered out the window and down at lush green fields spread in patchwork patterns as far as the eye could see, lined with trees, hedgerows and walls. She felt a rush of excitement; she'd wanted to come to England ever since she was a child.

As they came closer to London, the landscape started to

change and chaotic lines of mismatched buildings, new and old, large and small, stretched out below. From this vantage point, the city resembled the inside of a computer chip. It seemed completely disorderly, with tiny streets winding in opposite directions. But as the plane banked over the muddy Thames, soaring through the air above the heart of the city, Joey drew breath. There was Big Ben and the Houses of Parliament, London Bridge, The Eye! She drank in the images, her face inches from the window.

✳   ✳   ✳

Tink was still drowsy when Joey picked her up, so she left her in her crate for the cab ride. But an hour later, as the driver navigated the roads leading to Henry and Sarah's home near Notting Hill, the sedatives had clearly worn off, and Tink let Joey know in no uncertain terms that she'd had just about enough of being cooped up.

"Hush. Bad girl!" Joey said sharply, to no effect. They were rounding the perimeter of Holland Park, and Joey could barely pull her eyes from the passing scenery: the crisp geometry of the park's designed gardens, the gracious townhouses bathed in cool morning light.

"Forty-eight, you said?" the driver asked.

"Yes, Forty-eight Holland Road."

"Here we are, then."

"This…?" Joey stared out the window. The house was enormous: a distinguished Georgian three-storey jewel. Potted spruces in enormous planters lined the steps up to the door. Surely Henry and Sarah couldn't own the *whole thing*! It looked like a small hotel; they must have a duplex of some kind. Even a family with four children didn't need this much room. And Henry couldn't possibly have *this* much money…

As the driver unloaded Joey's bags from the boot, Joey

hurried up the front steps and rang the doorbell. From within, she heard the sound of its chimes. The next moment, the door flew open to reveal a girl and boy, breathless, as though they had just come to a skidding halt.

"Wait. Wait," the little girl said, then screeched "Mummy!" There was a bustle inside the door as what appeared to be a whole clutch of children assembled, grinning and fumbling with something large and white.

As the cab driver slammed closed the door of the boot, the children unfurled a large homemade banner that read: "WELCOME, AUNT JOEY!!!"

The banner, on sheets of white paper that had been haphazardly taped together, featured rainbows, birds, flowers, stick figures with smiles and other objects familiar to preschool art teachers everywhere.

"It's beautiful!" Joey cried, feeling suddenly completely overwhelmed.

"Hold on a sec, just let me take care of this." Joey set down Tink's crate, hurried over to the cab driver, and paid the fare with pounds she had swapped for her dollars at the airport. She pocketed the receipt and turned back to the children, who by now had been joined by an older boy and were on hands and knees in front of Tink's crate. Tink was barking frantically.

"Oooh, he's so sweet! Can he come out? What's his name?" The questions flew fast and furiously.

"It's a she. Tink. Sure." The older boy struggled with the catch on the crate, so Joey lent a hand. She worried momentarily about Tink running off, but Tink loved being the centre of attention and would be unlikely to bolt when so many hands were petting her. Sure enough, after zipping over to a tree for a quick squirt, she reclaimed her spot at the heart of the happy throng.

Something now caught the corner of Joey's eye and she glanced up to see a frumpy middle-aged woman in an apron on the front steps. She was shocked by the realisation that it was Sarah.

Her hair, streaked with grey and still very long, was held up with some pins, in a style that was painfully close to Sarah's mother's ubiquitous old-lady bun. As eight-year-olds, Joey and Sarah had dubbed it "the nest". Now, Joey bit her lip to keep from laughing. All she could think of was her and Sarah as kids, in the back seat of Sarah's family car, sticking toothpicks into hair-sprayed bun in the front seat. Her mother wouldn't notice, or would pretend not to notice, clambering out of the car with a bun full of toothpicks. Sarah and Joey would be almost sick with the effort to contain their hysterics.

Joey now looked fondly at the woman who stood before her. She had on a loose skirt that fell to mid-calf, over clogs worn with heavy woollen socks. Her turtleneck, all but covered by a large, floury apron, was worn and stretched, as though she had worn it straight through four pregnancies. Joey sought to hide her dismay at how much older and well, *staid* her old friend now looked.

"I know, I'm a mess," Sarah disarmed her by announcing.

"No you're not," Joey cried.

Sarah came down the steps.

"You've always worn your feelings on your face."

"It was just — *the nest!*" Joey burst out.

Sarah's hand flew to her hair. "Oh, I know." Then she started to laugh. "I've been cooking," she cried defensively.

Joey immediately felt guilty. This was *Sarah*. Her dearest pal. Who cared what she looked like?

"Sweetie!"

"Honey!"

They flew into each other's arm and hugged tightly for several long moments, then drew back and stared into each other's eyes.

"You look wonderful," Sarah said. "I hate you – you're so skinny!"

"I am not," Joey protested. The truth was, Joey hadn't gained a pound since she was twenty. And she worked at it, running, eating as little as she could, always keeping an eye on the scale.

"It was having kids that did me in," Sarah teased. "You'll see."

Joey wasn't sure she would. Kids definitely belonged in the *maybe someday but not any time soon* category.

"You must be exhausted," Sarah said. "Let's get you inside. Christopher, Timmy, give us a hand."

Two of the boys stood up and helped Sarah and Joey lug the bags into the house.

"Henry's in his study talking Aggie through the set up of her new computer on the phone," Sarah explained "He'll be free in a little while."

"Who's Aggie?"

"Oh, I can't believe I didn't mention her. Aggie is Henry's mother... Lady Howard." She raised an amused eyebrow. "She lives right by Stanway. It's extraordinary, isn't it? Small world... You're going to have to meet her."

Sarah's anglicised accent was even more pronounced now they were talking in person. There was barely a rising tone at the end of her statements at all.

An hour later, Joey and Sarah were sitting before a fire blazing in a sleek modern gas hearth in the living room. Following a tour of the house and all their rooms, the children had somehow been banished from their company.

The house wasn't a duplex. They lived in the whole thing.

It had nine bedrooms and six baths, although the grandeur of the outside was not exactly continued within. Antiques were scattered throughout the rooms – old desks and bookcases and chairs that needed re-caning – along with a selection of sturdy, middle-of-the-road family furniture that Joey could only describe as a triumph of comfort over style.

To begin with, Joey was a little surprised at the haphazard feeling of the interiors; then again, Sarah had never been interested in decorating or clothes. If an article of clothing fit and was clean, she wore it, with a carefree insouciance that allowed her to pull it off. But she was younger then. And slimmer.

Sinking into the soft leather of the sofa, Joey helped herself to the delicious-looking lunch Sarah had brought in on trays. There was brown bread, a good farmhouse cheddar and a rough pâté. Joey had vowed to drink only one glass of the Sancerre that Sarah had poured, and not to eat so much that she got even sleepier. She really wanted to stay awake! They had barely begun to swap stories of what had been happening over the years, in the broadest of outlines, with hardly any of the important details that held all the meaning. But the warmth of the fire, the soothing familiarity of Sarah's voice, the wine and the sleepless night on the plane soon conspired to bring a premature end to the reunion.

Joey's head nodded. She did her best to rouse herself and concentrate. But her eyes just would not stay open, no matter how hard she tried.

"All right, you," Sarah finally said. "Off to dreamland."

"I'm so sorry – I think I just need a little sleep, then I'll be fine."

"I know. Come on."

Joey barely remembered climbing the stairs, or slipping into bed.

As Sarah closed the shutters and the room fell into darkness, Joey fought off her drowsiness and struggled to a sitting position.

"Tink!" Joey whispered. "I forgot about – "

"Got it covered, baby," replied her friend.

Chapter 5

Joey opened her eyes. She had been trying to ignore the yelling, the slamming of doors and the clattering and pounding of children's feet up and down the stairs and hallways, but it was no use. How did Sarah and Henry put up with this level of noise? She rolled over and checked her BlackBerry; it was nearly three o'clock. She had been asleep for over two hours, but the nap had not restored her. She felt grumpy, disoriented and sluggish.

She sat up and looked around the room. It was cheerily papered in green stripes and had two tall windows with deep sills and creamily painted interior shutters. Joey got up and opened one pair of shutters. Dusk was already gathering, but she could just make out the contours of the back garden: a stone patio bordered with decorative urns, a line of mature trees, now bare of leaves, enclosing a small lawn crowded with bikes, a swing set, a wheelbarrow filled with gardening supplies, and some kind of playhouse erected under one of the trees.

She heard a noise and turned. The bedroom door was being eased open by two of the children, whose names she still wasn't sure of. The girl was round and blonde and her older brother, taller by at least six inches, had a discerning face that made him appear thoughtful beyond his years.

"You should knock before you come in!" Joey said sharply,

34

wondering why Sarah hadn't taught her kids this basic rule of etiquette and thanking her lucky stars that she was dressed.

"Mummy!" the blonde one bellowed. "Mummy, she's up!"

"Zoë! Christopher!" Sarah's voice floated up from downstairs. "Leave her alone. Don't wake her up."

The children stepped back into the hall, slamming the door behind them.

"It's okay," Joey called. "I was awake." She crossed the room, opened the door and peered out. "Sarah?"

Joey could hear sounds of a video game being played at full volume in an adjacent room. An argument seemed to have broken out between the two girls, one of whom was now screeching and racing up the hall stairs, clutching a ratty Madeline doll. Joey ducked back into the bedroom. She would change her clothes, put on some lipstick and march downstairs to meet the rest of the day.

She was just slipping on a sweater when a soft knock came at the door.

"Joey?"

"Come in! I was just coming down."

Sarah stood in the doorway carrying a gleaming silver tray.

Joey hurried across the room to help her with the door. "Oh, my gosh, what's this?"

"I made you something." On the tray was a small silver bowl covered with a fancy service lid. Sarah carried the tray over to the bed and set it down. Joey kicked off her shoes and climbed back onto the bed.

"You ready?" Sarah asked.

Joey nodded then gingerly lifted the lid of the silver-service, exaggerating her anticipation, as though she was half expecting something to jump out. Instead, the air was suffused with the aroma of something warm and deliciously sweet, hot and chocolaty. Joey peered closely; in the bowl were three gooey black and white clumps of tightly compacted mush. She looked even more closely, took a sniff and burst out laughing,

"Sarah, no! Chocolate Rice Krispy treats? I haven't had these since college!"

"No kidding!" Sarah said. "Look at you. What are you, a six?"

As if to deny that she gave any thought to her figure, Joey picked up a massive candy clump. She couldn't believe she was actually going to eat this. She never ate sugar if she could help it. She popped it in her mouth.

"Oh my God," she said. "I'd forgotten how great these are!"

Sarah ate the second clump of chocolate and insisted that Joey have the third. Then Sarah stood up abruptly and said, "Come on down. I've got a pile of these on the stove."

❈   ❈   ❈

The walls of the staircase were lined with dozens of framed pictures of babies, beaming, toothless children, a gradually widening Sarah, and a remarkably unchanged Henry. He looked as trim and fit as he always had.

At the bottom of the stairs, Joey was clipped by a fast-moving mop of blonde hair. There was a riotous scramble of feet and two more children skidded around the corner, slipping on the highly polished floorboards. Behind them came the boy who had opened Joey's bedroom door. He seemed to be trying to collect himself.

"Aunt Joey," he said. "I'm Christopher."

"Just call me Joey. Just Joey's fine."

Christopher stuck out a hand politely and waited for Joey

to grasp it. He was clearly trying hard to be grown-up.

"Pleased to meet you – again." Joey said, taking his hand. He shook hers firmly.

Two of the children came screeching back.

"Auntie Joey!" the small blonde girl sang, wrapping her arms tightly around Joey's thigh.

"This is Zoë," Christopher said.

"Auntie Joey!" Zoë squealed, squeezing harder. Joey struggled to keep her balance.

"Just Joey is fine," Joey repeated firmly.

They started laughing and chanting, "Just Joey, Just Joey!"

"Okay, that's enough," Joey said.

"Just Joey, Zoë just turned four," said Christopher. "Just Joey and Zoë, it rhymes."

"It does," Joey said, tiring of the refrain already.

"And you know Timothy, Just Joey." Christopher indicated a boy wearing a hooded jacket like a cape.

"I'm not Timothy," said the boy crossly.

Christopher gave Joey a conspiratorial look. "*Superman* is eight. He's twins with Matilda. She's shy. She's out in the garden."

My kind of kid, Joey thought. *Somewhere else.*

"How old are you, again, Chris?" Joey asked.

"I'm going to be ten in June."

"Right. Of course." Joey said. "Is your mum in the kitchen?"

"I'll take you to her," Christopher replied. "This way, Just Joey."

Christopher took the lead and Joey and the others fell in behind him. Zoë and Timmy gave a strange sort of salute, Zoë's more like a fumbled wave. After zigzagging through a series of gloomy corridors – Joey suspected that she was being taken the back way – they all burst into the sunny kitchen.

"Here you are," Sarah said. She bent down to kiss Timmy on the nose and handed Christopher a saucepan with the scrapings of the sticky candy.

"You guys can lick the pan, but take it out into the garden."

"It's freezing outside!" Timmy protested.

"Then put on a jacket," Sarah instructed him calmly. "And it's not freezing. Matilda's out there in just a T-shirt."

Zoë ran to the window. "She is," the girl confirmed.

"All for me!" Chris teased, swooping away with the pan of candy. Timmy and Zoë howled in protest and raced out after him.

The kitchen was large, airy and modern. A wide oak table, surrounded by black metal chairs, took up much of the room and gleaming stainless steel appliances, all industrial strength and size, lined the walls. Sarah, now wearing a blue and white striped apron, was standing at the stove, stirring another mucky mess of melting marshmallow and chocolate.

"A friend of Timmy's is having a birthday party and these always go down like the proverbial hot cakes," she explained. "I just made tea. It's in the pot."

Joey stepped up to the counter, reached for a mug sitting on one of the open shelves and poured herself some tea. "Are they hard to make?" asked Joey, opening the fridge in search of cream or milk. She stood staring at the most packed refrigerator she had ever seen as Sarah rattled off the recipe.

"Easy as anything. Melt the marshmallows and chocolate with half a stick of butter, stir in the Rice Krispies, press it all into a pan and let it cool. Or make them into clumps with your fingers. That's it!"

As Sarah measured cereal and poured it into the pan she

had been stirring, Joey glanced around the room. On closer inspection, the kitchen was quite a mess. In one corner sat what looked like a pirate island, encircled by a fleet of plastic and wooden ships and strewn with plastic figures, most missing legs and arms. On the opposite side of the room was a child-sized pink pedal car and a wall dedicated to children's drawings and paintings. Joey carried her mug across the space and examined the art: boats on the sea, trees laden with apples, animals of undeterminable species.

Timmy suddenly barrelled back through the door, and noticing Joey perusing the paintings, skittered over to her side.

"That one's mine," he said proudly, pointing.

"A – rabbit?" Joey guessed.

Timmy's face fell. "It's not a rabbit. It's Mindy," he said, looking offended.

"*Mindy?*" Joey said sheepishly, looking to Sarah for help.

"Our cat," Sarah said.

"You know, I kind of thought it was a cat," Joey said quickly. "I almost said, cat."

Timmy had fixed her with a reproachful look, but Sarah saved the day by announcing that yet another pan was available to be licked. She handed it to Timmy, and with that, he was gone.

Sarah plopped a bowl of the marshmallow mixture down onto the table, poured herself some tea and motioned Joey over. They both sat down.

"So."

"So," Joey echoed.

"Where were we?"

"Where were we when?"

"When you fell asleep on me!"

Joey knew exactly where they had been: approaching the

treacherous topic of her love life. She *so* didn't want to go there, but there was no way to avoid the subject.

"I don't know," Joey said evasively, sipping her tea. "Where were we?"

Sarah gave her a look, but pressed on. "Are you seeing anyone?"

Joey shook her head.

"What about that guy who worked at Lincoln Center?"

"Jonathan? Sarah, that was *years* ago."

"Well I haven't *seen* you for years. We haven't really *talked* in years, not about this. I thought you really liked him."

"I did like him, but – "

"But what?" Sarah asked.

"He was too – too – "

"Too *what?*"

"Short."

"Short? You broke up with him because he was too *short?* You're not serious."

"Well, it wasn't *just* that. He had no sense of humour, he was cheap, and all he liked to do was go sailing. I hate sailing. Anyway, that was light years ago."

"No, you're right. Hang on... I remember more recently you mentioning some guy at work," Sarah said. From the tone of her voice, Joey assumed that she must have told Sarah the relationship with Alex had to be kept super-secret.

"How much did I tell you?" Joey asked.

"Not enough," Sarah said, sighing. "I want to hear everything. It's heavenly having you sitting right here." Sarah reached into the bowl and pulled off a little clump of candy, which she popped into her mouth.

"Well, it's over," Joey said simply. "He dumped me."

Sarah chewed slowly, waiting for Joey to go on. When she didn't, Sarah asked, "What happened?"

"I was stupid," Joey said. "I should never have gotten involved with a partner at work."

"Who started it?" Sarah asked.

"*He* did. He picked me to be on his team for this big redevelopment project, and the next thing I know, we're working late every night, having food delivered... "

"Et cetera?" Sarah prompted.

Joey nodded.

"Did the people at work know?"

"Not at first. I think some might have suspected, but then one of the secretaries, a major blabbermouth, saw us in a restaurant in April. He broke up with me not long after that."

"Because he didn't want the relationship to become public?" Sarah asked.

"That's what he said. That it would be bad for him and disastrous for me. But about a month later, I found out that he'd been seeing this woman out in the Hamptons for eight or nine months."

"You're kidding."

Joey shook her head, suddenly feeling miserable. Images of their days together flashed through her mind: her and Alex vacationing on Nantucket, skiing in Vail, cooking pasta in her apartment, making love in his flat on Central Park West. She was silent for several moments. Sarah sipped her tea, gazing across the table sympathetically.

"You really liked him, didn't you?"

Joey came back to the present moment. And then surprised herself by welling up with tears. She nodded as the tears spilled over. "I was so stupid."

"You weren't stupid," Sarah said quietly, pulling her chair closer and reaching across the table for her friend's hand. "You were willing to open up your heart to him. *He* was the stupid one."

Joey shook her head, fighting to bring her tears under control.

"Yes he was," Sarah insisted. "He was an idiot. And he'll live to regret this."

"I doubt it," Joey whispered.

"I don't," Sarah said decisively.

They sat quietly for several moments. Sarah pushed the candy bowl toward Joey, but Joey shook her head. She'd already had more than enough.

"Why don't you go for a walk?" Sarah suggested. "Get some air before dinner. The kids can show you around. They'd love to."

Joey shrugged. The candy had turned to lead in her stomach, and she suddenly felt tired again. All she wanted to do was to go back upstairs and be alone.

"Maybe," she said. "But I'll go by myself."

Sarah looked up quickly. "The kids would love to take you. They've really been looking forward to your coming."

"I don't think I have the energy for – the whole gang."

Sarah's smile faded slightly, but when she spoke there was softness in her voice.

"All right. Whatever you want."

Chapter 6

When Sarah had referred to "giving the children their tea," Joey had pictured the four little Howards seated around the kitchen table sipping milky Earl Grey and munching on marmite sandwiches and digestives. She hadn't realised that this term meant *supper*, and that rather than having a long evening meal reminiscing with Henry and Sarah, the children tucked happily out of sight somewhere, they would all be eating dinner at the kitchen table at the uncivilised hour of six.

Henry had opened the door to her when she got back from her walk, and the pictures on the wall hadn't lied: he seemed hardly to have aged at all. He had always reminded Joey of Colin Firth, and he still did. She found herself wondering why a decade of family life had affected Sarah's appearance the way it had, yet exerted virtually no effect on Henry's. Was it the result of Sarah having borne the children, of her spending too much time in the kitchen, of not having a work presence in the world and hence a work wardrobe to fit into, or of just not caring about her appearance any more? Whatever the reason, Joey vowed that if she ever did have children, she wouldn't let herself go this way.

"You look fabulous," Henry said, after sweeping Joey into a warm embrace, and leading her down stairs.

"Don't give me that," she teased, glancing in Sarah's direction. "I look jet-lagged and ten years older."

Henry smiled and poured her a glass of wine. At least she wasn't going to be expected to drink milk.

"Go wash your hands," Sarah called from the stove, where she was dishing up bowls of steaming potatoes and vegetables. Zoe and Timmy were already at their places at the table.

"I did," said Zoë.

"You did not," Timmy countered.

"I did, too!" Zoë screeched.

Henry calmly walked to where Zoë was sitting and held out his hand. She offered up her palms for her father's inspection. "Clean enough," he pronounced.

Matilda appeared and slipped quietly into the chair beside Joey's. Joey glanced over and smiled, but the shy little girl could barely make eye contact.

Sarah set serving dishes on the table while Henry removed a roast leg of lamb from the oven and transferred it to a carving board.

"Where's Chris?" Sarah asked.

No one answered.

"Where's your brother, Timothy?" she asked again.

"Upstairs."

"Well, go get him!" Sarah looked damp and her tone bordered on irritated.

"Why do I always have to go? Make *her* go!"

Timmy shot a resentful glance at Zoë.

"I'll get him," Henry said.

"You will not," Sarah replied sharply. "That lamb needs to be carved *now*." She turned to Timothy. "*March*, mister. And if I hear another word out of that fresh little mouth of yours, you'll be going to bed without supper."

Whoa! Joey thought. *You go, girl!* These kids could use a bit more of firmness like this in her opinion.

"Ha, ha!" taunted Zoë.

"Shut up!" Timmy snapped as he slid out of his chair.

"What did you say?" Henry asked in a steely tone. "Timothy Snowden Howard!"

"He said 'shut up'," Zoë tattled gleefully.

"Did I ask you?" Henry replied. "No, I asked your brother."

Timmy had turned at the sound of his father's voice and now stood miserably by the back stairwell. Taking pity on the guilty boy, or perhaps just hoping to end all the bickering, Henry said calmly, "We don't use that kind of language in this family. Now, go and tell your brother that dinner is ready."

Relieved to be spared the punishment that seconds before had seemed inevitable, Timmy clambered up the stairs without another word.

✳   ✳   ✳

The catching up that Joey had hoped to do with Sarah and Henry happened later, once the kids were upstairs, supposedly in bed. Joey could hear talking and running around on the second floor until nearly ten o'clock. She wondered why neither Sarah nor Henry made an effort to enforce bedtime, but she wasn't going to ask. They were clearly capable of cracking the whip when they wanted to, but as they all sat in the living room sipping wine before a blazing fire, both parents turned a deaf ear to the sounds of their children's hijinks upstairs.

"So let's talk about what you're really doing here," Henry had said when they sat down.

"Henry!" Sarah squealed.

"I meant about work! We're thrilled to see you, of course."

When Joey mentioned Stanway House, Henry arched an eyebrow. "Ah yes, the *development...*"

"Henry, don't wind her up," Sarah said. "You might actually be of some help in the whole thing."

"You're right. I'm sorry," said Henry, settling back in his chair and taking a sip of wine. "The first thing we need to do is get you introduced to my mother. Benbrough is just a few miles down the road from where you're going to be working. She knows everyone in the area. "

"Yes, Sarah told me," Joey laughed. "So you *do* all know each other! Is that where you grew up?"

Henry nodded. "Been there for generations. Mother wishes we were still there, all of us."

"No, thank you," Sarah said, smiling. "I adore her, I really do. She fantastic. But I'm a city girl. London's not New York, but it's better than – "

"The sticks?" Henry supplied cheerfully.

"Exactly!"

"I'll get you there yet," he teased.

"Good luck," Sarah shot back.

Joey smiled. She felt a little guilty about thoughts she'd had during dinner, when she wondered if Sarah's changed appearance ever made Henry think of – straying. It was Europe, after all. Didn't Europeans, and especially aristocrats, which Henry definitely was, tend to treat the issue of marital fidelity a little more casually than Americans? But this gentle teasing and even the easy give-and-take they'd manifested during dinner spoke of an affectionate relationship characterised by humour and mutual tolerance.

"You mentioned you might be able to help?" said Joey. "Is there something I should know about?"

Henry and Sarah exchanged glances.

"Nothing Mother can't help you solve, if she wants to," Henry said.

"Oh, go on, Hens," Sarah replied. "You're making more of it than it is."

"More of what?" Joey asked.

Henry motioned to Sarah. Since she apparently thought that he was being too dramatic, he would let *her* tell the story.

"It's nothing," said Sarah. "Really."

"You're making me very nervous," Joey said, holding out her glass for more wine.

"I'm teasing, Joey," Henry went on. "I've just heard that some of the old farts down there aren't happy that Stanway's going to be done up and turned into a hotel. They wanted it to remain in private hands. They're afraid it's going to become Disney World." Henry now slipped into parody, imitating a pompous old man: "There have been rumours about – a *spa*."

"It will have a little spa," Joey said. "But a spa as in Baden Baden, not the Equinox Club."

"What's the Equinox Club?" Henry asked.

"Never mind!" Sarah said. "The point is, everybody loves Aggie – she's the most down-to-earth person you're likely to meet. If she's on your side, and we know she will be, you're halfway there."

❋ ❋ ❋

The house was quiet when Joey awoke in the morning. She had stumbled off to bed about eleven thirty, and between the wine and the jet-lag, she had slept soundly. She glanced at her BlackBerry: nine thirty. She dimly remembered a lot of noise and bustle earlier in the morning – Sarah getting the kids up and out of the house – but she had nodded off again as soon as the house quieted down. Now, all was silent.

She got up and dressed quickly, then headed down to the kitchen. The breakfast dishes were still on the table, but neither Sarah nor Henry was about. Sarah had mentioned a children's birthday party. Maybe she would be helping there all day long.

That was fine with Joey. A good guest didn't hang around the house waiting to be entertained. There was nothing worse than having a lot to do and feeling responsible for a visiting friend who had nothing to do. And, she was in London! She'd read quite a bit about the St. Pancras Station redevelopment in the architectural press back home and had wanted to see how they'd handled it. This was the perfect opportunity.

She wondered briefly whether she should do the breakfast dishes before she left. She didn't want Sarah to think she was critical of Sarah's housekeeping skills. Maybe it was better to leave them. Anyway, she didn't know where anything went.

She did have to check on Tink, though. She glanced into the crate that had been placed under the windows by the breezeway. Tink was curled up on her blanket at the back, fast asleep. Joey thought about just leaving her to doze the day away, but she didn't know whether she had been outside yet. She unhooked the crate and took Tink out into the garden. When she came in, she scraped the children's leftover eggs and sausage onto a plate and placed it on the floor. Tink gobbled the food greedily and then was surprisingly happy to be put back in her crate.

❊　❊　❊

An hour and a half later, Joey was standing in front of Sir George Gilbert Scott's marvel. People had often described it as the most romantic building in London. But she had never understood what they meant by *romantic*.

Now she did. It was in the detail: the hundreds of windows framed in Gothic arches and columns, the glorious clock tower with its elegant steeple, the varied tones of the brick and stone. Detail. That was it. Layer upon layer of articulation, of framing, of contrast, of presentation. And yet it didn't look fussy. How in the world had they managed that?

Inside – well, one could only describe it as being surrounded by gorgeousness. What had once been exterior taxi stands were now enclosed and transformed into sweeping lobbies of glazed red brick and ironwork. The Grand Staircase had Joey transfixed. It reminded her of the St. Chapelle in Paris, the private chapel of King Louis IX. For a king's chapel, yes, but to lavish this exquisite detail on a staircase? The ruby walls, the soaring arches, the glorious star-patterned panels that formed the ceiling of the winding staircase. And the tall, mullioned, stained glass windows, like those in a cathedral. This *was* a cathedral, Joey concluded. It was an overwhelming monument to beauty and architectural ambition.

As Joey finished touring the areas that were open to the public and headed toward the gift shop, she felt her spirits wilt. Would she ever design anything with even a fraction of this beauty? Maybe not. But there were still lessons to be learned here. Maybe there was a book on the building. She wanted to remember these ideas in detail.

In the shop, she found exactly what she was looking for, a book tracing the history of the building, formerly the Midland Grand Hotel, all the way up through its renovation. She wanted to buy a gift for Sarah, too, but nothing for sale in here felt right. She'd passed a nice clothing store a few blocks away. She would head over there before catching a cab back to the house.

❄   ❄   ❄

"Where were you?" Sarah cried as she flung open the front door.

"I went into town. I went to see St. Pancras."

"I've been worried sick. I came back home and you were gone."

Joey shrugged. "I figured you were busy. You said there was a children's birthday party."

"Well yes, but... why didn't you leave me a note?"

"Why didn't you just call me?" Joey asked. "I had my BlackBerry with me."

"I don't have your number. Have I ever called you on your BlackBerry?"

They were still standing in the doorway.

"No," Joey said. "I'm sorry. I figured you had things to do. I didn't want you to feel you had to entertain me."

Sarah pulled Joey in by the arm and slammed the door behind her. "*Entertain* you? You're my oldest friend in the world and I haven't seen you in ten years. *Entertain* you? There's nothing I want to do more."

"I'm sorry, I..."

"I had lunch reservations. I planned to take you to my favourite restaurant, then my favourite bookstore, then my favourite boutique and my favourite bar! I had everything all set up."

"But you didn't say anything. How was I supposed to know?"

"You weren't! It was a surprise. I figured you'd be out cold until noon. And at eleven o'clock I walk in, and you're gone."

Joey sighed. "I'm sorry. I really am. I was just trying to stay out of your hair." Not knowing what else to do, she handed Sarah the pink bag she was carrying.

"What's this?"

"A present."

"What is it?"

"A silk blouse."

Sarah now looked as though she was about to cry. "Nice try," she said, releasing the garment from its wrapper and holding it up in front of her.

"But wrong." Joey concluded.

Sarah nodded sadly.

Chapter 7

Joey stared out at the passing scenery as images from the previous evening floated through her mind. Sarah trying on the blouse, which was at least three sizes too small. Chris complaining about the supper menu and Henry angrily banishing him to his room. Zoë dissolving into tears because Timmy wouldn't stop looking at her. Tink throwing up on the kitchen floor.

All in all, it had been an evening she'd be glad to forget. To make matters worse, she had coped with the tension in the household by drinking too much wine, so as the driver now wove his way along the bumpy country roads that led to Stanway House, Joey was nursing a killer headache. All she wanted was to *get there*. Besides, there was no use obsessing about yesterday's spoiled plans and the strained feeling that hung over the evening. She hadn't meant to hurt Sarah's feelings. She hadn't meant to do anything but be a good guest. Fortunately, she'd be seeing everyone again in a few days. The children took riding lessons at a stable close to Benbrough House, and there was a pony club rally at the weekend. Sarah, Henry and all the children were coming to the country and Joey and Sarah would have half a day to themselves. Joey hoped she could repair the damage.

Up a last hill, through a crooked avenue of trees, and then the car turned in to a drive. Past the gatehouse, and suddenly, there it was: Stanway House. The driver turned off the engine as Joey gazed at the structure she had longed for so many months to see and experience for real. Jacobean in design, it was built from a local stone known as Gulting Yellow. The arch in its centre was flanked by bay windows and embellished at the roofline with stones carved in swirls.

"Well, here we are," the driver exhaled.

Joey jumped out of the car and stared rapturously up at the house, which had turned a golden yellow in the late afternoon sun. She couldn't resist walking up to it, and, running her hands slowly over the ancient stones, felt a rush of warmth emanating from the building. It spoke to her.

The driver retrieved Joey's bags from the boot and interrupted her communion to ask for his fare. She carefully counted out the notes and handed them to him. It had been expensive, hiring a taxi to bring her all the way out here from London, but there was no way she could have rented a car. She had a licence, but she rarely drove, and she certainly wasn't going to get behind the wheel on the wrong side of the road. As the driver pulled away, Joey carried her bags to the portico. Then she freed Tink from her crate and snapped on her leash.

They wandered along the path that wound away from the arch toward a stand of ancient trees. After months and months spent on this project, Joey felt as though she already knew this place. It was strange, like meeting a family member you've only known through photographs.

Behind the trees was a path lined on both sides with thick, dense rhododendrons, and a walkway that led off toward the house's water garden, one of the finest in England.

As Joey turned and headed back to the front of the house, she saw a girl standing in a doorway. A girl of perhaps fourteen, fifteen years, with sparkling emerald eyes and hair so lush and wavy that Joey couldn't take her eyes off it. It seemed as though half of the women in New York wanted fair hair and were willing to pay a small fortune every month or six weeks to pull off the pretence of being naturally blonde. But not even Marta, whom Joey considered a genius of a colourist, would be able to duplicate the subtle tones in this gorgeous mane.

She also wore a skirt so short that it brought to mind what Joey's father used to say whenever Joey had tried to escape from the house in a daring outfit: "That skirt's so short I can see what you had for breakfast!"

"Hello," she called. "I'm Joey Rubin."

"Hi. I'm Lily – Ian's daughter. We live in the gatehouse at the end of the drive."

Joey had been looking forward to meeting Ian Mc-Cormack, with whom she had spoken several times on the phone. Since Lord and Lady Tracy had relinquished the keys to the property and moved to their house in London, Ian had been the company's only on-site contact. She was hoping he could be persuaded to stay on and help manage the hotel and estate. It would help to have a local man in charge. And he probably knew the house and the grounds better than anyone.

"Where are *you* from?" the girl asked, giving Joey a thorough once-over.

"New York," Joey replied.

The veneer of adolescent disdain slipped away rapidly. "That's so cool. I'm moving to New York."

A man appeared in the doorway, and Joey knew it had to be Ian. The resemblance to his daughter was unmistakable, but it was his eyes – intelligent, watchful – that captivated her attention. He wore heavy canvas trousers and a wool shirt topped by a dark-grey Aran knit jumper that had seen better days. The cuffs and bottom ribbing were unravelling.

"Is that right?" he asked his daughter, a little dismissively. Now he gave *her* the once over, his disapproving gaze lingering on her skirt. "Where'd that get-up come from?"

"Oxfam."

"Where's the rest of it?"

"Dad!"

Joey bit her lip to keep from smiling.

"Go and change your clothes."

"Daddy!" she wailed.

"*Lily!*" he imitated.

With a helpless glance at Joey – a look that said, *Men! You understand, don't you?* – Lily turned on her heel and stomped into the house.

Joey had a vision of Ian styled for New York: close-cropped hair, cleanly shaved, a three-piece Italian suit. She did this to every man she met – imagined how they would look if she were allowed to manage every detail of their grooming and wardrobe. Today, though, she shook off the fantasy. Almost any man could look good in an Italian suit. There weren't too many that could look as good as Ian did in a worn out cabled sweater.

"I've been looking forward to meeting you," Joey said. She extended her hand.

Cute little crinkly lines did not appear at the edges of Ian's eyes, nor did he smile. He gave her a nod but did not reach for her hand. His restraint felt like a splash of cold water.

"I thought Wilson was coming."

"He was. He had an accident."

"Oh! Is he all right?"

"He will be," Joey replied.

"So *you're* in charge?"

"I am, yes. And I'll really need your help. We're starting

first thing in the morning. We have a walk-through with the contractor."

"What contractor? You've already hired one?"

Joey nodded. "His name is Massimo Fortinelli."

Ian gave Joey a disbelieving look. "Not *the Italian*..."

"What do you mean?"

"Jayses." Ian shook his head scornfully.

"But his references were fantastic. Everyone he's ever worked with here raves about him."

"Like who?" Ian pressed.

"Like – " Joey paused briefly, wondering whether it was ethical to relay the details of her confidential conversations, then realised that there was nothing whatsoever to hide. "Like – Alasdair Newell ... "

"Well, *sure*," Ian said. "*Newell*."

"Meaning what?"

"Meaning they're – " Ian held up two fingers, one wrapped around the other. "Like this! Of course Newell is going to be in the guy's corner."

"But they wouldn't be friends if Newell didn't respect him, would they? They've done three or four projects together."

"Precisely," Ian shot back. "Well, suit yourself. The flat's ready."

"Thank you," Joey whispered. "I thought I'd look around for a while."

"Do as you like. You don't need my permission. The place is yours now."

"I *wish*," Joey answered, trying to warm the distinct chill in the air. "*My* place would probably fit in one of the bathrooms."

Ian was not charmed. He stepped inside and returned a moment later with a ring of keys.

"Thanks, " Joey said.

He nodded, and walked off down the drive towards the gatehouse.

❋　❋　❋

An hour later, Joey was busily unpacking in the gracious apartment she would occupy for the next few weeks. It had been the private quarters of Lady Tracy's elderly aunt, Margaret, who the previous winter had suffered a fatal stroke at the age of ninety-one. The apartment had one large living room and a generous bedroom and bathroom. The elderly woman had taken many meals with the Tracy family and had others served to her privately in her rooms by the household staff.

Joey was going to have to get by without a kitchen, but apart from that, she couldn't imagine a lovelier place to stay. She had been happily surprised to learn that the apartment was still furnished, as many of the other rooms had been emptied of their objects at the time of the sale. Stanway House might be going public, but there were dozens of Tracys scattered about Great Britain and they had all been determined to carry off as much as they could of the portable property. She wondered why none of them seemed to have raided these rooms. Regardless, Joey was thrilled to stay in the house itself, rather than at a local inn or B&B. She would really be able to get the feel of the place, at all times of day and night.

As she drifted around the apartment, inspecting the well-polished furniture and lovingly maintained accoutrements, she felt a surprising wave of sadness. At first she thought it was because the woman who had lived here was so palpably absent – the abruptness of her departure could almost be felt. But it wasn't really that, Joey realised. Her sadness had its roots in the apartment itself.

The cushions bore hand-worked crewel, the framed

photographs were personal and informal, the counterpane on the bed had been crocheted by hand. There wasn't an object in the rooms that didn't seem to express some kind of personal thought, desire or significance. It was as though the rooms were filled with memories, and all the objects in them were talismans of places that were loved, people who were loved, times that had been alive with affection and connection.

Joey thought of all the things she had got rid of in the process of gutting and renovating her own apartment. She had been determined to make it feel like *hers*. Her mother had been so sick there for so long – and, to have the floors refinished, the walls ripped out, the kitchen and bathroom completely redone, to generally heal the place had felt vitally important at the time.

But in her zeal to make a whole new start, she had divested herself of many of the very things that made the apartment feel homey and welcoming: hand-crocheted afghans, framed snapshots, mismatched little odds and ends that had been gifts or heirlooms. Now, she found herself thinking of particular cups and saucers they had used when she was growing up. She had packed them all into a Goodwill box when she bought new saucepans and dishes. Maybe she shouldn't have been quite so hasty.

Joey dug out her make-up bag and sat down at the dressing table in the bedroom. She lifted the glass stopper from an old perfume bottle and inhaled the scent: it was heavy and dark, a glamorous, old-fashioned perfume. She dabbed some behind her ears, leaned in to the large oval mirror and stared at her own reflection.

She looked tired. She was tired. There were lines at the corners of her eyes that she hadn't noticed before. "Sunburst lines" she'd heard someone call them, trying a little too hard. They were crow's feet. Crow's feet! She would have to focus on not smiling automatically. She would have to remember to smile only when she really meant it.

Joey glanced over at Tink, panting happily beside a reading chair. Tink chose just that moment to roll over onto her side and let out a deep, contented sigh.

How can you be tired, Joey thought. You've been sleeping for two days!

Her thoughts floated back to her encounter with Ian. She hadn't been *trying* to be charming, but it was unsettling that she had not managed to prise even the slightest smile or the most banal pleasantry from his lips. What was the guy's problem? No one was kicking him out of his house. Yes, his life was going to change, but that's what life did: it changed. He had a good job waiting for him if he wanted it.

A worrisome thought flitted into her consciousness. Maybe he found her unattractive – too efficient, too *foreign*, too pushy? Not that she was *trying* to be attractive to him, but usually there was a little reaction, a little spark – of some sort. He had acted as though he couldn't wait to get out of her presence.

There was only one solution to this unsettled, jumpy feeling. She needed to go for a good long run.

Chapter 8

The sun, low in the sky, bathed the gardens as Joey passed in a divine, milky light. Vines, which would have been green and thick with leaves in summer, were now bare. The dark brown vegetation covering the building looked like thousands of tiny veins and arteries. Yes, even in the dead of winter, there was beauty, Joey thought. The densely clad facade looked like a Jackson Pollock canvas – dripped paint seeming at first to have no pattern or reason, but which, on reflection, appeared to say something after all.

Setting off at a sprint from outside the gatehouse arch, Joey felt the icy cold hit the back of her throat. It felt pure, as though she were breathing filtered, oxygenated water, fresh from the mountain springs.

She ran through a series of country lanes, keeping track of her lefts and rights. Ten or fifteen minutes passed without her seeing another human soul. She could not think of another time in her life when she had been outside for so long without company. No matter where you went in Manhattan, there were always people.

The solitude felt unnerving at first. She could have screamed out here and no one would have heard her. But as she jogged on, she felt an exhilarating freedom. She'd even left Tink behind, much to the dog's disgruntlement. She could do exactly what she wanted. She could sing at the top of her lungs or launch into an impromptu little cha-cha and there was absolutely no one to raise an eyebrow. She had to savour this moment.

The scenery, as if compensating for the utter absence of human life, was dazzling. Every field, every plant stuck out against the azure of the sky. The lane — one could hardly call it a road — had old stone walls on either side. Some parts were crumbling and some had been recently restored. As she entered the village, she passed a row of cottages with thatched roofs and gardens flanked by potting sheds.

She came upon a small stone post office and what looked like an ancient inn, "The Pump House". Through the inn's leaded-glass windows, Joey glimpsed faces animated in conversation. Batting off a wave of loneliness — she would *not* give in to her usual self-pity — she looped around the centre of the village and headed out towards the rambling farmlands beyond. A couple of hundred yards on, she turned off the road on to a muddy track, bordering fields, which looked as if it would take her back in the direction she had come. The terrain was uneven, and she kept her eyes firmly on the ground in front of her. Which was why she nearly collided with the ram.

He stood smack in the middle of the track as Joey stopped just a few feet away. Adrenaline racing, she drew in a sharp breath. What was this creature? Was he going to charge her? Impale her with his horns? It didn't seem so. He eyed her with indignation. He had no intention of getting out of her way. It was a stand off.

The ram stared at her, his long face impassive. Joey sidled to her right, pressing close to the hedge to try to squeak by. The ram stepped toward her. Joey stopped. The ram stopped.

She moved to her left, sinking her new running shoes deep into a puddle. The sheep shook out its ears and moved forward to join her. Joey paused again. The ears were the most disconcerting part, she decided; whenever she moved, they seemed to track her like little satellite dishes.

"Shoo!" Joey said.

The ram stared. He rotated his ears.

"Shoo!" she said more forcefully, this time with real feeling. "Go on – shoo!" The animal did not respond.

"Please! Damn it, let me through!" At that moment, something caught Joey's eye in the field to her right. Forgetting her stubborn challenger entirely, she walked up to the hedgerow and edged along to a gate to get a better look.

The field was populated by bulky black and white cows, some standing, some lying down. But in the distance there appeared to be an expanse of water. It looked like a large pond with a small island in the middle, from which grew a stand of fledgling birches. Something was moving in the water. Not just moving, thrashing about. Joey squinted into the deepening light. Something was wrong.

"Hello?" she called, her voice too thin in the cold air. There was no response. "Hello?"

She saw the movement again, and this time she realised what it was: the rising and falling of a flailing arm. She threw the gate open and tore across the field. The pond was a good distance away and the mud and grass slippery and soft.

"Hold on! I'm coming!" she yelled at the top of her lungs. Cresting a gentle rise in the pasture, she got a clear look down to the water. There, midway between the bank and the tree-lined island, was an elderly woman. She seemed barely afloat, listlessly treading water. Without another thought, Joey raced down the hill to the side of the bank, kicked her trainers off, and with one athletic leap, cleared the reeds and broke the surface of the pond.

The cold stunned her with a sensation like that of falling

into a bed of knives. She surfaced, raised her head above water and broke into a fierce crawl. The woman was a matter of yards away, still struggling in the murky water. *She must be freezing*, Joey thought, swimming as fast as she could and thanking her lucky stars that she had happened to pass by in time.

"I've got you." She wound her arm around the woman's waist, pulling her furiously toward the bank. The woman was thrashing her arms, clearly panicked and unable to process the fact that she was being rescued.

"It's okay. You're okay." It was hard to talk and swim and breathe at the same time, but Joey gave it her all. Man, the old girl was strong! But she would have had to be, to have kept herself from going under for however long she was in the freezing water. As Joey kicked them both toward the bank, she caught a glimpse of what looked like a shocked, incredulous face framed by white hair. Of course she was in shock. She'd nearly drowned! She seemed to be trying to say something, but Joey couldn't focus on that now. She had to get them both to shore.

Finally, they reached water shallow enough to stand in. Joey helped the woman to her feet, surprised at how heavy she was on land, and then by the fact that she was wearing — a bathing costume? Together, they staggered through the reeds and then collapsed on the safety of the bank. Panting, Joey turned to face her.

"Are you okay?"

The woman was coughing and spluttering. In her mind, Joey began to run through the steps of artificial resuscitation.

One, clear the victim's airway of any obstructions...

The woman had stopped coughing and was blinking rapidly at her. "You got a little water in my throat there."

Well, *that* was an odd reaction. The woman gave one final

cough then calmly said, "Thank you dear. I meant to do just ten minutes, and I probably *was* closer to fifteen. But I wasn't expecting such a dramatic reminder that it was time to come out!"

Joey froze. The woman was smiling. Clearly, she was mad.

"You sound American," the old woman commented. "Oh, dear, look, you're shivering!"

With remarkable agility, the woman skittered up the slippery bank toward a small neat pile of clothes stacked on top of two large towels. She wrapped one of the towels around her waist and threw the other down to Joey.

"I always bring an extra," she said, smiling kindly. "I'm so sorry, dear. I've given you quite a fright."

"I thought you were drowning," Joey said simply, feeling her face growing hot. Now it made sense. She couldn't believe she'd made such a rash assumption. Then again, she couldn't believe that anyone in their right mind, let alone a frail old lady, would think of paddling around in an icy lake in January.

"You must be Josephine."

Once again, Joey found herself mute. This was all too weird. She had humiliated herself by sprinting through cow pats to save a woman who didn't want or need to be saved, but at least she had figured that no one would find out about this. She was in the middle of nowhere; it wasn't as though she had leapt into Central Park's boating lake. But this woman knew her name...

"Yes. I'm – Joey." She tried to stop her teeth chattering. She was shivering wildly now. She didn't think she had ever been so cold.

"Well, delighted to meet you. I'm Aggie, Sarah's mother-in-law."

Aggie? Joey thought. *This* woman was Henry's mother, Lady Howard? Surely she wouldn't be swimming in icy ponds in the middle of winter... She'd be – reading Trollope and serving on the hospital board and overseeing a house run by maids and butlers.

"Sarah told me you were coming here today," the woman went on. "I was going to drop by Stanway House this evening." She smiled again, flashing bright turquoise eyes. Aggie finished drying herself, stepped into her trousers and pulled on a turtleneck and sweater. Then she sat down on a stump and pulled on a pair of waterproof boots. She stood up and grabbed her towel. "We'd better get inside or you'll catch your death."

Joey now trotted along behind Aggie, growing ever more awed. Of course Joey might have recognised her if she had attended Sarah and Henry's wedding, but that was yet another trip she'd had to cancel at the last minute. Now, she couldn't remember why. Something had come up at work, something that had seemed so important at the time.

Joey glanced up at the woman, striding purposefully up the rise toward the trees in front of her. This woman had a title. She had lunch, on the odd occasion, with the Queen! How this squared with the oversized muck boots and swimming alone in the dead of winter, Joey just wasn't sure. But the bone structure of her face was definitely regal and her gait strong and dignified. And if behaving with grace while under pressure signified a healthy dose of class, the title was well earned. Joey herself would have hauled off and smacked any lunatic who came after her the way she had come after Aggie just moments earlier.

"I'm really sorry," Joey began, finding her voice at last as the two of them hopped over the stile at the end of the field, "I'm mortified."

"Don't be absurd," Aggie chided. "There's not many a girl who'd have jumped in to save me."

"I should have seen the clothes. I shouldn't have just assumed – "

Aggie smiled and patted her arm, "It was very noble. We'll say no more about it."

The two continued in silence for a couple of minutes, Joey wishing she didn't have soaking wet clothes, racking her brain for suitable subjects of conversation. What did you talk about with a Lady? Were there subjects that were totally off limits? Were there rules?

As they turned toward the village, their path was blocked by a cow. A cow with friends. So many, in fact, that they blocked the road, preventing Joey and Aggie from moving forward, sideways or any way at all. In the middle of the herd was a red-faced farmer wielding a stick.

"Oh dear," Aggie murmured under her breath. The man pointed his stick accusingly at Joey.

"You!" he bellowed over the chaotic mooing. "I saw you run by. Right through my gates, right through my fields, leaving everything open for all damnation to break loose. Look..." He swept his stick about, gesturing at the bovine chaos. "All this, because of *you!*"

Joey struggled to remain upright while pressing herself up against the wall at the roadside to keep out of the animals' way, wondering whether cows, like horses, might kick out. The countryside was wild; anything was possible.

"Gordon," Aggie's voice soared above the mayhem. "It is entirely my fault. I asked Joey to meet me for a dip and completely forgot to instruct her about your gates. I'm so sorry, I don't know what I was thinking, but Joey, who has just arrived in the country as our guest, couldn't possibly have known."

The farmer's face turned from red to near purple. "It's common sense! Just common sense, pure and simple."

"I'm so sorry," Joey echoed. She was genuinely embarrassed. How many social codes could she break in one day? "I really didn't know."

Aggie grabbed Joey's arm and steered her through the stragglers, now that the cows were gradually being herded back into the nearest field.

"Gordon," she said, "I must make it up to you. I have a new bloom of orchids. You must let me share them with you. I'll come by tomorrow and drop some off."

To Joey's surprise, the farmer appeared to relax. "There's no need for that," he said slowly, pushing the last of the cattle into the field with his stick. They were sturdy animals, Joey noticed, making a mental note of this in case of a future encounter; they didn't seem to mind a good prodding. "But actually it's Tillie's birthday on Monday, you see, so that'd be all right." He swung a metal loop over the gate, securing it tightly.

"Then it's settled," said Aggie. "I'll leave them in your potting shed. They can be *your* surprise. Good evening, Gordon." Aggie had remained utterly dignified, despite her sopping hair and damp, creased clothes.

"Evening to you."

"Gordon's a dear," Aggie whispered when they were out of earshot, "but perhaps not the type to remember his wife's birthday. Maybe he'll win a few points." Aggie hurried Joey along the lane. They eventually arrived before an imposing stone structure seated deep in a grove of mature trees.

"Benbrough House," Joey guessed.

Aggie smiled. "You must come in and warm up, darling. I can't have you catching your death of cold on my behalf."

"Oh, I'm okay, really."

67

"Come along. I am not going to have you laid up with hypothermia. You've got a big job ahead of you and I, for one, am excited to hear about what you plan to do."

Inside, Aggie announced that she would speak to Anna about tea and fetch some dry clothes for Joey to borrow.

"I'll meet you in the library," she said, pointing down a long, shadowy hall.

"All right."

Joey made her way down the hallway. Quietly, she pushed open the heavy, carved door, which squeaked on its hinges, and found herself in a large, square room decorated with an old world grandeur usually reserved for museums. The ceilings were high and embellished with mouldings. The darkly varnished wooden floors were covered here and there with deeply coloured Oriental rugs. Joey was relieved to see that a fire was glowing quietly in the grate. She was freezing.

Most striking of all were the bookcases that reached from the floor to the rafters, packed to overflowing with books old and new: paperbacks, hardbacks, some frayed and peeling at the spine. Joey made the circuit of the room, peering at travel books from all places and ages. Books on Egypt, the pyramids, the deserts, books on African jungles and the rainforests of Borneo, and historical accounts of China and the territories beyond.

Joey couldn't imagine visiting this many places; she'd barely left New York. And here were shelves filled with literature, novels by Austen, Wilde, Hemingway, murder mysteries, encyclopaedias and dictionaries in numerous languages. The number of books was simply dizzying and Joey took a moment to absorb it all. She reached for a leather-bound tome.

"Beautiful, aren't they?" Aggie breezed into the room, carrying an armload of garments. "Here. Put these on. There's a bathroom off the hall."

Joey ducked into the bathroom, peeled off her wet running clothes and dressed in what appeared to be Aggie's tracksuit pants and a soft cashmere jersey. When she went back into the library, Aggie had pulled two armchairs up close to the crackling fire.

"Anna's bringing us tea," Aggie announced, "but we'll have a little of this first to warm the cockles." She reached for a tumbler, one of several on a nearby tray, poured Joey a drink from the decanter on her desk and handed it to her.

"Cheers," she said.

Joey sniffed the drink and sipped it. "It's amazing."

"It's a Cockburn's Special Reserve, 1963, but don't tell Henry. He thinks I'm saving it all for him." Aggie's eyes twinkled.

And I was worried about crow's feet? Joey thought. This woman could not be more beautiful.

Aggie sipped her port, then hopped up abruptly like an excited child.

"Are you into computers, dear?"

"I guess everyone is these days."

"This," announced Aggie, picking up a shiny new laptop from the desk, "was my Christmas present. Isn't it marvellous?"

"I love Macs," Joey said.

"Me too. Henry has just helped me get it all set up. The best thing is that I can get all my pictures on it," said Aggie delightedly, opening up her photo album so Joey could see her photographs of her grandchildren. "I love to keep up with the children. I adore them all. But, I want to show you something else."

Aggie tapped at her computer slowly, like someone just getting used to a new instrument. Finally, she came to a scene of the whitest snow, spread across a small field surrounded by trees, their branches heavy with frost. In the centre was a grey pond, icy clear and deadly still. Joey knew at once that this must be *the* pond – the scene of this afternoon's embarrassing incident.

There in the photo, lined up on an ice-covered jetty, their eyes shining in the winter cold and their swim-caps pulled all the way down on their heads, were five ancient-looking women – all of them dripping wet.

"Lilia, Viv, Gala and Meg," said Aggie.

"Your friends swim in the winter, too?"

"For more than fifty years." Aggie's short dip made more sense now. "You must come with us sometime."

"I'd love to," Joey answered politely, simultaneously thinking, *not in a million years*. Still, it was pretty impressive, friendships lasting fifty years, sustained in part by a shared ritual that many people would consider crazy. Joey wondered whether she and Sarah would still be friends in forty years. Their friendship seemed to have survived nearly a decade of casual neglect, but you couldn't ignore your friends for ever, not if you wanted to have any kind of meaningful relationship. And given her recent track record with her own university room-mates, Eva, Susan and Martina, Joey was going to have to rethink some of her priorities if she wanted to grow old in the intimate company of close girlfriends.

"You're lucky to have such great friends," Joey said quietly.

"Luck has nothing to do with it, dearie. We decided to become friends and to stay friends, through thick and thin, warts and all. You'll no doubt meet them soon. Here, this one is Lilia, Ian McCormack's mother-in-law. He's the caretaker at Stanway House. Have you come across him yet?"

"Yes," Joey said.

"Lovely man… Sad."

"Sad?" Joey gazed at the older woman.

"Ian's wife, Lilia's daughter Cait, was killed in a car crash." Aggie flicked through to the next photo. "Nine or ten years ago, now. Left a little girl, and Ian." Aggie broke off, shaking her head. "Hard. Awfully hard."

"Lily's mother? That's terrible."

"Lilia never talks about Cait. Swims away her pain. This one here – that's Meg Rowland. A great writer and historian." Aggie pivoted around and pulled a dark volume from a shelf behind her chair. "She wrote this."

Joey took the book and glanced at its cover. It featured a sepia photograph of five young boys dressed in the play costumes of swashbuckling adventurers.

"What's it about?" Joey asked.

"J.M. Barrie."

"You're kidding! I've been reading all about him. *What* a fascinating life."

"You know, then, that he often spent his holidays at Stanway. Those boys on the cover, they're the Llewelyn Davies boys – the sons of the family who owned it. Barrie was like a father to them, after their own father died."

"Yes, I've been researching that; we want to honour Barrie somehow in the building."

"Honour him? How?"

"We'll probably design a special room in his name, something that evokes his spirit."

"That sounds… well, lovely. It will certainly please – some people in town…"

"Is the book a biography?" Joey asked.

"Barrie was friendly with the Asquiths, Cynthia and her family," Aggie explained. "Meg got access to all their letters, and she put together a fascinating history of those years. Barrie liked to swim himself, until poor Michael drowned."

"Michael?" Now Joey was confused. Wasn't Michael a character in *Peter Pan*? "From the book?"

Aggie gave an enigmatic shrug. "That's one of the connections she draws, between the 'lost boys' of Peter Pan and the five Llewelyn Davies boys. Barrie was especially close to Michael, who drowned at Oxford just before his twenty-first birthday. Tragic."

"So that's what the book is about?" Joey asked.

"In part," Aggie said. "Give it a go."

"Who's this one?" Joey had another sip of port and pointed at another image on the computer.

"Gala Goldstein."

"There's a name and a half. Gala Goldstein, it sounds like a new hybrid apple."

Aggie laughed. "It does, doesn't it?" Then her expression grew serious, and her next words made Joey regret having joked about the name.

"Gala was in Auschwitz. She saw her entire family killed before her eyes. She was only eight years old at the time. A remarkable woman. Remarkable."

"You're all remarkable," Joey said quietly.

"Remarkably old!" Aggie teased, just as a woman appeared at the door carrying a tea tray. As Aggie stood up to place her computer on the desk, Joey picked up the book to make room for the woman to set down the tray. She opened it to Meg's dedication page.

"*For the J.M. Barrie Ladies' Swimming Society*", she read.

❋ ❋ ❋

Lily must have heard Aggie's car on the gravel, because the Bentley had no sooner deposited Joey and headed back onto the road than she appeared in the doorway of the gatehouse. Joey marvelled again at the colour of the girl's eyes, but Lily wore a look of disapproval.

"Your dog was crying," she said.

"She was?"

"I could hear her when I passed the house."

Joey untied the key from her shoelace and slid it into the lock as Lily crossed the gravel. "Crying or howling?" Joey asked her.

"More like howling," Lily clarified.

Joey nodded and grinned. "She's mad at me. She's letting the world know what a cruel and neglectful owner she has."

"Why?" Lily asked coolly.

"Why what?" Joey pushed open the heavy front door.

"Why is she mad at you?"

"Because I didn't take her running with me."

"Do you usually?"

"Yeah, but she was a little sick last night. It might have been a plate of sausage and eggs I gave her, but I figured I'd let her sleep."

Lily nodded and appeared to be lingering, as though she wanted to keep the conversation going. "Can I come in?" she asked.

Joey paused and turned. "Sure, if it's okay with your dad."

"Why wouldn't it be? I'm not five years old. Anyway, you're not pervy, are you? Or an axe-murderer?"

"Nope."

Lily shrugged. "All right, then."

"All right, then," Joey echoed, as they stepped inside and she closed the door. "I'm sure you know the place a lot better than I do."

"I do," Lily said. She followed Joey into the entrance hall, then paused and glanced around. She shook her head, her expression darkening. "Everything's gone."

"The Tracys took almost everything when they moved out."

"I *know*. I was *here*." Lily gave Joey a very direct look.

Joey held her tongue. As hard as it must be for Ian to deal with the changes that were coming, it had to be even harder for Lily. Lily's tone said she didn't want to be treated as a child, but Joey could sense the pain beneath her adolescent fractiousness.

"Were you close to them?" Joey asked.

"No," Lily fired back. After a moment, she added, "Not to Lord Tracy, anyway. He was always cross about something. Lady Eleanor was okay."

Joey nodded, watching Lily's gaze take in the nearly empty hallway. Joey had thought of the elderly Tracys and all their grown children, grimly packing up everything that meant anything to them and leaving their home to strangers. But this house had been part of Lily's childhood, too.

They crossed the hall to the great staircase. Lily caught her breath.

"What?" asked Joey.

"The princess painting." She pointed to an empty spot over the landing, where the painting in question must formerly have hung.

"Princess Who?" Joey asked.

"She wasn't really," Lily said dismissively, suddenly a teenager again. "Just a girl in a fancy dress. With gorgeous red hair."

"*You're* the one with the gorgeous hair."

"I despise my hair." Lily paused on the steps and turned to Joey.

"What? *Why?* Women where I come from would kill for your colour."

"I'm dying it black next year, when I turn sixteen. When Dad can't stop me."

74

"No!" Joey screeched. "You can't. You have no idea the lengths people would go to to have your highlights – those auburn streaks. Promise me you won't touch it!"

"No way!" Lily said, but Joey thought she caught just the hint of a smile.

They reached the upstairs hall and headed toward Joey's apartment. Tink, having heard footsteps approaching, threw herself into a frenzy of barking. Joey and Lily paused before the door to the apartment.

"Did you know Lady Margaret?" asked Joey.

"A bit."

Hearing their voices, Tink redoubled her barking.

The dog flew out of her crate the moment the door was open and Lily folded herself down onto the floorboards, genuinely smiling for the first time. Tink lapped her face and tried to climb into her lap.

"She's so... *lovely*. So friendly."

Joey smiled. "She likes you. Look, do you mind if I have a two-second shower? I've got pond scum on me."

"Pond scum? You weren't swimming with Granny, were you? She's mad. All those ladies are crazy."

"Your grandmother wasn't there. I'll tell you all about it in a minute."

Lily nodded, glancing around casually, then followed Joey into the bedroom.

"Oh my God," Lily said. "Are those yours?" She dropped to her knees and picked up one of Joey's suede Fendi boots. "I love these boots! I would *kill* for... "

"Try them on," Joey smiled.

"Really?"

"Sure."

Lily slipped out of her trainers and socks. "What size are they?"

"They're a US eight. So … perhaps, seven?"

Joey headed for the bathroom. "I'll make it quick."

"Take your time," Lily said, eyeing Joey's clothes and make-up scattered about.

The shower felt wonderful, and when Joey returned to the bedroom, towel drying her hair, she was surprised to find Lily sitting at the dressing table, experimenting with pots of cream and tubes of colour. She was also wearing Joey's boots.

Lily turned to Joey. "How do I look?"

Like a beautiful little clown, Joey thought.

"Don't ask my opinion if you don't want the truth," Joey said.

"I do!" Lily cried.

Joey nodded, then came over and sat down beside Lily on the vanity bench. She took Lily's chin in her hand and turned her face toward the window, so she could see the make-up in more natural light. She thought for a moment before speaking.

"The liner's too harsh. You need one with a greenish-grey or a plum tint, to bring out the green in your eyes. And the black mascara's too – black. With your colouring, you'd do better with a dark brown."

Lily nodded trustingly, glancing back toward the mirror. "What about the lipstick?" she asked.

It was Joey's new Chanel shade, and it was all wrong on Lily.

"It's not perfect," Joey said kindly. "The cooler tones in this make you look pale, but a coral shade would really bring up the colour in your complexion."

"It would?"

"We could go make-up shopping some time if you like. It helps to have an objective opinion."

"Really? When?"

Joey shrugged. "Any time. How do the boots fit?"

Lily glanced down. "Too big. But I'll grow into them."

"Dream on," Joey teased.

Chapter 9

The Fiat pulled through the archway and in front of the house. Massimo Fortinelli unfolded his generous form from the car and hurried across to greet them. His hair was unruly and streaked with silver, of a length that could either mean that he'd been too busy in the past couple of months to get a haircut *or* that he was intentionally cultivating his resemblance to a sexy Italian movie idol. By contrast, his olive jacket and supple leather boots were rather understated. But they nevertheless whispered a very unambiguous message: when I buy something, I buy the very best.

'Hello, Hello!" Massimo cried, juggling tubes of blue-prints, a phone and a small day planner of cognac-coloured leather. "You are waiting, I'm so sorry. Forgive me!"

"You're not late," Joey said. "You're right on time."

Massimo held up one finger. "First, we turn off the phone." He turned off his phone with a flourish and put it in his pocket.

"What if your office needs to reach you?" Joey asked.

"They wait," Massimo said decisively. "I never take a call when I am with someone else. Well, once in a while from one of my children, if I know it is very important. But now, Miss Rubin — at last we meet."

He kissed Joey warmly, first on one cheek and then on the other. Joey found herself smiling broadly.

"Do you know Ian McCormack?"

"I do not," Massimo replied, taking Ian's hand and pumping it enthusiastically. "But I know what people say of him."

"And what's that?" Ian asked guardedly.

Massimo appeared to regret what he had just thoughtlessly babbled, but he threw up his hands in mock resignation. "That he may be the only person in fifty, no a *hundred* miles, who could have managed both Stanway House –" and here Massimo leaned in as though to whisper in confidence – "and its owners. Pardon me if I am speaking out of turn..."

Ian couldn't help softening slightly. "Not at all."

"A *wonderful* family, wonderful." Massimo continued. "Generous to the schools, magnanimous to the town... but maybe, just possibly a *little* – careful with the wallet, no? When it came to such an important architectural monument?" He gazed rapturously at the house.

"They didn't waste money, I'll say that of them," Ian confirmed.

"Though," Massimo continued, "to be fair, they also did not *do* things we would have to *undo*, correct? So for that – " and here the contractor brought a hand to his heart and raised his eyes skyward – "we give thanks."

Joey smiled and sighed, casting a sideways glance at Ian, who was now staring curiously at the effusive Massimo.

"I thought we could set ourselves up in the kitchen," Joey suggested. "I've got coffee on and I've made a list of all the things we need to discuss. We could get ourselves organised, and then, maybe, Ian, you could give us both the master tour?"

Ian shrugged, willing to go along.

"How many items on the list?" Massimo asked with a grin.

"At least a hundred!"

Ian groaned.

"Not all today," she added quickly. "We have you for two days, right, Massimo?"

"You have me for as long as you need me," he replied courteously, making Joey wonder how she could have ended up employing two such different colleagues. Ian and Massimo were like the proverbial chalk and cheese.

Ninety minutes later, having finished their coffees and prioritised a two-page To Do list, Ian, Massimo and Joey were inspecting the first of the outbuildings slated for reconstruction: what had once been a stone dairy barn at the farthest edge of the estate. This was to be converted into four rental suites.

"There's a lot of rot in that far corner and along the back wall," Ian said, pointing. "The foundation back there is crumbling. And sinking."

Massimo frowned and nodded, crossing the space. Glancing out of a window, he noted: "The stream is so close. The ground is exceptionally wet." He turned to Ian. "How many years since the building was used?"

"Oh, ten, fifteen at least. They used to store farm equipment in here, but when the roof started to go..."

Massimo and Joey glanced up. The roof wasn't threatening to come down on their heads, but patches of grey sky were visible through holes of varying sizes.

"Of course you know what they secured the roof stones with, don't you?" Ian asked. "The original ones?" He eyed Massimo a little suspiciously, and Joey wondered if the question represented a test of some kind.

Massimo smiled. He had a hunch. But he motioned for Ian to explain it to Joey.

"Sheep's vertebrae."

"In Italy, the same," Massimo concurred.

"*What?*" Joey glanced at Massimo, who nodded. "How would that work?"

Massimo nodded toward Ian, letting him explain.

"The shape of it formed a wedge, locking the heavier stones in place. If we took that roof down right now, you'd find the individual vertebrae lined up right along it."

"This man," Massimo said, tapping his temple and nodding at Ian. "I have never met another man in England that knew that. We're lucky to have his help, Joey."

Ian, a little embarrassed, shook off the praise. But Joey thought she glimpsed on his face the hint of a smile.

❋　❋　❋

At two thirty, Massimo had insisted that they all break for lunch at one of his favourite restaurants in the local town – "They serve real Italian food." Ian had tried hard to decline. Lily would be getting back from school in an hour or so and would wonder where he was. But Massimo would accept no excuses. He promised that Ian would be back by four o'clock and proceeded to call the restaurant right then and there to beg them to stay open, and place a lunch order. He was a regular, judging from his ebullient chatter.

Now, though, as Joey and Ian waited for him to join them at the table, his office seemed to have caught up with him. Massimo was pacing on the pavement in front of the restaurant, talking exuberantly with whoever was on the other end of the line. Three plates of appetisers had already been placed on the table: a salad of tuna, egg, olives and potatoes, a bowl of wine-simmered mussels and a toasted ciabatta heaped with tomato, basil and onion. Joey was sipping a glass of white wine and Ian, having eventually given into the idea of a restaurant lunch, had broken down and ordered a glass of Chianti.

"So what do you have against Massimo?" Joey asked quietly.

"I've got nothing against the man," Ian replied, spooning a helping of salad onto his plate.

"That's not the impression I got."

Ian shrugged and had a bite of salad. He shook his head.

"Is there something I should know? *Please!*"

Ian chewed silently for several moments, scanning Joey's expression, before silently putting his fork down and clearing his throat.

"He does very good work," Ian stated flatly.

"Okay. And —"

"And everyone likes his wife."

Joey waited for him to go on. "I'm sensing there's a 'but' coming... Please. I'm asking for your help here."

"All right, all right! It's just that — some of the fellows have had to close up shop."

"Other contractors?"

Ian nodded.

"He forced them out of business?"

"Well, not intentionally. In fact he hired a couple of them — Lucian Bride and Harry Douglass."

"What happened to their companies?"

"They couldn't compete. Everyone started using Fortinelli. Well, not everyone — many of the locals remained loyal — but the new money, the people fixing up second homes, weekend blow-ins from London, he got all that work."

"But why? Was he a lot cheaper?"

"No, I don't think so, not a whole lot, anyway."

"Faster?"

"Faster, yes. And everyone says he keeps a beautiful worksite."

"Meaning?"

"Well, if you drove by at night, it would be all swept up, the rubbish collected and put out of sight, everything just spit-spot, even in the middle of construction."

"I heard that, too. So they just resent him, because he had the *nerve* to be good at what he does? That's his offence?"

"He advertises on the internet."

Joey couldn't restrain a small chuckle. "God, throw the man in jail!"

Ian didn't smile. "It's a small town, Joey. The Douglasses and the Brides go way back. And suddenly, out of the blue, men who've been supporting their families are having to close up shop and go to work for – someone who barely speaks English."

"That's not true, Ian, come on." Joey had a sip of her wine and spooned several mussels onto her plate.

The silence was uncomfortable for several moments. They ate slowly and thoughtfully, not speaking.

"Let me ask you something," Joey finally said.

"Fire away."

"If you had been in charge of preserving and restoring Stanway, if it had been up to *you* to make the decision – " Joey leaned forward, hoping Ian would catch her drift. If he did, he didn't let on. "Would *you* have been confident that Douglass or Bride could handle the job?"

Ian sat back in his chair. "On their own?"

"Or working with sub-contractors, either way. Would you have entrusted a job of this scale to them?"

Ian looked away, uncomfortable at being put on the spot.

"Please," Joey said. "I value your opinion, Ian. If I'm making a mistake here, I really need to know before it's too late."

Ian let out a long sigh. "You're not making a mistake. Around here, he probably *is* the best man for the job. But people still feel bad for Luke and Harry."

"I understand," Joey whispered as Massimo, beaming broadly, appeared at the door and hurried over to their table.

"I'm so sorry. You are eating, I see. *Buono!*" Massimo slid into his seat. "We have no more business during lunch. Not a word. Bad for the digestion."

Massimo unfolded his napkin and laid it in his lap. He took a sip of wine. "We talk only about our lives, everything else but work. Joey, you live in New York, no? Where is your home?"

"On the Upper East Side. Do you know Manhattan?"

"Not so much. But I love it! Have you visited, Ian?"

Ian shook his head.

"You have a house, or an apartment?"

"An apartment. It's the one I grew up in. My mom died a while ago. My father remarried and moved to Florida."

Massimo made a sad face. "So you are all alone in the city? But you have brothers? Sisters, no?"

"My work keeps me pretty busy."

Massimo nodded, smiling. He seemed to find this unusual, if not a little odd, but professional decorum prevented him from asking more personal questions. He nodded, glanced at Ian for several moments, then back at Joey.

He served himself some mussels then passed the plate around. "So delicious," he said. "I am reminded of my honeymoon on Lago di Garda. Now there is a place you *both* must visit!"

Chapter 10

Joey pulled closed the heavy front door and locked it. She had already put in a good day's work and the long lunch had left her feeling full and sleepy. Tempted as she was to go to bed for a nap, she knew she would wake up groggy and grumpy. She decided to go for a run.

She glanced up at the low, grey sky. The cold in England felt different to the cold in New York. She wondered if this was because in New York, she was always in and out of cabs, or sheltered from the worst of the winds by the tall midtown buildings. In any case, the cold here felt damp, penetrating. She took a deep breath and set off at a warm-up pace.

She felt a little guilty leaving Tink behind again, but she'd already taken her out twice today and she wanted to be alone. There was so much to think about: all the subjects that she, Massimo and Ian had discussed during their lunch. Running had always sorted things out for her, without her even being aware that it was happening. Maybe today, it would help her sort out all the conflicting feelings she was having toward Ian. He could be so negative and sarcastic, yet he clearly had a sense of humour. She often felt resentment coming her way, but once in a while, he'd make a comment that suggested he thought she really knew her stuff.

Joey felt her muscles warming and loosening as she picked up the pace, the various knots and kinks starting to soften and relax. The cold, which had at first seemed bitter, soon ceased to bother her at all. She had been running for close to three miles, she figured, glancing at her watch, when she realised she was in the area of Aggie's pond.

She had come to it by a different route, approaching the pond from the north-east rather than the south-west, so she hadn't understood her location at first. But she recognised the field just off to the left and knew she had to be close.

Joey paused, breathing out little clouds of steam. In the near silence, her ear caught the sound of laughter floating on the wind. On impulse, she set off along the well-trodden path that led from the road into a dense stand of trees. The laughter and voices grew louder, and soon she was gazing at the pond from the top of a little hill that overlooked it.

Yesterday, propelled by fear and adrenaline, she hadn't really seen it. All of her focus had been on the woman she believed to be drowning, and after she and Aggie got out of the water, she was too consumed by her own embarrassment and confusion to take in the details of her surroundings.

Now, though, she caught her breath. What stretched out before her almost seemed like a glorious mirage, shimmering and otherworldly. Ringed by green and golden browns and glistening in the few rays of sunlight that had broken through the clouds, the expanse of water, covered in certain areas with a very thin layer of ice, was so still that Nature appeared to be holding hold her breath. Birches and willows stood in attendance.

Joey felt an irrational sense that it was all a dream, that if she ventured one more step, the pond would vanish into thin air. But the voices were real, she was certain of that. And if they were real, then this glorious apparition also had to be.

She headed down the hill, negotiating shrubs and over-hanging branches until the full magnitude of the pond came into view. Joey spotted Aggie immediately. Propelled by powerful crawl strokes, she crossed an ice-free expanse with an elegant glide, a swimming companion by her side. Nearer to the shore, where an ancient, moss-covered dock bobbed in the water, a pixie-like woman ducked and dived. Joey paused and smiled: they looked like three mermaids, playing in the tide. A few steps on, she spied, off to her right, a short, stout woman, breaking up thin sheets of ice on the water's surface with a pole. So that was how they did it.

On a bench near a rough-hewn hut sat another woman, with faded red hair, bundled in something that looked more like a bedspread than an outfit. She seemed to be knitting – a line of thick, cherry wool trailing upward from a bag.

"A jumper," the woman said, as though reading Joey's mind. Only then did she pause in her knitting and look up. "I'm sorry. Are you lost? Can we help you?"

"No," Joey said. "I'm a friend of Aggie's. I was just – "

"The American girl? The one who's going to *ruin* Stanway House?"

Joey was taken aback. "Not ruin it, no, we're just – "

"I was teasing, dear. Of course you won't ruin it! You're bringing the old place back from the brink! I'm Viv, by the way. And you are – ?"

"Joey. Nice to meet you." Joey thought that Viv looked surprisingly young to be one of Aggie's companions. She seemed to be in her early sixties.

"Joey!" Aggie called. Joey turned to see that Aggie had paused briefly and was standing in the water. The elfin lady had also come ashore and was now heading toward them.

"It's positively hot in there today," said the elf casually, as she unbuckled the chin strap of what looked like an ancient bathing cap and peeled it off her head. She extended her hand to Joey.

"Meg," she said, "Meg Rowland."

"The writer. I started your book last night," Joey replied. "I'm really interested in the time Barrie spent at Stanway House."

"Chapters fourteen, sixteen and seventeen," Meg said. "Fourteen is about his relationship with the family, after the First World War, and sixteen and seventeen involve his cricket team, the Allhakabarries. It was quite the crew."

"Really?" asked Joey. She knew that Barrie had been responsible for the construction of a cricket pavilion on the grounds of the estate, but she hadn't known there was a team.

"Oh, yes, all the literary luminaries: H.G. Wells, Conan Doyle, A.A. Milne, P.G. Wodehouse."

"Enough!" said Viv abruptly, finishing her row with a flourish and turning to face Joey. "The girl is here to swim, Meg, not discuss literature. You *are* going in, aren't you?"

"Me? No!... I don't have a suit," Joey replied, grateful for the excuse.

"Don't worry about that," Viv replied. "There are three or four suits inside. We never know when we're going to have visitors."

Joey glanced down at the water. Aggie was back to swimming her seemingly effortless laps. It did look enticing, and the air seemed to have warmed up a little with the appearance of the sun. It *would* be an unforgettable experience. And if five old women were doing it, how hard could it be? She had already braved the water once, when she dived in thinking she was rescuing Aggie, and she didn't remember the water being all *that* cold.

And then there was the *real* reason she found herself actually contemplating going in. Could Joey really back away from this challenge, when women nearly three times her age took it on almost daily?

"Chicken!"

Joey turned, startled. It was the woman with the pole who had shouted this, and now she was grinning.

"That's Gala," Viv explained. "Gala, behave yourself. Give the poor girl time to think!"

"She'll never do it," Gala called, not realising, or maybe knowing full well, that this amounted to a dare. And Joey never refused a dare. "Watch me," she shot back.

She marched to the lapping waters. She could feel an icy breeze skimming the pond's surface. She dipped her hands into the water, and it was all she could do not to screech out loud. These women were out of their minds! The water was so cold that Joey was surprised that it wasn't frozen solid.

Meg was now right beside her. Joey struggled not to show her shock at the temperature of the water.

"Did you know," Meg said, her impish face contorting in thought, "that when an extremity – like the hand – is immersed in cold water, the temperature of the other hand falls in kind?"

"No," Joey replied, "I didn't know that." She wondered idly if a person could get frostbite from being in freezing water.

Meg continued her cheery commentary. "The cold water takes so much heat from the body, that it affects the internal organs through the nervous system. The nervous system responds by sending the same signals to the opposite limb."

Joey looked at her in bafflement. Was Meg trying to talk her out of going in?

"When you're completely submerged," Meg went on, seemingly oblivious, "your lips turn blue, your breathing goes into spasms and your pulse races. That's when all the blood really accumulates in the internal organs. And if you're really, really lucky – and your body can take it – you'll feel a sudden rush of joy and exhilaration. It's pure and utter bliss."

Oh, so that was the point of the story, Joey thought.

"*Of course* her body can take it," Viv scoffed. "She just ran over here! When was the last time you went running, Meg?"

Meg shrugged.

Viv turned to Joey. "Go for it! At the very least, it'll be good for you. I haven't had a cold in forty years!"

Joey threw Viv a sceptical glance.

"Is this truly wise?" A rumbling Scottish burr reached Joey's ears. The final member of the club, who had to be Lilia, had emerged from the hut to join the conversation.

"It's not the North Pole, Lilia," Viv chided.

"She's too thin," Lilia shot back.

"You're just jealous," Viv volleyed.

"I am not!" Lilia replied grandly. "I like a woman who looks like a woman."

"Body mass does make a difference," Meg continued. "What's your BMI, dear?"

"My what?" Joey answered.

"BMI. Body Mass Index. Ration of lean to fat."

"I have no idea," Joey said. "I guess I'm – normal."

"I thought all you Americans were obsessed with numbers; good cholesterol, bad cholesterol! And all the while eating yourselves into early graves!"

"Gala!" Viv admonished. "That's a terrible thing to say!"

"It's true," Gala retorted. "Have you ever been to Florida?'

"It doesn't matter if it's true! It's still rude!"

"I didn't say *she* was fat," Gala protested, pouting.

"Well I should hope not!" Meg had apparently taken on the role of Joey's defender. "Look at the size of her! Anyway, we're supposed to be encouraging her, not scaring her to death."

Joey looked from Meg to Lilia to Gala to Viv. She glanced

down at the water, where Aggie was still in motion. If they could do it, so could she.

"I'll go get a suit," Joey said primly as the ladies broke into cheers.

She walked into the hut, followed by Gala. It was warm inside, with a pleasant smell which came from a wood-burning stove in one corner. Pushed up against the far wall was a small wooden table, and along both sides were rough wooden benches, on which sat piles of the ladies' clothes. For Joey, there was something almost poignant about the sight of these neatly folded piles.

"The suits are in that box," Gala announced, pointing to a wooden crate under one of the benches. She leaned her pole against an old beam and began to undress.

"So you're the official ice-breaker," Joey mused, pulling out of the box one old, misshapen suit after another.

"It doesn't take long to freeze," Gala explained. She removed her long johns, then crossed the floor stark naked. She opened the door of the woodburning stove and loaded several logs into its interior. Joey pretended to concentrate on the suit she had chosen, a stretched-out red tank with blue stripes down the sides. She peeled off her own damp layers and wiggled into the bathing costume. But she couldn't stop stealing glances at Gala's naked body.

Joey had seen plenty of older women without their clothes on at her health club – well-toned, well-preserved, and often professionally sculpted by the surgeon or the trainer – or both. But she had never seen an *ancient* woman naked before. She was positively fascinated. Gala's skin was stretched and thin, and her ample flesh rolled over her hips, sagging down from her belly. Her arms were freckled and strong, yet padded with soft flesh. Her breasts, once obviously bounteous, were sagging, pale, used. Yet Gala's stride was strong and hearty, and she seemed more secure and comfortable in her body than did the nervous, self-conscious socialites in the locker room at home.

Joey pulled her arms through the straps of the suit.

"It's now or never," Gala said, looking up.

"Now!" Joey said energetically.

She followed Gala outside. Viv and Meg cheered as they made their way down to the water's edge and climbed up onto the dock. Lilia was now in the water with Aggie. Joey was debating – dive in headlong or slip into the water gradually?

Gala dived in and swam off. Joey decided to slide in slowly, adjusting to the arctic temperature a little at a time. She sat down on the dock and slipped one foot into the water.

HOLY! SHIT!

"You don't have to if you don't want to," Gala said. She had circled back to the dock and was now treading water about ten feet away. Joey shook her head. *She was doing this!* She shimmied over to the edge of the dock, stood up, took a deep breath and jumped.

The effect was stunning. Joey felt as though she had fallen into a massive container of broken glass. She felt her throat close up and her muscles jerk tightly, her mind freezing over in panic. The water was worse than ice; it was like liquid death. The pain was so intense, like the stabbing of a million ice picks. She couldn't hear. She couldn't speak. All she could do was kick furiously and try to keep her head above water.

For an endless, awful moment, she thought she might drown right then and there. In an English pond, thousands of miles from home. And for no good reason. For a stupid reason! Because she wouldn't walk away from a dare! Because she didn't want to be called a chicken!

She concentrated on breathing steadily, keeping calm. Her panic subsided and her mind began to clear. She began to swim and then to relax into her strokes. Gradually, she felt brave enough to go totally underwater, where she felt a new sensation: the firmness caused by cold water tightening her body. It gave her an immense feeling of strength. She felt like a kid again.

She kicked her way upwards, breaking the surface in a shower of pure ecstasy, her whole body swelling with joy, recklessness, glorious abandon. She shouted to Aggie and the others, but she didn't know if they heard her. Had she ever felt this wonderful before? She didn't think so. She swam out from the shore with a steady stroke, heading for the far bank. She felt wildly, euphorically happy.

She felt at one with the water, with the breeze, with the sky and the day, at one with her life, and with all of life. Everything she could see – the birds, the trees, the sun, the grass – seemed suddenly bright, sharply defined, newly crisp.

She looked up at the moving clouds, the changing shapes. a rabbit, a lion, a bear! She thought of her mother, and of them lying together on a beach, picking shapes out of the clouds. Joey was overcome with a sense of peace, of space, of lightness and freedom. The high she got from running was nothing compared to this. The rush of a business deal, the elation of orgasm, these were pale imitations of what she was feeling right now.

"Joey?" Meg called.

Aggie had finished her swim and was now on the bank with a towel wrapped tightly around her waist. Concern clouded her expression.

"I'm amazed that she's lasted this long," Lilia said frankly, sipping tea from a thermos.

"How long has she been in?" Aggie asked.

"I don't know ten, fifteen minutes."

"It's longer than that," said Meg.

"Joey!" Aggie shouted. "Joey! Come back!"

Joey heard Aggie's voice and turned to see her waving from the bank, the others at her side. They were motioning for her to return to shore. But Joey didn't feel like coming in yet; she fought a fleeting wave of annoyance as she turned and began to swim toward the shore. First they badger her to get in, and then, the minute she's in, they're badgering her to get out!

"Time to come OUT, Joey. Now!" Aggie yelled.

Meg jumped to her feet. "Now! Hurry. You could lose a hand!"

Joey didn't hear their words, but she sensed their anxiety and understood that it was urgent – no, *extremely* urgent! – that she get out of the water right away. Could there be a shark? No, that was crazy: this was a pond, not the ocean. But *something* was wrong. She started to feel panicky as she struggled to reach the shore.

She was suddenly dead tired. She seemed to be in a dream, trying desperately to make progress with limbs that would barely move.

All of the women were clustered on the dock when she finally placed one foot on the ladder and reached for the rails. To her dismay, Joey found that neither arm nor foot responded to her will. Looking down, the foot she had attempted to place on the stepladder was hanging uselessly in the water. She reached for the rails, but her arms grazed the metal with all the force of a gentle caress. Somewhere, in the distant nerve endings of her fingers, she felt the metal of the pole, but even as she tried to close her hands around it, she found herself pitching backward into the water.

This, she realised, was not right. She now could feel absolutely nothing.

"Aggie," she gasped, in a voice that came out in shivers. She had no control at all. Everything was backwards. Her face muscles contracted whenever she tried to speak, but in her arms and her legs, she could feel nothing.

"Aggie! Help me!"

At once, the women were organised like an aqua-rescue team. Aggie and Lilia in the water, Gala and Viv prepared to receive Joey on the dock and Meg on her way to the hut for blankets and towels. Within moments, Joey was safely in the clutches of strong arms, and then she was on the wooden platform. Together, the women all but carried Joey to the hut, and sat her down on one of the benches.

Meg wrapped her in warm towels. As the women fussed and chattered around her, Joey found it hard to concentrate. She felt removed, but also almost exhilarated with exhaustion. As she sat before the burning stove, a slow tingling sensation started creeping up her toes, then her feet, then her legs "That stinging," Meg said, as Joey shook out her hands, "is just the nerve endings. It means everything has survived, and your limbs and all your digits are still healthy. That's how they test for frostbite. If your fingers and toes didn't sting, they'd be headed for the chopping block."

Aggie wrapped another blanket around her shoulders. "It was a grand thing to do, my dear, staying in that long."

"It was a foolish thing to do," Lilia added curtly, handing Joey a cup of tea. "You could have died if we hadn't got you out when we did!"

"I didn't know," Joey whispered. "I had no idea. It felt – wonderful."

"Let's not be overly dramatic, Lilia," Gala said. "We should have warned her. If it's anyone's fault, it's ours."

Viv handed Joey the lid of a flask. "Drink this, darling. It'll do you the world of good."

Joey took a sip of hot whisky. God, did it feel good. Gradually, her skin and muscles were reawakening in the soothing warmth.

"I'm sorry,' Joey said. "I didn't know."

"And that is our fault, not yours," Aggie decreed.

"It was completely amazing," Joey whispered. "It was like – nothing I've ever felt."

Aggie nodded.

"We know," Meg agreed, and the others nodded in unison.

Joey gazed at each in turn, wondering how they could be so calm in the face of the profound experience she now shared with them. "It's the most extraordinary sensation I think I have ever had."

"No it isn't, dear," Aggie said evenly.

"It is!" Joey insisted. "You need to keep this a secret! Or tell the whole world! I'm not sure which."

The women giggled and smiled.

"We'll keep that under consideration," Lilia announced.

"We'll take a vote," Meg added.

"We will *not*," opined Viv, pouring a little more hot whisky into the cup and handing it to Joey. Joey sipped it gratefully, its warmth spreading within her. She gazed around, and for a moment she saw in the women around her the twenty-year-olds they once had been: brash and beautiful, proud, vain, anxious to live passionately and with purpose, desperate to love and to be loved.

Had life favoured them with luck? Yes and no. One could hardly call internment in a concentration camp a stroke of luck. One could only label the loss of a child, even a grown child, a stark and utter tragedy. But they had loved, these beautiful, proud, ancient women, and they had been loved. *That was something*, Joey thought.

Maybe the most important thing.

❋　❋　❋

Aggie threaded her arm through Joey's as they walked across the great field.

Behind them, Viv, Gala, Meg and Lilia weaved their way through the frozen grasses.

"Thank you, all of you," Joey said, stopping at the edge of the field. "I haven't felt this good in – maybe ever."

"How sad!" Viv quipped, mimicking a glum face. "You need to be having more fun!"

Aggie gave Joey's arm a squeeze.

"Look at her skin," Meg said. "She's just glowing."

"I'm hooked," Joey responded. "I really am. I can't wait to do it again. Are you there every day?"

"Rain or shine," Aggie replied.

"Or snow!" Viv said brightly. "It rarely amounts to much."

"Then – maybe I'll see you – tomorrow," Joey suggested gently. She hoped to hear a chorus of "Yes, please, join us!" but Lilia seemed to be ignoring her and Gala was distracted by some mallards winging their way over the distant hedgerows.

"Lovely, darling," Aggie said. "Shall I give you a lift to Stanway House?"

Joey's first impulse was to refuse, but she felt chilled and a little shaky. The sensation had returned to her arms and legs, but she didn't have the energy to run home and certainly didn't relish the idea of making her way back to the house, wearing only her lightweight running clothes. She glanced around at the women and wondered whether they were going home to husbands, companions or empty houses. The thought that they might be facing long evenings alone caused her to blurt out impulsively:

"I have an idea. Could I take you all to dinner? If you don't already have plans, I mean. I'd love to repay your kindness and – well, I'm pretty sure I owe you my life."

"You don't owe us a thing," Lilia snapped.

"I never eat in restaurants," Gala announced. "I don't trust other people's cooking."

"*You* don't trust other people, period," Meg replied.

"I most certainly do," Gala said grandly.

Meg shook her head. "I don't tend to eat proper dinner any more. I don't feel it's good for the constitution. I have tea and two seven-minute eggs at half six, hot chocolate before bed, and a ploughman's breakfast, every morning."

"Thank you for the full report," Viv teased, a note of irony in her voice. "Would you care to tell us how you sugar your tea?"

"I don't," Meg crowed with satisfaction. "You know that."

"As you can see, we'd probably kill each other if we spent any more time together," Viv confided with a grin.

Lilia snorted, "Speak for yourself."

"You'll come again," Viv said confidently to Joey. "We can do our visiting by the water."

She seemed to be speaking for all of them, as they nodded and waved and trudged toward their waiting cars, parked at skewed angles just off the road. It was late afternoon and the gathering darkness made it feel, once again, like mid-winter. Joey slid in beside Aggie and was grateful when the car began to warm.

Chapter 11

Saturday dawned clear and cold. Sarah and her family had arrived from London late the previous night. Perhaps wanting to avoid any further missed connections, Sarah had called Joey at about ten the night before to finalise plans for their morning together. A leisurely lunch wasn't going to be possible, given the schedule of the pony club rally, but they'd have a good two or three hours in the morning to visit a couple of places Sarah really wanted Joey to see.

Joey would just as soon have whiled away the morning in a cosy village café, drinking coffee together, but Sarah seemed determined to play the role of tour guide. Maybe, thought Joey, Sarah wanted to prove that she still cared about things other than the feeding of four little Howards.

By the time Joey heard the crunch of Sarah's tyres on the gravel out front, she had been up for over two hours. She had taken Tink for a long ramble in the woods behind Stanway House, a jaunt enlivened by Tink's pursuit of several squirrels who'd been unwise enough to dart into sight.

On hearing Sarah's knock, Joey hurried down the winding staircase and pulled open the heavy front door. Sarah was smart in wellingtons, soft wool trousers and a green Barbour jacket. She wore a faint dash of mauve lipstick that brought some colour to her cheeks.

"You cut your hair!" Joey screeched.

"You like it?" Sarah asked uncertainly.

"It looks fantastic.." And it did. While Sarah hadn't gone so far as to add any tint or streaking, the shoulder-length bob was gracefully layered in waves around her face. "Turn around," Joey ordered.

Sarah turned, a little self-consciously.

"I love it, honey. It really looks great."

"I was so embarrassed."

"About what?"

"The nest." Sarah looked hurt.

"I'm so sorry. I should never have said that."

"No. You *should* have! That's what real friends do. So, as you can see, I've made a bit of an effort."

As though to cut off any further discussion of this obviously painful moment, Sarah stepped into the hallway and glanced around. "This is where Aggie was married, you know."

"She was? Here?"

"Well, in the estate chapel. But the reception was in this room here."

Sarah led Joey across the stone expanse and into a large room lined with mullioned windows.

Joey gazed around and could instantly imagine it all — hundreds of candles flickering in the candelabra and sconces, the strains of chamber music echoing through the cavernous space.

"They used to have Manorial courts here, too," Sarah said quietly.

Joey moved about the space, her running shoes squeaking on the floor. It was majestic. She could easily imagine Aggie gliding around the room in a beautiful dress, rays of sunlight catching the motes of dust high above.

"People think it's bad luck, though."

"What is?" Joey asked.

"Getting married here."

"Really?" This wasn't good news. The Apex Group, she knew, were hoping to market Stanway House as the perfect place for a wedding. They'd drawn up all sorts of packages, from renting the entire manor and the services of its staff for the weekend, to having a simple ceremony and reception in one of the smaller rooms. Smaller being a relative term.

"Why?" Joey asked.

"There've been a lot of weird stories. Like this one couple, who got married here some years ago. They were friends of Alasdair Tracy. The bride's first husband was killed in a car crash and she met this new guy. It was a gorgeous day. The sun was out and the guests were scattered across the lawn with their champagne glasses, then, right at the end of the reception, the bride looked out towards the fountain, where everyone was gathered, and she saw the ghost of her dead husband. Just standing there, silent and watching. She ran through the crowd, but by the time she got to where he was standing, he'd disappeared. And ever afterwards she was convinced he was living with her and her new husband, always in their house. It was like there were three of them in the marriage."

Joey looked pensive, but, despite her best efforts, began to laugh.

"You don't actually believe that," she said.

"I most certainly do!" Sarah replied.

❈   ❈   ❈

"Aggie swam the Channel?" Joey cried in disbelief. She and Sarah had left the car by the side of the road and were making their way along a path that led to a thicket of trees.

"She didn't tell you? She was seventeen. She's done it twice since then."

That explains some things, Joey thought. Now if that had

been Joey, she mused, she would have been broadcasting her achievement from the rooftops.

"For their first anniversary," Sarah went on, a little out of breath, "Richard – that was her husband – hired a yacht and had them taken across the Channel, along the exact route Aggie followed when she swam it."

"That's so romantic."

"He was. Runs in the family."

They ducked under an arch formed by trees and brambles, and emerged onto open ground. Sarah pointed to a spot on the top of a nearby hill.

A great Gothic tower composed of grey stone stretched up from the earth. Even from this distance, Joey could tell that it was at least three storeys high. Turrets adorned its jagged parapet, and from one, a colourful flag fluttered gaily.

"That's amazing," Joey said.

"Over two hundred years old."

"Looks as solid as a rock." Joey scrambled up the hill. "It amazes me how well these builders understood their materials, the physics of the job, the stresses of exposed locations like this. They were geniuses."

Sarah hurried to catch up with her. "Henry brought me here just a couple of weeks after I arrived," she said. "It was up there – " she paused, pointing to the tower – "that I knew I was in love with him. And with England."

"Who built it?" Joey asked as they reached the heavy vaulted door.

"The sixth Earl of Coventry."

To Joey's surprise, they were able to push the door inward and enter the tower.

"They just leave it open like this?" Joey asked.

"Aggie made a call. Officially, it's closed until April."

"What was it used for?" Joey asked. "A lookout?"

"The Earl's fiancée lived some miles away," Sarah explained. "During their engagement, he built it so he could burn a fire on the roof that she would be able to see from her house. It was his way of letting her know that he was thinking about her."

Joey stared up at the ancient stone, the polished wood. Sarah headed for the curving interior stairway that would bring them to the top of the tower and Joey followed.

"And while she's a county away," Joey said, "locked up in her father's house, gazing off at the fires, he's right here having a final fling, whooping it up with all the fair young maidens."

Sarah stopped on the stairs and turned, narrowing her eyes.

"You are such a cynic."

"No, I'm not," Joey smiled.

"You've been living in New York too long."

"You've been living in Camelot too long!"

Sarah gave Joey a wry grin then led her up the rest of the stairs and into a large, beautifully furnished room.

"This," Sarah said grandly, "is the Morris room." She headed straight for the doorway on the far side, "Named after William Morris, the writer and designer. He used the place as a country retreat, did some of his best work here. You should see his designs, he was one of the greatest Pre-Raphaelite — "

"I know who William Morris is, Sarah," Joey said, struggling to contain a hint of annoyance.

"You do?"

"I *did* go to design school. You can buy note cards of his motifs in virtually any stationery store. They still use his wall-paper patterns."

"Right, sorry..." Sarah reached the doorway that opened

onto a balcony. She beckoned Joey over. "Look, you can see the whole county from here."

Joey crossed the room and stood in the doorway. Bends and dips of land stretched out before her, green fields and trees with crimson leaves, rolling streams bisecting the landscape and what, from this height, looked like toy towns nestled neatly between the hills.

"Nice, huh?" Sarah threaded her arm through Joey's and drew her close. "Henry brought me right to this balcony. I'd been here a couple of weeks; I was really missing New York, missing you."

The wind stung their cheeks and made Joey's eyes water as she gazed out across the fields.

"I missed you, too," she said, acutely aware of what an understatement this was. From the time that Joey was four years old, when she and her parents moved into her current apartment, Sarah had been like Joey's other half. Except for the two weeks every summer that Joey spent at camp and the two that Sarah spent on the Delaware shore, they were rarely apart.

After Joey inherited the apartment, Sarah all but moved in, cooking them delicious casseroles that filled the place with the smell of home. And after Sarah left for London, for good the last time, Joey had drifted tearfully around her silent flat for days, inconsolable. Losing Sarah had been almost as hard and disorienting as losing her mother.

"We stood right here," Sarah said. "Henry told me the story of the lovesick Earl and I asked him, 'Would you do the same for me, Hens?'"

"You didn't!" Joey said wryly. "You should never ask a man something like that. Either he'll lie, or he'll give you an answer you don't want to hear."

"Would you shut up and listen?"

Joey grinned, turning her face back to the wind.

"'No,' he said, just like that. 'No, I wouldn't – '"

"I told you," Joey crowed.

"'*Because* I refuse to be that far away from you. Ever. Don't go back to New York, please. Stay. And marry me.'"

Joey shook her head and grinned.

"You really are made of stone!" Sarah cried.

Joey laughed, pulled away and walked toward the edge of the balcony. "Most people I tell that story to think that it's the most romantic thing they've ever heard."

"Most people you tell that story to are country bumpkins. With husbands who *didn't* take them to the top of a tower to soften them up before they popped the big question."

For a moment, Joey thought Sarah was laughing, too, but when she turned to look at her friend, she realised that she was anything but amused.

"You think Henry felt that he had to flatter me? Tell the ditsy little woman a pretty story before going in for the   ?" Sarah broke off.

"No, I'm not saying that. It's just that, well, Henry *is* a lawyer, Sarah. He knows how to make a case."

Sarah glared at her. "I don't get you sometimes, Joey. You're your own worst enemy." Abruptly, she turned to head back inside.

"What do you mean by that?"

Sarah paused and looked back. "You give people so little credit. You're always questioning everyone's motives, as though you just can't imagine someone doing something out of simple human kindness or generosity of spirit." Sarah wheeled around and disappeared into the darkness of the tower.

"Sarah!" Joey followed her inside. "I'm not criticising Henry. I love Henry!" And now a dark thought occurred to her. "Is everything okay with you two?"

Sarah stopped walking and looked Joey in the eye.

"It's more than okay. This is not about Henry. Or me."

"Then what *is* it about?"

"It's about you!" Sarah shot back. "I want to see you happy."

"You think I don't want to be happy?"

"I want to see you – *with* someone. And you don't make that easy."

Now tears pricked at the back of Joey's eyes. Did she *really* have to spell this out? Could Sarah possibly *not* understand what she had been through in the past six months?

"*He* left *me*, Sarah," she blurted out.

"I know. I understand what you've been through. But if you wall yourself off from every well-meaning gesture and innocent pleasantry, you might scare away the real thing."

"I had the real thing," Joey insisted.

"No you didn't," Sarah said softly.

❋   ❋   ❋

They were quiet on the drive to Snowshill Stables. Once again, without meaning to at all, Joey had managed to upset her friend. In Sarah's defence, Joey thought, gazing out at the passing countryside, it would be hard *not* to be romantic when surrounded by hills and trees and fields so vibrant that they looked like an illustration from a children's book.

Of course, Sarah had been influenced by the ancient beauty of the landscape. Who wouldn't be? Her old friend hadn't disappeared; somewhere inside the jolly, competent British "mum" had to be Joey's "New York Sarah", the Sarah who sat around in her pyjamas, laughing at corny love stories on late night TV and picking peanut brittle from her braces. Joey sighed as she gazed off at the dusky hills. She missed that person. She hadn't even realised how *much* she missed her until she arrived in England and met not the old pal she was hoping to see, but someone else entirely.

They pulled into the car park of Snowshill Stables, where the children had spent the morning riding. The wind had got up, blowing ominous clouds over the expansive grounds. Joey had been dreading this all morning. She would have given anything to get out of it. Apart from Tink, who was probably starting to get restless back at Stanway House, Joey was not a huge fan of animals, or of standing around in the freezing cold watching small children ride them.

Joey trudged behind Sarah with all the enthusiasm of a woman on her way to have a root canal. They wove through the huddles of parents and grandparents, all dressed against the cold. Few looked happy, Joey noted; she obviously wasn't the only one who would have preferred to be inside with a hot cup of tea — or something stronger — in front of a roaring fire.

The atmosphere was alarmingly tense as pint-sized equestrians put their ponies and horses through their paces. She could hardly stand to watch as children who looked no older than four held on for dear life while their mounts cantered, trotted and pranced. Joey glanced around at the spectators, half hoping that a little altercation might break out and relieve the oppressive tension. But good manners seemed to be holding the crowd in check.

"Henry!" Sarah called, glimpsing her husband at the edge of the ring. She grabbed Joey's hand and pulled her through the people to where Henry was standing. Joey felt embarrassed, being dragged through the masses like one of Sarah's children, but she didn't protest.

"We didn't miss it, did we?" Joey scanned the faces of the children in jodhpurs and riding helmets.

"Chris is doing the two foot six course," Sarah explained,

having located her son at the other side of the ring. "Matilda and Timmy are trying the mini round."

Henry bent down and produced a wide homemade banner with the kids' names scrawled across it. This struck Joey as embarrassingly hokey and partisan. Weren't grown-ups supposed to cheer for all the children, and not just their own?

"Kill it, Chris! You can do it!" Henry screamed.

"You're number one!" Sarah chanted. "You're number one!"

Joey glanced around uncomfortably and took a couple of steps backward as Henry and Sarah continued to cheer and holler. She would have died if anyone had done that to her when she was a kid. Between the shouting and the banner, she wouldn't be surprised if the kids refused to get in the car with them for the trip back home. At a moment when Sarah was shouting so passionately that it looked as though she might burst a vein, Joey slipped back through the crowd, searching for a spot on one of the benches near the barn.

"Had enough?" she heard someone ask. Peering at the tall, elegant woman in the headscarf and muddy boots, Joey realised that it was Aggie. She smiled, headed over and sat down beside her.

"You're a good grandmother," Joey said.

Aggie rolled her eyes and shook her head. "I adore the children, I really do. And I like coming out to support them. But the shouting and screeching is so ludicrous. I can't stand to be in the middle of it."

"I thought it was just me," Joey said.

"No, it's not," Aggie replied. "And the whole rigmarole is *endless*. One thinks it's nearly over and another lot trot up! I've been here for three hours… I really should have my head examined."

Their conversation was interrupted by a sudden gasp from the crowd. Joey and Aggie stood up to see what was going on. A horse had refused at a jump, and its young rider had landed bottom-first in a puddle. Joey drew in a sharp breath and felt her stomach muscles tense.

"She's fine," Aggie said. "It's terribly good for the character, all this mucking about in the wet and the mud. I'm all for it. I only wish I didn't have to sit here and watch."

"Your ears must have been burning this morning," Joey said as they both sat down.

"How so?"

"Sarah told me you swam the English Channel. I can't believe you didn't mention it after I all but *drowned* you trying to — *save* you!"

Aggie gave just a hint of a smile. "It's not the sort of thing I mention when I first meet someone."

"That's really impressive. Three times!"

"You run, don't you?" Aggie asked.

Joey nodded. "Almost every day. I love it."

"Have you even run a marathon?"

"I think about it, every so often. I've just never wanted to devote that much time to training. It's like having another job."

"It would be a thrill, though, wouldn't it?" Aggie asked. "To set a goal like that for yourself and achieve it."

"It would. No question. I should think about it."

"You should," Aggie said, turning to focus again on the action in the ring.

They sat in companionable silence. At the age when Joey had been choosing her major and foisting herself on anyone who could help her build a network of connections, Aggie had been striking out from the white cliffs of Dover, all greased up and ready to go. Joey could hardly imagine navigating the choppy, freezing shipping lanes of the English Channel. Then again, Joey had always had to work for a living and Aggie had not. There were a lot of adventures one could have in life when one came from a background like Aggie's.

"Did your husband really charter a yacht on your anniversary so you could sail along your route?"

"He did," Aggie answered simply. She smiled at the reminiscence and sighed.

"It was fabulous, as was he. I never saw myself marrying, really. Or rather, I should say, I had never given a moment's thought to it, one way or the other.

"But you can't control everything, all of the time. Sometimes fate just throws you something – or someone – out of the blue." Her eyes twinkled. "I take my hat off to Independent You. Unfortunately, we can't all of us be fabulously single. Times were different when I was young."

Before Joey could react, they both caught a glimpse of Sarah jumping up and down like a rabbit, and Henry cheering by her side.

"Looks like we'd better get up there," Aggie said, rising with ease from the bench and moving toward the crowd of spectators. "After all this time waiting, we don't want to miss the five minutes that matter."

Joey followed her toward the crowd, puzzled by the tone of Aggie's words. Did she regret her marriage and family life? Joey peered over the heads of men and women as Aggie manoeuvred toward the front.

It was Matilda who had cantered out proudly. She looked tiny in the ring, as her fat little pony gave a swish of its tail. As her name was called, she kicked her pony forward.

Her face was pale and tight with concentration. Sarah let out a cheer and Henry called out his daughter's name. A woman in the front row, who, in Joey's opinion, looked rather horsy herself, turned around and scowled. Joey scowled back.

"Go, Matilda! Come on, girl. We love you, honey!"

Sarah and Henry were shouting at the top of their lungs. To Joey's surprise, far from dying of shame, Matilda looked up, scanned the faces in the crowd, found her mother and father with their horrendous banner, and broke into an enormous grin. Then, with a swift kick of her foot, she goaded her pony into motion.

They all held their breath as Matilda began her routine. So did the crowd, it seemed, and soon Joey understood why: all of the other parents and grandparents, aunts and uncles, *wanted* Matilda to fail. There was an audible groan each time Matilda cleared a hurdle. Henry and Sarah, intentionally oblivious, just cheered more loudly.

Joey watched it all with a strange feeling of detachment. It was not that she wasn't happy for them all, just, this wasn't her world, this cosy little universe of family. It was so — embarrassingly intimate.

And yet.

There was something so openhearted and genuine about Henry and Sarah at that moment. They would have done anything to support their little girl, to support all of their children. And was this not what it was all about, really? Not just cooking and nursing and overseeing homework, scolding and washing and teaching and guiding. Most importantly, it was about this kind of affection and love.

Matilda was a good little rider. Even Joey, who knew nothing about showjumping, was wowed. Having cleared three jumps, a white gate and a cross-bar, she and her pony cantered the length of the ring toward a tricky double.

Joey glanced over at Sarah, who looked like she might actually burst with pride. Henry was concentrating fiercely, as though he could will Matilda to success. Aggie grinned from ear to ear.

Oh God, Joey thought, as Matilda turned to face the jump. Don't let her hesitate. Let her make it.

The crowd had gone silent. Joey could almost feel the hostility of the crowd and could barely keep herself from shouting, "What is *wrong* with you people? She's a baby!"

In truth, though, there was nothing baby-like about Matilda at this moment. Features set, eyes on the final bar, she kicked her pony toward it, and with a precise thwack of her crop, sailed over it, landing safely on the other side.

Henry and Sarah burst into wild cheering. Joey joined in the clapping, and Aggie beamed and waved toward her grand-daughter. The rest of the crowd applauded half-heartedly.

Matilda grinned at her parents, slid off the pony and led him by the reins to the edge of the ring closest to where Sarah, Henry and Aggie were standing. Joey drifted away. She wasn't a member of this family. Until two days ago, she could have passed Matilda on the street and not known who she was. This was a moment that belonged to the family, whether Joey liked it or not.

She felt for her BlackBerry in her pocket. What had people done before the invention of personal technology to make themselves look busy in awkward situations?

She had two or three dozen new emails. She scanned the subject lines quickly: almost all were from work and could wait until tomorrow or the next day. Her hopes were raised by several addresses she recognised but couldn't immediately place, but none of these emails turned out to be very interesting. An acquaintance she had little in common with was inviting her to join a book group. *No.* Another was requesting – for the third time! – that she sign up for Facebook. *Arrgh*. There was a reminder that she had an appointment to have her teeth cleaned in three weeks. *Great.* And spam that had somehow gotten through her filter: ads for rodent removal, drugs for female "pleasure enhancement" and offers of deep discounts on online photo reproduction.

"Joey, I simply cannot believe you!"

Joey looked up to see Sarah glaring in her direction. Sarah's nostrils were flaring as they had when she was a teenager and was about to have a tantrum.

"You're checking emails?" Sarah screeched. "For God's sake, do you ever stop thinking about yourself?"

Joey was shocked. She hadn't been thinking about herself, she had been trying to look busy. And what did Sarah expect? They'd been hanging out in the bloody cold for close to two hours. Was this Sarah's idea of *fun*?

But before she could reply, Sarah turned away, shaking her head. Joey put her BlackBerry in her pocket, but she knew her cheeks were reddening. She had been stung by the bitterness in her friend's voice. She retreated to the bench near the barn, and in moments, Aggie was settling in beside her.

"Hot toddy, dear? You look like you could use it."

To Joey's surprise, Aggie extended the lid of a flask to Joey and produced a small plastic cup for herself. "Down the hatch!" she ordered. Joey obeyed, feeling the warmth spread from her mouth to her throat to her chest.

"Ignore her," Aggie said. "She gets tense at these things. I can see how close you two are."

Joey gave her a look. *Close?* She felt a million miles away from her friend.

"You are," Aggie insisted. "You fight like sisters. No holds barred. Mere friends don't fight that way."

Joey was grateful for her words and would have liked to have talked with Aggie about this, but she wasn't sure she felt comfortable discussing Sarah with her own mother-in-law. If anything she said got back to Sarah, Joey would have even more problems on her hands than she did now. She felt it best to change the subject.

"You sounded – *mixed*. Before."

"Mixed?" Aggie said. "About what?"

"Marriage," Joey whispered.

Aggie nodded and paused to think before she spoke. Finally she turned and looked at Joey fondly.

"I loved my husband. I love Henry and Sarah and I adore the children. I can barely imagine what my life would have been like if I had never married. But I rather think I would have liked being a working girl in the big city."

"It has its joys," Joey said quietly. "And its difficulties."

"Like everything in life," Aggie mused. "What made you choose the work you do? I gather you're very successful."

"Oh, it looks that way, does it? Well, I'm glad."

"No false modesty, dear," Aggie chided. "Don't diminish your achievements."

Joey looked up quickly. "I answered an ad in the *New York Times* the week after I graduated from NYU. I had student loans to pay off and I had to support myself. I came in at the ground level of my firm, as an assistant to one of the partners. I've been there ever since."

"But how did you get into what you're doing now?"

"They paid for me to go to graduate school. I took two courses a semester, for five years. Got a combined architecture and design degree."

"Impressive. I admire a woman who's worked her way up. You must be very proud of yourself."

Joey shrugged. "I work hard – and sometimes, I have to admit, I resent the fact that I seem to have to work harder than the men in my business just to stay at the same level…

But I really like what I do. I get restless if I'm not busy. I don't like that about myself, but it's true. I don't do well on vacations."

"No, I can see that."

"Really?"

Aggie nodded kindly. "You remind me of myself."

"I'm flattered. But to be honest, I don't see the resemblance. I'm a bit of a loner."

"So am I."

"I think I sometimes scare men off." The words had slipped out before Joey had time to censor herself. What had made her say this?

"Many men like to be or to think that they're smarter than their women," Aggie responded.

Joey smiled. "I'm really happy at work. I love seeing old spaces and figuring out how to preserve the beauty of what they have, what they are. It's creative, yet really grounded in the world. I can't think of anything I'd rather do."

"You're lucky to feel that way. And they're lucky to have you."

Joey grimaced.

"And is there a special someone in the picture?" Aggie surprised her by asking. "Man or woman. I don't care a whit either way."

Joey paused before answering. "There was. A man."

"Past tense?"

"He fell in love with someone else."

Aggie glanced over, compassion in her eyes. "Well, the heart wants what it wants. Or perhaps another organ."

"Exactly!" Joey squealed.

Aggie shook her head, as though she were not at all surprised. "His loss, my dear. But I'm sorry he hurt you. I know what that feels like."

"You do?"

Aggie nodded seriously and remained silent for several moments before speaking. "When I swam the Channel, the first time, it was the culmination of a long – relationship. He was the first person I'd see in the morning – at five am – every day, up and training in the dark and the cold, all through the winter. He was my coach, my teacher, my inspiration. He told me I could do it and I believed him. Until I learned to believe in myself.

"In the aftermath of all the excitement, I came to realise that the man had changed. The glow in his eyes was gone. All his enthusiasm for our joint project – and for me – just evaporated. Turned out it had never been about *me*, or us. It had all been about him. He described for the press how he had plucked me from obscurity, a woman with no natural talent, no aptitude at all. He was Henry Higgins and I was Eliza Doolittle – a mere project, a lump of clay. Three weeks later, he found himself a new protégée."

Joey shook her head. "You're kidding."

"I'm not. I used to wonder whether I married Richard to get away from him. I stopped swimming. I didn't go into the water for years. But now I realise how much I learned from that narcissist. I learned to tell the difference between a man who loved me for *himself*, and a man who loved me for *me*. Richard didn't care about what I *did*. He cared about who I was."

"But you swam the Channel two more times. What got you back into the water?"

"My friends."

"The ones you swim with now?"

Aggie smiled. "The very same."

Joey had assumed that Sarah and her family would be spending the whole weekend at Benbrough House, and that one way or the other, she would be folded into the plans for dinner at Aggie's or out at a restaurant. But as soon as the pony trials were concluded, Henry and Sarah packed everyone into the Range Rover for the two-hour trip back to London. They'd spent nearly every weekend in the country since October, Sarah explained, and she and Henry had plans for Sunday in town. Joey wasn't sure she believed her. She couldn't shake the feeling that the abrupt departure had more to do with the tension between her and her friend.

"I'm sorry," Joey had whispered as Sarah turned for a goodbye hug.

"Me, too. I'm sorry I got mad."

"I was trying to stay out of the way," Joey explained. "It was a family moment. I didn't feel I belonged in the middle of it."

Sarah's bittersweet expression only grew darker. She shook her head.

"What?" Joey pressed. "What is it?" When Sarah didn't respond right away, Joey felt her frustration rising. "I feel like I can't do anything right. No matter what I say, you get upset with me. Everything I do is wrong."

"You were always like — my sister," Sarah said haltingly. "My one and only. And I thought I was yours. If that doesn't qualify as family, I don't know what does."

They hugged each other tightly, both aware that whatever had to be resolved between them was not going to be resolved here and now. Not with a car full of hungry, bickering children and a husband who appeared anxious to get on the road.

"I'll call you," Sarah said as she stepped into the car and

closed the door. Joey nodded and waved until the car was out of sight, then accepted a ride from Aggie back to Stanway House.

Chapter 12

On Monday morning Joey settled down to do some work on the building plans. She needed to adjust some of her drawings to take in certain changes suggested by Massimo on his last visit. And she needed to do some thinking in preparation for a trip she was making to London the following week, to meet the English management company who were handling the renovation of Stanway on behalf of the Tracy family. They'd been pressing her for resolution on the concept for the Barrie Suite. It was going to be central to their marketing scheme, the opportunity for guests to stay in the room where he might have slept.

Happy to be able to throw herself into work as an antidote to her confusion and unhappiness about Sarah, she began to research J.M. Barrie online and also to read some of the books she had brought from New York. Joey had long loved *Peter Pan*, but not until now had she seriously started to understand the man behind the book. She learned that James M Barrie lived alone; he had only been married once, for a brief time. But his world was rich and filled with love and kindness and friendship. His life had truly been a brilliant design for living.

Among his friends was Sir Arthur Conan Doyle, whom he had met when they were at Edinburgh University together, long before they became famous writers. Coincidentally, they both ended up spending a great deal of time in the Cotswolds, and Doyle was on Barrie's cricket team. One time Barrie had been commissioned to write an operetta and then had fallen ill. He was desperate and anxious to deliver the work and called his friend for help. Conan Doyle immediately came to his bedside and helped Barrie finish his commission. It was called *Jane Annie, or The Good Conduct Prize*. Although written by two of the greatest authors in the English language, it was an utter and complete disaster. George Bernard Shaw wrote a scathing review saying it was " the most unblushing outburst of tomfoolery that two responsible citizens could conceivably indulge in public!" However, a few years later, Barrie, a man with a great sense of humour, repaid Doyle's unconditional help with a special gift: a spoof of Sherlock Holmes, called *The Adventure of the Two Collaborators*. The plot involved two men who asked Sherlock Holmes to solve a mystery – why their operetta had not been a huge hit.

Conan Doyle once wrote of Barrie that he was a man "about whom there is nothing small except his body". Joey hadn't known Barrie was so short – just five-foot-one. He must have looked himself like the boy who never grew up! The more Joey discovered about James M Barrie, the more she liked the sound of him. Barrie loved his friends and they became his family. Joey couldn't help but think of Sarah. Would they manage to achieve what Barrie and Doyle had – friendship for ever?

❋ ❋ ❋

At about three o'clock, unable to read any more, Joey decided to walk over to the pond. The next thing she knew, she was piling her clothing neatly on the bench of the hut and adjusting the straps of her suit.

She wrapped herself in a towel, pulled on her windbreaker

and made her way down to the edge of the water, where all the ladies were sitting on a blanket spread out on the grass. She gently eased herself down, as Meg silently poured her a cup of tea and handed it to her. The noon sun was unseasonably warm; steam rose gently from the surface of the water.

"No ice to break today, eh, Gala?" Joey said.

Gala looked over and shook her head.

Joey sipped her tea, listening to the women chat about a widower in town, someone called Mr. Walmsley, who had been seen in the company of a woman twenty years his junior.

"Thirty!" Viv shrieked.

"Maybe it was his niece," Meg suggested.

Lilia sighed in exasperation. "Honestly, Meg, sometimes I think you don't have the sense God gave an ant."

"Ants are brilliant," Meg said. "Have you ever read E.O. Wilson?"

"I have not," Lilia replied.

"Well you should," Meg said quietly. "It'll change your opinion of ants."

"I don't want my opinion changed," Lilia responded. "I know everything I need to know about them."

"Which is obviously very little," Meg chirped.

Joey glanced around at the other women, who were smiling. She concluded that this gentle teasing must be business as usual.

"It's warmer today, isn't it?" Joey said.

"It's like 1969," Aggie replied, glancing around at the others. "Do you remember?"

"Of course," chorused Gala and Viv.

"It was the hottest January on record," explained Lilia.

"All my orchids died," added Aggie. "One doesn't forget a winter like that."

"And I, for one," Gala announced, "am taking advantage of this splendid thaw. Nothing feels better than nothing at all. No suit for me today."

"Nor me," said Viv. "Just give me a moment."

Joey was afraid that Gala and Viv were going to strip right then and there, but the old women hauled themselves to their feet and tottered off toward the hut.

"I agree," said Aggie, who did proceed to remove her suit right then and there. "Joey, dear, a day like this is a gift. You'll notice that the water's much warmer."

"But it was freezing last night," Joey said cautiously.

"That was last night," said Meg, who had also begun to remove her suit. "Today is today. The pond is surprisingly shallow. It heats up quickly."

Gala and Viv came trotting back, wrapped only in large towels. Aggie and Meg had already shed their suits and now Lilia was peeling aside her straps. They all smiled at Joey. Was she going to strip off the ugly red tank suit and come skinny-dipping with the rest of them?

She guessed she was. A little self-consciously, she slipped off her suit and joined the procession of pale naked females heading for the water.

"Don't give us another fright today," Meg cautioned, as they slid off the dock and into the water. "Fifteen minutes at the most."

"Okay," Joey said, before sliding underwater.

They had all been right. The water was so much warmer that it was hard to believe she was swimming in the same place. Ribbons of warmth and pockets of heat caressed her body as she swam through the cool pond. Again, she felt rejuvenated and clear. Her skin began to tingle and grow taut, and waves of pure energy flooded her body, as though the pond was electric and was somehow recharging her.

Her forearms and legs felt strong as she swam the crawl. She slid underwater, opening her eyes in the murky brown, pulling herself through the alternating waves of warmth and cool. When she surfaced, the sun was bright above her. She floated on her back, staring up at the cloudless sky, and felt suffused with a great sense of peace and calm.

Out of nowhere, she thought of her mother.

She's here, Joey felt, with utter certainty. Mount Carmel Cemetery, with its rusty iron fence and sad little plastic bouquets left by people without the means to keep the graves adorned with real flowers, suddenly seemed irrelevant. Her mother was here, with her, and with the sun and the wind, the water and the sweet, bracing air.

Joey turned over and scanned the surface of the water. Aggie, Lilia, Meg, Gala and Viv were splashing each other like children at play. She swam toward them, these five ancient women who had been, up until a few days ago, complete strangers to her. How could she explain the effect they had had and how important they now felt to her? It made no sense at all.

She was a working girl from New York. She wasn't religious or philosophical. Her thinking was logical, concrete, as sturdy and enduring as the skyscrapers of her hometown. If someone had said the word *angel* to her, claiming that their life had been somehow "touched by angels", Joey would have laughed in their face. Until now.

"Isn't it great?" shouted Aggie as Joey swam toward her.

"You're sure there aren't any men around here?" Joey called.

"No men. Ever!" Gala said. "We're *freeee!*" Gala dived under the water and soon appeared by Joey's side.

Joey nodded eagerly. As an American, Joey had always taken freedom for granted. The word would have special significance for Gala.

Lilia had been swimming toward them. "Not everyone wants to be free of men, Gala," she said. "Many women feel comfortable being taken care of, being a helpmate to the man they love."

"Maybe so," replied Meg. "It's certainly an easier choice, in some ways. Freedom can be lonely. One pays a high price to maintain one's independence."

"A higher price than to relinquish it?" asked Viv.

They were all treading water. Joey thought it would make far more sense to continue this conversation on land, but she wasn't going to be the one to suggest it.

"Think of our families," Aggie said reasonably. "If every woman did exactly as she pleased, there'd be no families, no children."

"Oh yes, there would!" Meg maintained. "There'd be millions of children! And no one to take care of them! Their mothers would be off making more!" She laughed wickedly.

"Well, that's what men do, isn't it? Sow the seed and leave the rest to us ladies? Not all men, of course, but down through history…" Aggie said.

"Richard wasn't like that," Gala put in.

"No, he wasn't," Aggie replied. "He would have done anything for me, and I would have done anything for him."

"Anything?" Meg piped up, "*Anything?* That sounds like enslavement to me!"

"Meg!" Aggie cried. "I never was and never would be a slave to anyone, family or friend, in deeds or opinions!" Aggie shot Meg a baffled look. "How could you think that of me?"

"You're certainly a slave to your work, Meg." Lilia pointed out. "So where's your freedom?"

Meg laughed, refusing to be offended. "I freely choose to be a slave to my work. So there!"

Joey had been watching and listening, but she wasn't going to wade into this hornets' nest. These girls really kicked it around!

"Are you married, Joey?" Viv asked suddenly.

Joey shook her head.

"Not yet," Aggie said kindly.

"I work pretty long hours," Joey explained, hoping to change the subject.

"That's no excuse," Gala put in. "You know what Freud said, everyone needs both work and love."

"Freud said no such thing!" Viv protested.

"He most certainly did!" Gala said grandly.

"I was going out with someone," Joey said softly, "but it didn't work out."

"His fault or yours?" Meg asked bluntly.

"I don't know," Joey replied. "I guess I didn't make him happy. Or happy enough."

"No one can make another person happy," Viv opined, "if they're not happy within themselves. That's why so many marriages fail."

"*Is* it?" asked Meg with a grin. "How about that — you've got it all figured out! You should write a book."

"I should!" said Viv cheerfully.

"I agree with her," Gala said.

"I'm not saying that married people can't be happy *together*, can't bring joy to each other and comfort and security, but no person can cure another human being's fundamental unhappiness."

"What if people are unhappy because they're lonely?" Aggie asked. "And then they get together and they're not lonely any more. Hasn't one person cured the other's unhappiness?"

"That's not the same thing," Gala said.

"Yes it is," Aggie insisted.

Viv shook her head. "I'm talking about deep-seated unhappiness within oneself. That's not the same as loneliness."

"Speaking of lonely," Gala sputtered, "I hear you're staying at Stanway House. Have you met the caretaker?"

Aggie shot Gala a warning glance, but Gala seemed oblivious.

"You mean Ian?" Joey asked.

"Handsome man, isn't he?" Gala went on. "And that Lily is a beauty. Just like her grandmother."

Joey turned to look at Lilia, whose face was like stone.

"Now *there* is a man who seems lonely," Gala said gently. "Maybe —"

"Ian is married," Lilia whispered. She turned suddenly and made her way to the ladder and climbed out of the water.

"*Was* married, Lilia. It's been seven years. You have to remember that."

Lilia paused at the top of the steps. She seemed barely able to speak. "You don't need to remind *me* how long it's been. I'm aware of every day I live in this world without my daughter."

"No, don't go!" shouted Gala. "Please. I'm sorry."

Lilia turned and stared, her naked flesh white and stark. "You can be so hard sometimes, Gala. I know it's what helped you to survive the trials in your life... But why do you turn it on your friends?"

"I want Ian to be happy again," Gala cried. "I want you to be happy."

"That will never happen, " Lilia said. "For me, or for Ian."

"He *can* be. So can you. I let go of *my* ghosts."

"Then you're a stronger person than I am," Lilia said resignedly, scooping up her towel and heading for the hut.

Gala scrambled out of the water.

"Let her go, Gala," Aggie said quietly.

But Gala wasn't listening. She moved toward Lilia as quickly as her old legs would carry her and threw her arms around her just as her friend reached the entrance to the hut. Gala pulled her into a tight embrace. Resisting at first, Lilia finally softened, and buried her face in Gala's shoulder.

Chapter 13

The high, shrill whine was like nothing Joey had ever heard. Dusk was closing in and Joey was walking Tink by the woods that bordered the park behind Stanway House. She had let the dog off her leash, slightly against her better judgment – she didn't trust her not to run off, excited by sounds and scents far more primal and commanding than the ones she routinely encountered in New York, but equally she couldn't resist giving her the chance to sniff and dig at the edge of the woods.

She heard the horrible whining and wondered what it could possibly be. She assumed it was some kind of animal in distress, but it never occurred to Joey that it could be Tink. Then Joey saw her at the edge of the woods, pawing at her snout, whimpering. Joey raced toward her.

Tink seemed oblivious to her presence when Joey knelt beside her. She was bleeding, from her nose, and snout, letting out the most pitiful wail Joey had every heard. Her head was caught in what looked like a roll of barbed wire. Joey was paralysed for a moment, sick with fear and revulsion. Coaxing Tink, she set about pulling her free of the thick metal thorns.

The difficulty was keeping the dog still enough to be able to complete the task without hurting her further. It was an agonising process. When she was finally done, she picked her up and ran with her to the McCormacks' cottage.

She pounded on the door. It felt like hours before the door opened, revealing an irritated Ian.

"I need a vet," Joey blurted out.

"Jesus Christ," Ian said.

"I didn't know there was barbed wire in the woods!" Joey was nearing tears.

"There shouldn't be," Ian replied calmly. He came in closer and put his hand on the back of Tink's head. "Some fence builders must have left it there."

"What do I do? I don't have a car."

"You don't need a car. But you do need to calm down."

Lily appeared behind her father. "Oh, no!" she said, coming forward.

"Put some water on to boil, love," Ian said gently. "And bring me some towels."

"What are you going to do?" Joey asked.

"I'm going to bathe the wounds. Get the dirt out. Check whether she needs stitches. I'll need your help."

"Do you know how? Do you know what you're doing?" Joey immediately regretted her words.

Ian appeared to take a deep breath, and to struggle for control.

"Yes, Miss Rubin," he finally said. "I know how."

Fifteen minutes later, Ian pronounced the job done. There was a nasty cut below Tink's left eye, but he didn't think she required stitches. Lily put down a deep bowl of water, which Tink emptied.

In her relief at realising her dog was going to be fine, Joey embarrassed herself by bursting into tears.

Ian responded by silently crossing the room to the sideboard, pouring her three fingers of whisky and quietly handing it to her. She didn't know how she could thank him. He had been so kind, so gentle with Tink and yet able to ignore her whining so as to focus on the task at hand. The dog would be fine by morning, he said.

"Thank you so much," Joey blubbed, wiping away her tears.

"You're welcome."

"I don't know what I would have done — I — I — "

"Drink your whisky," Ian said.

Joey did as she was told. Lily was sitting by the fire, stroking Tink, who was clearly exhausted.

"Leave her here overnight," Ian said. "I'll keep an eye on her."

"That's okay. You've done enough."

"Leave her here," he said firmly. Joey looked over at Lily, who nodded.

"Okay," she said, taking another deep sip of her drink.

❋ ❋ ❋

There was a note taped to Ian's door when Joey went over in the morning.

"In the back barn. Dog fine."

Joey tried the handle and found the door open.

"Hello?" she called. The only response she got was Tink trotting happily toward her, tail wagging.

"Baby!" Joey cooed, kneeling down and smothering her with kisses. "Poor baby!"

Tink seemed fine. Joey noted that there was half a bowl of water and an empty bowl of — something that had been completely devoured — beside the stove. She scooped Tink up in her arms, resolving to get to town later in the day to buy Ian a nice bottle of — something. She crossed to the sideboard and looked at the bottles. She rarely drank hard liquor herself — until she had come here, anyway — but he seemed to favour Scotches. She would ask at the off licence for a really nice bottle.

An hour later, with Tink sprawled at her feet, Joey was able to get down to work. The first part of the challenge involved hanging out in each of the rooms of Stanway House and thinking about renovations in a very general way. The grander spaces would be left almost as they were. They were sumptuous, atmospheric and irreplaceable: the chapel, the entrance hall, the ancient refectory where the monks had dined. The wiring in these soaring spaces would have to be updated, the mahogany panelling refinished, the floors re-glazed, but Joey wanted to change as little as possible.

That left the rest of the house: sixteen bedrooms, twelve baths, a library, six semi-private sitting rooms, a breakfast room, a very large kitchen, a laundry and a dozen or so more chambers that had served various purposes down through the centuries. The outbuildings would be dealt with later in the process. There was a Tithe Barn, a stone edifice traditionally used to store the tenth of the produce produced by the estate's farm, donated annually to the Church. There were several "guest cottages" in dire need of repair, having sheltered no guests for at least a hundred years.

There was also a long, plain stone dormitory where the monks of Tewkesbury Abbey had slept. Self-contained and overlooking a small, private pond, this could be an amazing retreat. The Tithe Barn could also work for small private parties or intimate weddings, and the guest cottages could be repurposed as self-contained rental properties. All were close enough to be serviced by the kitchen at Stanway House.

But in her excitement, Joey was getting ahead of herself. She had to figure out a plan and to work through the spaces methodically over the next couple of weeks. An hour later, she had divided the spaces into eight groups, one of which she would tackle each day. That would leave some time at the end of her trip to organise her findings and proposals and to make preliminary inquiries about construction permits and building supplies. Joey then decided that she would work from the largest spaces to the smallest. She loved decorating more than anything, but that was the fun and easy part. The harder tasks she would tackle first.

She worked steadily through the afternoon, breaking only once to take Tink out. By five o'clock, she had completed a thorough inspection of the kitchen facilities and had formulated her ideas into a rough proposal. Over the decades, the kitchen had been carved up and adapted to suit the purposes of several generations of Tracys. Originally designed to turn out hundreds of meals a day, it was now an intimate and idiosyncratic kitchen, one that had served the personal needs of a large extended family.

Everything would have to go, with the possible exception of the glass-fronted cabinets that stretched from floor to ceiling in an ample adjacent pantry. In the main body of the kitchen, they'd have to take it back to the studs. They would bring in an industrial kitchen designer, but in all likelihood, except for modern appliances and ventilation and safety equipment, the finished room would look much as it had done a hundred and fifty years ago: plenty of work space, traditional materials on the surfaces lining the extended walls, a long central refectory table for bread and pastry making, and for the plating of large numbers of dinners.

Joey glanced at her watch. It was five twenty. She had finished the work she'd carved out for the day. She wished she'd thought about dinner earlier, when she'd stopped at the shop to grab a sandwich after her swim. If she could make it back there before it closed, she could get an order of basics – and then perhaps take a cab home. She didn't need enough food for the next couple of weeks, but she needed her toast and coffee in the morning.

❋ ❋ ❋

The smell reached her as she was locking the front door. It was a strange, earthy odour, not one she recognised. There was obviously some kind of meat being cooked in the gatehouse but what was it? Not beef, she thought, but not pork or chicken, either. She crunched across the gravel, running through the possibilities in her mind. Lamb? Turkey? Something very English, like – goose? Or pheasant?

"Joey!"

Joey turned to see Lily in her doorway.

"Hi!"

"Where are you going?" Lily asked.

"Out to get some groceries."

"Now?" Lily asked, incredulous.

Joey nodded. "I should have thought of it earlier."

"I'm sure the shop won't be open now," Lily said, looking back to get her father's eye.

"If it's supper you need, Uncle Angus is coming over, and Dad's cooking his speciality..." Lily half-turned and called into the house. "Dad?"

Ian appeared at the door.

"I can't thank you enough – everything you did for Tink," Joey said.

Ian waved her thanks away. "How's she doing?"

"She seems fine. She's conked."

Ian nodded. "I'm glad."

"You sure knew what you were doing."

Ian shrugged.

"Joey's staying for dinner," Lily announced.

"Is she now?"

"She has nothing to eat, Dad!" Lily whined with exasperation. "The shop's closed!"

"I'm aware of that, Lily," Ian said evenly.

"I'm fine, really, I certainly didn't come round to invite…" Joey insisted.

"Dad!" Lily wailed, as though Ian had uttered a syllable. "What do you expect her to do, starve?"

Ian looked at Lily as though she were a raving lunatic. But it seemed to have been decided. Joey was joining them for dinner. And now she was walking through their door, wondering if this was really a good idea. The episode at the pond swam hauntingly to mind. There was no point her denying it to herself. She definitely found Ian attractive, and Lily was a real live wire. But judging from Lilia's extreme reaction to the mere suggestion that Ian might be – available – the situation was complicated. She had better proceed with caution.

Joey stepped inside. "Nothing like an unexpected guest…"

"We're already having Angus for dinner. We'll put you to work," Ian said, throwing a white apron her way. "Treat your guests like family and your family like guests. That's what my mum used to say."

He reached for a tumbler and poured Joey some wine. "Sit yourself down there."

Joey obeyed, glancing around. This was clearly the space in which Lily and Ian spent most of their time. Two over-stuffed chairs were pulled up to a woodstove and open shelves displayed a motley assortment of mismatched china and mugs. A lumpy sofa piled with cushions and draped with knitted throws dominated the far wall.

"What are you making?" Joey asked. "It smells great."

"Haggis."

"What's that?"

"You don't know what haggis is?" Lily cried. "You're kidding."

Joey shook her head. "I've led a sheltered life."

"*Right*. In New York," Ian said wryly.

"I'm not much of a cook," Joey admitted. "I *like* to, I just – never learned."

"No time like the present," Ian said, with a wry smile. He handed Joey the cookbook that had been open on the table. "It's the Scottish national dish. Give that a gander."

Joey set down her glass and perused the recipe to which Ian had pointed. She read the first few ingredients listed:

1 sheep stomach
1 sheep liver
1 sheep heart
1 sheep tongue
1/2 pound suet

Joey looked up. Surely he was joking. Wasn't suet *pig fat*? Ian, preoccupied with chopping herbs, didn't return her gaze. She read on:

3 medium onions, minced
1/2 pound dry oats, toasted
1 teaspoon salt
1/2 teaspoon ground black pepper
minced fresh herbs, to taste

Joey began to feel vaguely nauseous as she quickly skimmed the steps of the recipe. Soak the sheep's stomach bag overnight. Mince the heart, tongue and liver and mix it with the suet. Add oats and a little water and stuff the stomach with the meat/oat mixture. Sew the stomach closed.

Joey looked up and took a deep breath. *Sew the stomach closed?*

Horrified, she continued to read. Boil the stomach for three hours and, if the boiling stomach bag looks as though it's about to burst, pierce it with a needle.

Joey fought another wave of nausea. She gently slid the cookbook onto the table. "Wow," she said weakly. "That's what you're making?"

"It's all made," Ian said. "Just got to throw together a salad." He turned to Joey with a smile: "Don't worry, this isn't something we make regularly. A special treat once a year."

They were interrupted by the sound of someone knocking on the door.

"Uncle Angus!" Lily said, hopping up. She was back in a minute, followed by a roly-poly, redheaded man with a bushy ponytail and beard, and thick arms that reminded Joey of Popeye.

"Glad to meet ya," Angus bellowed, extending his hand, and shaking hers so long and hard that Joey thought it would fall off.

"Joey Rubin. Nice to meet Lily's uncle. "

"Ah, he's just a bum I keep fed so he doesn't starve to death," said Ian.

Angus grabbed Ian in a bear hug and proceeded to lift his six-foot-four-inch friend clear off the ground.

"Ian, my man!" said Angus, full of affection. He walked over to the stove, smelled the haggis, and looked nearly faint with happiness.

"Joey," he said, "this guy over here, he sure knows how to treat a friend right..."

Lily explained that Ian and Angus had met as school-boys in Scotland. And Angus had then followed Ian to the Cotswolds some twenty years ago. "Mum and Dad had to make him my godfather, to make it official," exclaimed Lily.

So, Angus and Ian were lifelong friends. Joey wondered what Angus might make of a new woman in Ian's life.

Angus grabbed a beer from the fridge and guzzled it down in what seemed like seconds. As he reached for another, Lily sidled up to him.

"Uncle Angus, can I…?" She nodded playfully at the bottle in his hand.

"What?" Ian bellowed. "Absolutely not!"

"Dad, come on! I have to learn to drink sometime, don't I?"

"Nice try," Ian replied coolly.

"That's how they do it in France. They let the kids have a little at meals, so it's no big deal when they're old enough to drink on their own."

"She's right about that," Angus put in.

"See?" Lily said.

"How about a small glass, Ian?" Angus suggested. "A third of my beer. Give us a cup there. It won't do her any harm."

Ian rolled his eyes and shook his head, then reached into a cabinet and pulled out an egg cup. He handed it over with a grin.

"Daddy!" Lily protested.

Ian then handed Angus a porcelain teacup, which Angus proceeded to fill.

"That's better," Lily said, accepting the cup with a broad grin.

Angus sat down in the chair by the stove and Lily followed him, depositing herself down on the floor beside him. They clinked their glasses.

"So, Joey, what do you think of our little village?" Angus asked. "Ian tells me you come from New York City. A bit different here, no?"

Joey was surprised but definitely pleased that Ian had mentioned her to his friend.

"I love it. It's so beautiful... and quiet... And no traffic noise, ever. Do you live nearby too?" inquired Joey, wanting to make small talk but also wanting to find out more about Angus and Ian. Know a man's best friend, know a man.

"I am over in Snowshill, about ten miles from here. I run the stables over there. Taught Lily how to ride when she was five years old," said Angus. "You ride?"

"I've been there, at the stables! I watched a competition of young riders, children of my friend," Joey said excitedly.

"Hey, dinner is almost ready," Ian called to everyone, "Come on."

Joey's spirits sank at the mention of dinner. Maybe she could just eat the salad. She honestly doubted that she would be able to swallow a mouthful of that vile mixture of organs, pig fat and oats. She would gag!

She busied herself helping Lily to set the table, averting her eyes as Ian fished the revolting balloon of sheep's stomach out of its boiling bath. She had to admit, though, it smelled – okay.

Ian prepared the plates on the sideboard, and when he set them on the table, Joey was surprised to see no evidence at all of the sheep's vile stomach. A loose, aromatic mound of what looked like soft meatloaf shared the plate with a fresh green salad and slim, roasted carrots.

"It looks – great," Joey said, hoping she sounded genuinely enthusiastic.

Ian handed her a basket of warm rolls. Where had they come from? It was looking more and more as though she could get through this meal without giving away the fact that she was utterly revolted by the thought of the main dish. She could hide what she didn't eat under the salad. She could conceal a bite she couldn't swallow in a roll.

Angus filled their wine glasses as Lily set out a slab of fresh butter. As Lily leaned over to set the plate down on the dining table, Joey noticed a long, jagged scar running the length of her upper arm. Had Lily also been in the car accident that killed her mother? Joey suddenly wondered. It was terrible to think of a young child enduring such a trauma, and Joey felt a sudden wave of affection for the girl. She was so spirited and lively, so full of curiosity and excitement about the future. If she had been in the accident, this certainly hadn't destroyed her zest for life.

They pulled out their chairs, sat down and shook out their napkins.

Angus raised his glass. "Slàinte mhòr agad!" he said.

"Slàinte mhòr agad!" Lily and Ian replied.

Joey smiled and clinked glasses with the others.

"It means 'good health to you'," Ian explained.

"Oh! Well, good health to you!" Joey said.

They all tucked into their dinners.

"Good God," Angus burst out, after tasting his first bite of the evening's speciality. "It's brilliant, man! Brings tears to my eyes!"

And to mine, Joey thought dismally. But she had to have a bite. It would be really bad form not even to try something made with such love and care.

Ian glanced over as she put a bit of haggis on her fork and brought it to her lips. She opened her mouth and tasted it and – it was phenomenal! It was fantastic! "Oh my God!" she said. "I've never tasted anything like this!"

Truer words were never spoken.

"I love it." she said, having another bite. "It's amazing! You're an amazing cook!"

"Isn't he?" said Lily. "I think he should open a restaurant."

Ian shook his head modestly. "I couldn't put up with the public," he said. "I do enjoy cooking, but only for people I like."

He glanced at Joey, almost inadvertently, and then quickly away.

Had he really meant that? Joey wondered. Had Ian actually tried to be friendly? She felt herself reddening, and suddenly felt painfully embarrassed.

Angus came to the rescue.

"So you're here doing what?" he queried Joey, reaching for the rolls.

"The architectural firm I work for is contracted to handle the building conversion of Stanway House."

"*Building* conversion?" Ian said wryly. "Bloody theme park, more like!"

Joey thought she could sense a bit of humour in his tone.

"We promise to take very good care of it!"

"Right," Angus put in. "And make a fortune while you're at it, catering to the swells."

"It always catered to the swells, didn't it?" Joey shot back. "Since the swells got it away from the monks."

"You're right about that," Ian conceded with a grin.

"Think of it as letting regular people in on a bit of the fun," Joey suggested.

"Regular people with insanely fat wallets," Angus said.

"Not insanely," Joey countered. "Just slightly – plump."

"How long will you be here?" Angus asked.

"A few weeks or so. I have to pop up to London for a day to meet the management company, the people we're working with."

"You're going to London?" Lily asked.

"One day next week. We haven't worked out the details."

"Can I come?" she asked, glancing nervously at Ian.

"Lily!" Ian said. "I'm sure Joey has enough on her hands without – "

"You *said* you'd take me make-up shopping!" Lily wheedled.

"It's fine with me," Joey replied, "but don't you have school?"

"Yeah, but Dad it's not just for shopping. There's this amazing play at the National which I really, really want to go. Mrs Ferns saw it the week before last and she said it was the most exciting play she'd ever been to. In her whole life!"

"We'll see," Ian said.

"*Daddy!* Isn't it more important, if one wants to be an actress, to actually see and hear living, breathing plays and not just read about them in stuffy old classrooms? Please? I know Mrs Ferns will agree, and I'll *die* if I don't get out of this sheep-town soon!"

"We'll *see*, I said," he responded firmly.

"You want to be an actress?" Joey asked.

"I am *going* to be an actress," Lily replied grandly. "I believe it's what I was born to do. That's why I'm going to move to New York. I want to be on Broadway!"

"Is that so?" Ian said, pursing his lips as he opened another bottle of wine and set it on the table. He returned to the stove to dish out for Joey a second helping of haggis.

As Ian's back was turned, Lily reached for the wine bottle and began to pour some into her teacup. Angus noticed and put his hand on the bottle, allowing Lily half a cup and no more. He shook his head. It was clear that he didn't approve, but he wasn't going to bust Lily in front of her father.

They passed the next hour in sociable chatter about

England and New York. But there was a change in the tone of the evening as soon as the subject of Stanway House was raised again.

"Our clients are very much hoping you'll consider staying on," she said to Ian.

"Oh they are, are they?" He took a sip of his wine.

"I'm supposed to try to convince you."

"Are you, now? I see. I get it."

"Get what?"

"The reason for your visit this evening."

"Tonight? Absolutely not!"

"No? Then why?"

"Because your daughter invited me."

Ian gave her a sly look, as though he didn't really believe her.

"*And* – I didn't have a crumb of food in the house."

"*Now* we're getting to it," he said, the warmth suddenly gone from his voice. He took his napkin from his lap and laid it on the table.

Had she offended him? What was she supposed to say, that she was starting to – like him? That she had felt a flush of happiness when he welcomed her into their home with that phrase about friends and family?

Was this her signal to leave? It certainly seemed to be.

"Can I help with the dishes?" she asked.

"No, no."

" – I'd like to…" Joey pressed, wishing the subject of Stanway House had not come up again, and longing for the warm and easy banter they had all traded over dinner. But the mood in the room had definitely cooled.

"Don't go," Lily pleaded. "We'll do the dishes, Daddy. Come on! Let us!"

As if to set in motion what she wanted to have happen, Lily

stood up and began stacking the plates. Joey sensed that Lily really liked having her here, or perhaps just having any woman around who wasn't Lilia's age, and she would have loved to have stayed on a bit, doing the dishes and getting to know this lovely, free-spirited girl as Ian and Angus relaxed by the fire talking their own stuff. But probably best to quit while she was ahead.

Angus was all warmth as she said her goodbyes, Lily full of reminders about taking her to London. But Ian was definitely subdued.

"Thank you again," she said at the door.

"You're welcome," he said formally, and then closed it firmly behind her.

Chapter 14

The weeklong negotiations that resulted in Ian allowing Lily to accompany Joey to London were contentious and intense. First of all, he didn't want her to miss school. Lily responded by bringing home a note from her English teacher, confirming that she would get extra credit for writing an essay on the play she was hoping Joey would take her to see.

"And what is that?" Ian asked.

"Mary Shelley's *Frankenstein*."

"*Frankenstein?*" Ian scoffed.

"It's on next year's reading list, Dad!"

"That sounds awfully convenient," Ian replied. "You've never mentioned it before…"

In the end, Lily succeeded in demolishing every one of her father's objections. When Joey dropped by the gatehouse to finalise the plans with Ian, she got the distinct impression that he had finally just given up, worn down by his daughter's relentless campaign.

"She's a teenager," Joey said smiling.

"A teenage girl," Ian said, shaking his head. "God help me."

At six fifteen on the day of the much-anticipated trip, Lily appeared at Joey's apartment door wearing a skirt that Joey recognised: the skirt that Ian had so clearly objected to when Lily had it on a week and a half earlier. They were due to leave for the train in half an hour.

"It's okay, isn't it?" Lily wailed. "Dad wants me to change, but he told me I could wear it if *you* said it was okay."

Joey forced herself to act blasé, as though she were really considering the question. She wasn't. Though Lily was a gorgeous girl who could pull off almost anything, the skirt made her look a little too — well, trashy. It was fine for kicking around the countryside, but Lily was going to be on her own for a while in London. Joey knew the kind of attention Lily would attract in this outfit and she wasn't sure whether Lily was ready to handle it. She stepped back and peered at the skirt.

"Turn around," she said.

Lily turned all the way around, a hopeful look on her face.

"Hmmm." Joey hesitated.

"*What?*"

"It's a little short, honey. Everything else looks fine, but you might just find yourself attracting some unwanted attention down there in the city. What about your black velvet jeans? Those are so great."

"With what?"

"Exactly what you have on. They'd be perfect."

"But I love this skirt!"

"I know. Another time."

"Okay," Lily said resignedly then headed down the stairs to change. A short time later, when Joey met Lily and Ian out in the driveway, Lily looked every bit the proper, hip schoolgirl. Ian nodded at Joey, a nod she interpreted to mean: *thank you.*

At 9:55, Joey and Lily were standing outside the offices of Churchill and Marks, the public relations firm hired to market the restored Stanway estate and hotel. Joey's meeting was scheduled for ten o'clock, and the plan was for Lily to spend the morning a few blocks away at the Victoria & Albert Museum. They had an exhibit running on the fashion icons of the fifties and sixties – Grace Kelly, Audrey Hepburn, Jacqueline Kennedy – and an installation devoted to Diaghilev and the Ballets Russes. Joey was curious to see what Lily would be drawn to.

Joey was sure she would be finished with her meeting by noon, so they decided that she would then walk to the museum to meet Lily. After her morning in the galleries, Lily was going to check out the Museum Café and see if it looked like a nice place to have lunch. If the menu didn't appeal to her, Lily would meet Joey outside at 12:30, at the museum's main entrance on Cromwell Road, and they would find another place to eat.

Afterwards, the plan was to go to Harvey Nichols where they would choose for Lily an age-appropriate array of make-up. Then a light supper, before the play.

Joey gave Lily a hug on the street and made her way into the offices of Churchill and Marks. There were only six people in the conference room when she was ushered in, and over a surprising spread of tea, cappuccinos and fresh croissants, Joey took the writers and strategists through a full presentation on the status of the project and the Apex Group's plans.

They spent the rest of the morning brainstorming about potential magazine pieces the writers and photographers could begin to develop for long-lead publications, features on the history of the house and its restoration. Joey, smiling quietly to herself, suggested a piece on Massimo: centuries of Italian craftsmanship being brought to bear on the effort to preserve one of Britain's most beloved architectural treasures.

Joey glanced at her watch as she stepped out into the

chilly air and wound her scarves around her neck. It was five minutes before twelve. The day was going like clockwork.

* * *

Lily was nowhere to be found. The plan had been that, if Lily *wasn't* waiting at the V&A's Grand Entrance when Joey arrived, they would meet inside at the Museum Café. But Lily was not in either place. It was now nearly one thirty and Joey was struggling to fend off a full-blown panic attack.

"That's odd," she said, returning to the hostess just inside the Café door. "You definitely didn't see a teenage girl wearing black velvet jeans and a dark red coat?"

"I'm afraid not."

"We must have gotten our signals crossed," Joey said. "If she does show up, would you ask her to wait here for me? I'll check back in a few minutes."

Joey tried Lily's mobile number again, punching the redial button as if trying to get more impact. She had made five missed calls — all of them going to voicemail. What on earth could have happened to her?

She hurried back down the hall, but she had no clear idea where she should go or what she should do. Should she go back outside? Check all the museum's galleries? She doubted they had a public address system here, and she wouldn't have wanted to embarrass Lily, anyway. But that was ridiculous! Who cared about embarrassment when Lily's very life might be in danger? Perhaps someone had started talking to her, a man, some lecherous old creep who hung out in museums just looking for sweet, naïve girls like Lily. What if she had left with him? What if he had convinced her to get into a cab with him and they were at this very moment on their way to — God knows where?

Joey was practically running down the hall now, ducking

her head into gallery after gallery, scanning the figures standing before the exhibitis or sitting peacefully on the benches. She should call the police! No, she should call Ian! No, she should call the police, because what could Ian do from so far away? He would positively freak out, and there was absolutely nothing he could do to help. The police could at least *do* something. They could fan out all over the area, searching every restaurant and store and alley until they found her. Oh God, please no... Joey steeled herself: she would not let her thoughts go to Lily being – in an alley.

She suddenly felt faint with anxiety. She forced herself to sit down on a marble bench. She had to think clearly.

She took a few deep breaths. *Why* the hell wasn't she answering her mobile phone? The minutes were ticking by. She had to do something. She decided to make one circuit of the outside of the building, in case Lily had got confused and was waiting at a different entrance. If she didn't find Lily in the next five minutes, she would call the police.

Joey headed outside. If anything happened to Lily, she would never forgive herself. She wasn't *totally* to blame, though. She and Ian had discussed this plan, and he had been absolutely fine with the idea of her spending the morning alone at the museum. Joey had turned up at the Grand Entrance early. She was right where she said she would be, right when she said she would be there. It was *Lily* who had screwed things up... If Ian had trusted his daughter to be mature enough for this, how was *Joey* supposed to know she wasn't?

None of this mattered now. What mattered was the fact that beautiful, vulnerable, headstrong Lily was nowhere to be found and the minutes were ticking by. Ian had entrusted her with Lily's safety and Joey had – had – *lost* her!

Joey hurried down the stairs of the Grand Entrance, scanning the street to her left and right. She let out a little involuntary shout when her gaze fell on Lily, huddled in the shelter of one of the museum's arches, looking pale and miserable in the icy wind.

"Lily!" Joey shouted, her voice edged with anger. "Where *were* you? I was ready to call the police!"

Lily's face crumpled when she heard Joey's scalding tone. Tears spilled down her cheeks.

Joey immediately regretted her outburst. Something *had* happened. This wasn't just a case of a missed connection. She also thought she smelled cigarette smoke in Lily's hair.

"Were you smoking?" she asked sharply, before she could stop herself.

Lily now burst into tears. Joey folded her into her arms, deciding that the smoking conversation would have to wait. "What happened? What's wrong?" When Lily didn't answer right away, Joey went on. "Where were you? Did someone — did somebody — ?"

Lily shook her head. "I got my — I started — my —"

"Your period?" Joey guessed, glancing at the bulky bag from Boots that Lily seemed to have acquired. "Oh, Lily... thank God!" Joey said.

"*Thank God?*" Lily said, outraged. "It was horrible. I didn't have anything — so I went to the Museum Store, but *they* didn't have anything, so I had to — and there was a *man* at the cash register, and — " A fresh round of tears spilled down her cheeks.

"You didn't know you were due?" Joey asked. "You didn't have anything in your purse?"

"I never had it before!" Lily shot back.

"Oh, honey," Joey said, softening. "You poor thing! Oh, my God! But it's not so bad... you'll see."

"Are you mad?" Lily asked.

Joey smiled. "I know how you feel."

"Terrible!" Lily retorted. "I want to go home!"

"I bet you feel – not ill, exactly, but not quite right," Joey said.

Lily nodded wretchedly.

"Kind of clammy? Jumpy?" Joey continued.

Lily sniffed. "I hate it! It's awful."

"It's just the hormones. It's all chemical."

"Yesterday, I felt like I was going to cry all the time. I thought I was just excited, but I guess it was – this."

Joey wrapped her arm around her. "Well, the good news is, once it actually starts, you feel better. It's the build-up that's the worst. Do you have cramps?"

Lily nodded.

"Okay, let's go back to Boots. We women may have to put up with this, but we don't have to feel like hell."

Lily looked up. The morning's bravado had slipped away, and she looked very much like a little girl in need of some sisterly TLC. "Don't we?" she whispered.

"Nope," Joey said firmly. "You just leave everything to me."

A couple of hours later, after a soothing hot chocolate, Lily was being pampered and fussed over by the beautician at the Lancôme counter. Joey looked on, smiling, as the saleswoman expertly applied Lily's make-up. She thought back to her own early experiences with make-up, grateful that she had had her mother around for advice on this front.

Her mother had never had manicures or pedicures. She and her friends coloured each other's hair and Leah visited the salon only a few times a year for blunt, stylish cuts that were easy to maintain. But on skin – Leah spent money. Four times a year she visited Basia, a woman who specialised in Eastern European-style facials. From the time Joey was fourteen years old, she and her mother had gone to Basia together, and the habits Joey learned from the gentle, sweet Polish woman with the porcelain skin had always stayed with her. Now, Joey felt a wave of sympathy for Lily. She was glad that she had been able to be with Lily today, of all days.

They didn't eat lunch until four, and then they stopped for gelato at an ice cream parlour. Later, as they took their seats at the National, and Joey began to read about the production they were about to see, she wished she had done a little more research before purchasing the tickets. They were going to be in for quite a wild ride.

"This is a pretty — mature play," Joey commented casually.

Lily smiled. "What do you mean?"

Joey struggled for the right words. "It's pretty out there. Benedict Cumberbatch — naked?"

"I know. This is the kind of theatre I'm interested in."

"Did you know about the nudity?"

"Yeah. Big deal."

"Did your dad?" Joey suspected she already knew the answer to this question.

Lily rolled her eyes and sighed in annoyance. "He could have looked it up. It's public knowledge. You could have, too."

"So he *didn't* know."

"I have no idea what he knows or doesn't know," Lily answered defensively. "Come on, Joey! I'm not a baby."

Joey sat back, took a deep breath and thought for a moment. Fine, they would stay and see the play and later, say as little as possible about it to Ian. If he found out and was angry, Joey would just have to deal with it as best she could. In Joey's opinion, a little nudity on stage wasn't going to scar

Lily for life. Joey would show Lily just how fair and open-minded she could be.

But on one subject, she wasn't open-minded at all.

"Okay," Joey said. "All in the name of art." She turned to Lily and gave her a forceful, direct gaze. "But I expect a truthful answer to a question I'm about to ask you."

"What?"

"Were you smoking today?"

Lily looked away.

"Lily?"

Lily nodded.

"Where'd you get the cigarettes?"

"I had them."

"You brought them? From home?"

Lily nodded sheepishly.

"So I'm assuming this isn't your first time?"

"Loads of people do it. Half my class…"

"Well, I'm not interested in 'loads of people', Lily. I'm interested in you, and I beg you not to take up a habit that you will spend the rest of your life trying to break. Hand them over. Come on…"

"What? Why?" Lily wailed. "They're mine."

"Hand them over. Right now." Joey was surprised by the firm tone of her own voice. When Lily didn't immediately comply, Joey went on.

"I mean it, Lily. Give me the cigarettes or we'll leave. We'll skip the play and head home."

The house lights were going down as Lily fished the crumpled packet out of her bag and handed it to Joey.

"You're too smart for this, Lily. I'm not cool with fifteen-year-olds smoking. Not cool with it at all."

"I'm sorry," Lily whispered.

"Don't try it again," Joey said, flexing a maternal muscle

she barely knew she had. "Smoking is a really, really stupid thing to do."

Chapter 15

"Off to bed with you now," Ian finally said. "It's very late and I don't want be hearing that you're too tired to go to school in the morning. Not after I let you bunk off today."

They were sitting in Ian's kitchen. Joey and Lily had no sooner got off the train and into Ian's warm van than Lily had announced that she was *starving*. This was not unreasonable. The last thing she and Joey had eaten was gelato at tea time, and it had been after midnight when the train pulled into the station at Cheltenham.

"Didn't you feed her?" Ian had asked, as he steered the van out of the car park and onto the road.

"Of course I did!" Joey exclaimed. "But we were trying to make the ten o'clock train and we didn't have time to stop for –"

"Joey!" Lily said.

"I thought we could get a sandwich on the – "

"*Joey!*" Lily snapped, cutting her off abruptly.

Joey glanced at Lily, who was seated between her and Ian.

"He was kidding," Lily said calmly.

And sure enough, there was a wry grin on Ian's face.

"Got your knickers in a bit of a twist there," he said dryly. "Anyway, what else is new? She's always starving."

"I am not!" Lily cried.

"I've never seen a girl put away the quantity of food that – "

"Daddy!"

"It's a wonder I don't have to haul you over to the school in a wheelbarrow!"

It was true, Joey thought, when they had got back to the house, Lily certainly had a carefree appetite. As Tink, who Jocy had left with Ian that morning, dosed contentedly by the kitchen stove, more at home in this space, it seemed, than in the apartment she was occupying, Joey tried not to stare as Lily wolfed down several pieces of buttered toast along with camomile tea with spoonfuls of honey, then a banana, then two plums, more tea, more honey. It was kind of wonderful to see an adolescent girl eat freely and even greedily. To hear people talk about it back in the States, girls of Lily's age were already hardened veterans of the diet wars.

Joey sipped wine, listening to Lily recount every twist and turn of the play's plot. She wisely steered clear of any mention of the nudity in the play, focusing on how great the costumes and sets were. Lily had spent much of her morning, before she'd had to make the emergency run to Boots, at the museum's fashion exhibit. It made Joey feel incredibly ancient to have to explain to Lily who Grace Kelly and Jackie Kennedy were.

"Anything else you've forgotten to mention?" Joey prodded as Lily carried her dishes to the sink.

"Nope," Lily said studiedly.

"No?" Joey goaded.

Ian glanced at Joey; he could tell she was alluding to something specific. He peered at his daughter curiously.

Lily shook her head. "Thanks for a great day, Joey. I had a wonderful time."

"Me too," Joey said. "We'll do it again."

"Can Tink stay here tonight?"

Tink, hearing her name mentioned, roused herself and looked up sleepily.

"Sure," Joey said, "if you want."

"Tink!" Joey called brightly. "Tink, come!"

Tink was on her feet in an instant.

Lily hugged them both then headed for the stairs. "Come on, Tink! Come with me!"

Tink bounded over to the staircase and began the climb, without so much as a backward glance.

"If I think of – anything we forgot to – mention," Joey called after them, "should I – ?"

"Sure," Lily said, racing up the staircase. They heard the slam of her bedroom door.

Joey took a sip of her wine.

"What was that all about?" Ian asked.

Joey sighed. "She had kind of a big day."

Ian cocked his head. If he was supposed to comprehend what Joey was being so elliptical about, he wasn't getting it.

"Today," Joey said quietly, then paused. She felt suddenly very gauche before this man she hardly knew. She had always despised the use of the word "period" to describe that portion of the female cycle. It was such a brusque and ugly word for something so organic and full of purpose. But how better to put it?

"Your little girl became a woman," she said finally – this phrase, too, sounding like something you'd encounter in a film made for school sexual health classes.

"Oh my God!" Ian said, looking suddenly stricken. "Really?"

Joey nodded.

"Is she all right? Is she — ?"

"She's fine. We had a bit of drama, but we got everything sorted out."

"Drama?" he asked.

"It happened while I was at the meeting. She didn't have anything with her."

"Oh, no! I should have — I just never — "

"What were the odds?" Joey asked quietly.

Ian got up and began to pace. He seemed to be having a hard time processing this information.

"If you ask me," Joey said, "I don't think it was completely accidental."

Ian paused and fixed her with a questioning look.

"I'm not saying it was under her conscious control, but maybe something in her subconscious felt free to — let go. Maybe it was easier for her this way."

"Because she was with you?"

"No no. Not *me*, necessarily. Just — another woman."

At this, Ian looked up sharply.

"Ian, listen, I wasn't criticising, I just — you're a fantastic father! And she's an amazing girl."

Ian responded with a wounded nod. "And she likes you. I can see that. I didn't mean to snap at you, I — "

Joey stood up, and moved toward Ian. In her wildest imagination, it would never have occurred to her when she walked through his door an hour earlier that it would feel completely natural and imperative that she kiss Ian with every bit of love and tenderness she possessed. But this is what she now did.

Ian relaxed into her embrace, kissing her back with rough, deep, pent-up feeling. Their coming together felt inevitable.

"Come back with me," she whispered.

"Back where?"

"Stanway House."

He shook his head.

"*Please*," she pressed, kissing him again, putting her hand at the small of his back and drawing him toward her. She pulled him to his feet and kissed him again. As he felt the pressure of her hips, he gasped. He kissed her more deeply, with more force and urgency.

"There's no one over there," Joey murmured.

Ian glanced toward the stairs, as though fearing that at any moment Lily would appear on the landing and find them entwined.

He took a deep breath. "I haven't been – with any one. Since Cait."

"I know."

Pain seemed to crinkle the corners of his eyes. "How do you know?"

"I don't, not really. I just assumed."

"Because of how I – ?"

"No!"

He shook his head desolately. "I can't," he said.

"Why not?"

"Because it's not right. It's not *fair*."

"To whom?"

Ian shook his head. He couldn't speak.

"To Cait?" Joey asked. "Ian, surely… "

She knew she was treading on dangerous ground. "You think this is what Cait would want? For you to be alone for the rest of your life? For you to be unhappy, and for that unhappiness to hang over your home, your *child's* home, *her* child's home?"

Desperation was in his eyes when he gazed at her, and she met that gaze with another kiss. This time it was a gentle kiss. When they finally drew apart, Ian extinguished the lamp on the kitchen table, took Joey by the hand, and led her across the living room to the front door. Something had changed. She wasn't sure how exactly it had happened, or even why – was he saying yes out of need, anger, dawning affection? But she knew that for reasons she might never fully understand, Ian had made up his mind. He was going to come back to Stanway House with her.

"Hold on," he said, tiptoeing up the staircase. He was back in a minute with a bundle of duvets and pillows.

"What's that for?" Joey asked.

"I'm not going up to that depressing apartment."

Joey smiled as they opened the front door, closed it silently behind them and tried to cross the gravel as quietly as possible.

The next three hours, until Ian kissed her one last time and went back to the gatehouse at four am, were among the most precious and delicious that Joey had ever experienced. They carried the bedding into the huge entrance hall of the house. There was a vast stone hearth on one side of the space, and just next to it a little recess in the wall which once must have provided a warming seat for visitors and new arrivals. They lay down there, bathed in the glow of the fire, and were soon entangled in the soft, worn duvets, their teasing kisses alternately fierce and tender.

Time slipped away. Was it three o'clock? Five o'clock? Had this closeness, this giddiness, this pure joy been going on for minutes? Hours? Joey had no way of telling. She was suspended in one glorious, ardent, blazing *now*, and more than anything she had ever wanted in her life, she wanted this not to end, not ever. Never in her life had she abandoned herself so completely to the essence and movements of another human being.

And then, it was over. They had been dozing by the

embers, and Ian gently detached himself from her embrace, wrapping her up against the air.

"I'll go now," he whispered decisively.

She didn't protest. He needed to go, and she felt that.

"I'll see you in the morning," she said.

"It is morning," he said, pushing a strand of hair away from her eyes.

Chapter 16

At about six o'clock, Joey gathered up the duvets and climbed the stairs to her apartment. She flopped down on her back on the bed and stared at the ceiling, where the paint had cracked into a map of tiny roads and byways, crisscrossing the expanse of yellowed plaster. Had it really been only twenty-four hours since Lily had pounded on her door, anxious for Joey to sanction the questionable outfit?

Lily! Tink! She had to get Tink! Joey sat upright, glad for a legitimate reason to cross the gravel to the gatehouse. Lily would be leaving for school before long, and Ian had been nice enough to take care of Tink so that they could make their trip to London. But Ian and Massimo had a full day of inspections planned, tedious and time-consuming assessments of the foundations, supporting walls and masonry of each and every building on the grounds. Joey really had to relieve Ian of the responsibility of the dog.

She stepped into the bathroom, turned on the light, and gazed at her reflection in the mirror. Her cheeks were bright pink, partly due to the roughness of Ian's beard, her lips plump and nearly crimson. She looked as fresh and vital as if she had just stepped off a ski slope.

She debated taking a quick shower and decided against it. She loved the smell of Ian on her skin, her hands, her hair, and she wanted to inhabit that glorious, redolent cloud for as long as she could.

She pulled on her jeans, and a thick wool sweater. She brushed her teeth, stepped into her boots and dabbed on a little lip gloss. Giving her reflection a final once-over in the mirror, she smiled. What was happening to her? Was she actually going to greet her new lover without carefully applying make-up and coordinating all her clothes to deliver just the right impression? She'd barely even registered the fact that her jeans were a little tight. No surprise, really, given the copious amounts of wine she had been drinking and her gradual forsaking of every single one of the eating habits that had kept her slender for twenty years. A leaf of lettuce hadn't crossed her plate in nearly a week.

Oh well, she thought. A few more nights like last night, and a pound or five didn't stand a chance in the world.

❋ ❋ ❋

Lily answered the door and gave Joey a spontaneous hug.

"How you feeling?" Joey whispered.

"Lousy," Lily replied. "Did you tell him?"

Joey nodded. Lily covered her eyes.

"What did he say?" Lily finally asked, peeking out from behind her fingers.

"Oh, you know your dad. Kind of the strong, silent type."

They were interrupted by Tink bounding across the room and jumping up on Joey. She rarely did this these days, and it signalled to Joey that Tink must really have missed her. This dog had such an uncanny sixth sense. Did she know something?

"Good morning," Joey said quietly.

Ian was standing at the stove, tending to a skillet of eggs and some kind of pork or bacon.

162

He turned and smiled warmly. "Good morning. Care for coffee?"

"I'd kill for coffee."

"That won't be necessary," Ian said, reaching for a mug from one of the open shelves and pouring the fragrant amber liquid from a thermos on the counter. He handed it to Joey. Their fingers touched, and then their eyes met. Joey winked. He winked back.

"And for some of whatever it is you've got going there," she said, pouring cream into her coffee and nodding toward the stove. "I'm really hungry."

"Coming up," said Ian, not rising to the bait.

They lingered at the table for close to half an hour, until it was time for Ian to drive Lily to school.

"What time's Massimo coming?" Joey asked.

He and Ian had spent the day together while Joey and Lily were in London, creating a master schedule for all phases of the reconstruction. Joey was going to be spared today's inquiry into the intimacies of the aged substructure. She was glad they didn't need her for this, as she had several important reports to submit to the folks back in New York and at least two dozen phone calls to make.

"Eight forty-five," Ian said, as Lily headed across the room to gather up her books.

Lily looked from Joey to her father, who had quickly got up and was carrying dishes to the sink. She glanced back at Joey with a puzzled stare. "What's so funny?"

"Nothing! *Really!*" But Joey couldn't keep from smiling. She looked down at her plate.

"Let's get this show on the road," Ian said brusquely.

❋　❋　❋

At about four o'clock, Joey decided to walk into the village with Tink to mail some documents at the post office. At least that was the official reason for the walk. The unofficial reasons were many: she was restless, she was sick of being inside, and Tink was driving her crazy, hopping to her feet every time Joey got up, staring at her sadly with moony eyes. Joey had almost nothing with which to make dinner, no wine, and no coffee for the morning. Secretly, she also hoped that if she poked her head out into the world, she might just happen to run into Ian and Massimo. But she didn't, and she didn't hear voices from the gatehouse as they passed. The house was closed up tight and Ian's van was gone.

Walking the mile and a half into the village, Joey admired the rosy streaks in the midwinter sky. She just made it to the post office before they closed, and when she stepped back out onto the pavement, she saw Aggie coming out of the bakery across the street.

"Aggie!" she called.

Aggie looked up and waved. Joey manoeuvered Tink through the cars parked at both kerbs, stepped up onto the pavement and gave Aggie a hug.

"Those look yummy," Joey said, admiring two crusty baguettes sticking out of brown paper sleeves.

"They are," Aggie replied. "You should get one."

"I should."

"Go in right now," Aggie suggested. "They only have a few left. I'll watch her."

"Thanks!" Joey handed Aggie Tink's leash, stepped inside and made a dash for the bread shelves. She stepped back out and reclaimed Tink.

"Well, there's a start," she said brightly.

Aggie gave her a puzzled look.

"On dinner," Joey replied.

"Your dinner? Are you – on your own tonight?"

Joey nodded.

Aggie hesitated, then finally spoke. "We're having a little supper party, at the pond. You're more than welcome to come along."

"Thank you, Aggie," Joey smiled gratefully. "But no, I'm not crashing your party."

"You wouldn't be crashing it. I'm inviting you."

"That's really kind..."

Joey was torn. She would rather spend the evening with the ladies than be alone, but — and she felt horrible admitting this, even to herself — if she had the choice, she would rather be with Ian than with the ladies.

"You know what they always say about special dinners," Aggie continued.

"No, what?"

"That there should always be at least one person everybody doesn't know very well — one wild card. It shakes up the dynamics and puts people on their best behaviour."

"I can't imagine any of you misbehaving!"

"Oh, you'd be surprised," Aggie said wryly.

"I'd love to if I can," Joey said evasively. "But there's a lot going on at the house right now. The contractor started work yesterday, and, well, I'm on the clock. "

"Suit yourself, dear," Aggie said. "We'll see you if we see you." She hugged Joey and headed off to finish her errands.

From that moment until the moment when Joey headed out the door to walk back to the village, she debated whether to go. She positively ached to see Ian again but felt that the next move had to come from him. And when she didn't hear anything from him or see him again all day, she began to worry — did he regret what had happened between them?

He might be exhausted. She musn't blow things out of proportion. He and Massimo had had a very full day, much of it out in the wind and cold. Given how little he had slept last night, he might be longing for a quiet evening and an early bedtime.

He might want to be with Lily. They hadn't been alone since yesterday, when, after all, she had reached a pretty big milestone in her life. Maybe one huge event happening in their tight little family of two was all that he could deal with right now.

He might be freaking out. It was one thing to succumb to the pleasures of their night together – and there had been many; quite another to contemplate this in the cold, hard light of day. Maybe he was racked with remorse, feeling he had betrayed his wife. He might be feeling he had made a mistake. There were presumably lots of reasons why he hadn't been with a woman since Cait died, reasons Joey might not ever know. Maybe his silence meant that he was slamming on the brakes, right now, before this could go any further.

Maybe he didn't like the way she kissed, or the way she –

No. *No way.* Joey wasn't going there. There wasn't a doubt in her mind that Ian had enjoyed every second of their time together. He might not want to take this any further, for any number of reasons, but *that* wasn't one of them.

✳ ✳ ✳

At seven thirty, Joey locked the door to Stanway House and tiptoed across the drive, trying to make as little noise as possible. She had debated taking Tink – Tink would have loved the pond and the walk into the village in the darkness – but she decided against it. It was an honour to be invited to spend time with the ladies, and Tink had not been invited. One couldn't just assume that everybody loved dogs as much as she did.

The gatehouse was all lit up, but the curtains had been

drawn against the evening's chill air and Joey couldn't hear any sound from inside. Using a torch as her guide, she walked into the village and made her way along the narrow path that led to the pond. The water was cloaked in blackness. The moon did little to illuminate the scene, but the hut was glowing with light and warmth.

Joey paused outside the door, listening to the women's voices within and the sound of – that had to be Edith Piaf singing in a rough, scratchy recording. Joey knocked on the door and it was thrown open by Viv.

"Joey! We heard you might stop by. Come in. We're just about to eat."

Joey handed Viv the baguette from the bakery and two bottles of Graves. She stepped into the hut. The ladies of the swimming society were gathered around an old wooden table adorned with a rustic linen cloth. The woodstove crackled merrily in the corner, and tiny white Christmas lights had been hung from all the rafters. The women wore shiny paper crowns. Joey suddenly had the feeling that this was more than a casual supper.

"It's so beautiful in here," Joey said, glancing all around as she sat down on the sturdy wooden bench. "Do you do this often?"

"Only on birthdays. Five times a year!"

"Whose birthday is it?" Joey asked, wishing Aggie had let her know the reason for the celebration, so she could have bought a gift.

"Meg's!" they all cried.

"Can't you tell by her crown?" Viv asked.

She saw now that Meg's paper crown was gold, and taller and more elaborate than the others.

"We used to celebrate birthdays at our houses," Lilia began.

"But our husbands were always ghosting around, acting all put out! *They* weren't *invited*? God forbid! So we decided to sneak away and have our little parties here."

"But now they're all — " Meg stopped abruptly in the middle of her sentence, a little afraid to finish it.

"Dead," Viv whispered. Then she giggled.

"Not that we don't miss them," Aggie said. "We do! Terribly!"

"We could go back to having the parties at home," Lilia said. "Perhaps we should."

"No!" Meg wailed. "This is much more fun!"

Gala set a heavy steaming pot in the centre of the table as Aggie handed around mismatched bowls. A bottle of Scotch, a brand Joey had never heard of, sat on the table, as did the baguettes that Aggie had bought. Viv added Joey's baguette to the pile as Lilia set down a saucer holding a big, square slab of butter. Meg reached for a corkscrew, hung on string on a nail in the wall, and proceeded to open one of the bottles of wine.

"Dinner is served," Gala said proudly.

"Chicken in a pot. My favourite!" Meg announced, smiling.

One by one, they all held out their bowls, waiting patiently for Gala to serve them.

"Where'd you learn to make this?" Joey asked.

"From my mother," Gala said quietly, "who learned it from her mother."

"Where did they live?" said Joey.

"Poland. A little town known as Bolimów. Known for its ceramics: beautiful, beautiful pottery. Not like this!"

She gestured with scorn to the ceramic pot in which she had cooked the dish. "This has no grace. The handles are too thin and the cover is too thick." She shook her head. But the memory of her mother – and perhaps other memories of what had eventually happened to her mother – caused Gala's expression to cloud over.

"*Zum Wohl*," she said quietly, when the last bowl was filled.

"If you could bottle this, you'd be a millionaire," Lilia whispered, closing her eyes to savour the complicated mixture of essences in the broth.

Joey sipped the creamy soup, thick with potatoes and carrots and laced with threads of chicken that just melted in her mouth. They all ate, quietly, almost reverently.

Later, they chatted happily through seconds, sipping Scotch and wine as they listened to the plaintive songs playing on the CD player. At a certain moment, Aggie and Viv exchanged a significant glance, got up and retreated to a dark corner of the room. Seconds later, Viv was carrying to the table a cake so adorned with candles that it appeared to be almost ablaze.

Viv's warbling soprano led them into song.

Happy birthday to you!
Happy birthday to you!
Happy birthday, dear Meg!
Happy birthday to you!

"If you live much longer, Megsie," Aggie teased, "we're going to have to use two cakes." Meg grinned as Viv swept the cake away to cut it.

"Or fewer candles," Gala said. "How about one for each decade?"

Aggie handed Meg a large white box tied with a beautiful blue bow.

"Didn't we decide on no birthday presents, ever?" Meg asked, taking the gift from Aggie all the same.

"When was that?" Gala called out.

"I believe it was 1967." Meg held the package up, admiring the beautiful bow.

"But it's your *eightieth*, Meg. I think we can make an exception!"

"Open it up." Aggie said excitedly. "You only go around once!"

"Speak for yourself!" said Viv. "I happen to believe in reincarnation."

"Don't be ridiculous," Lilia put in sharply. "When you're dead, you're dead. Game over."

"Ladies, ladies! It's Meg's night! Please!" Aggie chastised.

"I don't recall getting any eightieth birthday presents," sighed Gala.

"But you did!" Lilia protested. "That red hat! With the black velvet band!"

"Oh yes," Gala conceded.

Joey thought back to a celebration she had attended in New York, for the eightieth birthday of Alex's mentor, Richard Andrews. It had been a huge event with a twelve-piece brass swing ensemble, attended by over three hundred guests. Four thousand long-stemmed tulips had been flown in from Holland to adorn every horizontal surface of the Waldorf-Astoria ballroom. Richard's fourth wife, a former Victoria's Secret model, seemed ill at ease at the event, though Joey supposed that was to be expected, given the vintage of Richard's contemporaries. *Like mentor, like protégée*, she thought.

If she ever lived to be eighty, Joey mused, she'd rather have a party like this.

Meg gasped when the content of the package was revealed: a fragile copy of the London *Times* from 1958. She unfolded the paper and held it up for them all to see. On the front page was a photograph of three young women, apparently protesting at some kind of rally.

"Oh my God!" Meg said. "Look at this! It's us…"

"Wow!" exclaimed Joey, astonished to recognise the ladies' younger faces.

"The Aldermaston Marches," Lilia said. "It's how we all met. Viv and I were at that rally, too. We just didn't elbow ourselves into the picture!"

Meg carefully set down the yellowed newspaper. "Where did you get this?" she asked in amazement.

"I bought it online," Aggie announced proudly. "It's amazing what one can find with a computer."

"What were the Alderman Marches?" Joey asked, a little sheepish about not knowing.

"Aldermaston," Gala corrected. "The Campaign for Nuclear Disarmament."

"It took us four days, " Aggie explained. "We walked all the way from Trafalgar Square to the Atomic Weapons Establishment."

"The next year, they reversed the direction, so the protesters would end up in London," Meg pointed out.

"I marched every single year," Gala said proudly. "Sixe times in all."

"I marched twice," Lilia put in.

"Look at us!" Meg said warmly, scrutinising their younger faces in the photo. "I still feel exactly like that. I look in the mirror and I'm always surprised, because inside, I still feel like that girl."

When she looked up and around, there were tears in her eyes.

"Now, now," said Viv, "let's not get all weepy and morose! Ageing is a privilege! Not everybody's lucky enough to get to do it. Besides, we don't want to bore our young friend here. There's nothing worse than old people moaning and whining!"

"You'd never bore me," Joey said. "Sometimes I feel old, too. Old-er, anyway! Yesterday, I had to explain to Lily who Jackie Kennedy and Grace Kelly were!"

Lilia turned swiftly. "How did that come up?" she asked sharply.

"I took her to London, and – "

"My *granddaughter?*"

"Yes. I had meeting, so –"

"*You* took *Lily* to *London?* On a school day?" Lilia's eyes were flashing.

"She really wanted to go, and she begged Ian to let her take the day off."

Lilia said nothing, but from the look on her face, Joey could tell that the woman was enraged.

"I see," she said coldly.

She stood up abruptly and carried her uneaten cake to the side table. Perhaps in an effort to cut the tension that had suddenly filled the air, Viv hopped up, went over to the CD player and restarted the Edith Piaf disc.

"Wait! Wait!" she called. "We have to sing our song! It's not a proper birthday party if we don't sing our song! Lilia! Come on."

"I'm sorry," Lilia said. "I have to go." And with that, she crossed the room, kissed Meg and abruptly departed, slamming the door behind her.

"I'm so sorry," Joey whispered.

"It's not your fault," Meg said. "And it's not about you. Or London."

"It's Cait's birthday this week," Aggie explained. "She would have been forty this coming Friday."

"I'm sorry," Joey said. "I've ruined things."

"Not at all, dear one," Aggie said softly. "Sometimes Lilia just needs her — space."

Edith Piaf's signature song had just begun. Her raw, powerful voice soared out of the scratchy, crackling recording.

"*Je ne regrette rien*," Aggie sang.

"Not the good things, " Gala added. "And not the bad things!"

One by one, Meg, Viv and Gala joined in, clasping hands with Joey on the table as their beautiful ancient faces glowed in the firelight.

Non, rien de rien
Non, je ne regrette rien
Ni le bien qu'on m'a fait
Ni le mal, tout ça m'est bien égal
Non, rien de rien
Non, je ne regrette rien
C'est payé, balayé, oublié
Je me fous du passé

Chapter 17

When Joey took Tink outside first thing in the morning, she discovered that a warm front had moved in during the night. The air smelled positively spring-like, and she wondered whether here, as in the American north-east, there was a regular "January thaw". There hadn't been snow since she arrived in England, though the air had been damp and often bone-chilling. But today, she could smell the loam and the grasses, and not just wood smoke from all the chimneys. Where had this warm air come from? she wondered. The Mediterranean? The Irish Sea? She even thought she could detect a hint of salt in the air, though that hardly seemed possible, given how far inland they were.

Tink reacted to the thaw as she always did when spring came to New York; her urge to sniff went into overdrive. She strained at her leash, doing everything she could do to drag her mistress into the carnival of scents that beckoned from the woods. Joey steered her instead toward the body of water called the Gravity Pool, which lay at the top of the cascading water terraces that fed Stanway's famous fountain. A one-room stone structure had been built on top of the pond's outlet. Capped by a steeple that gave the building its name – The Pyramid – it afforded exquisite views of the surrounding countryside and the intriguing sensation of being in an open room at the top of a castle's turret.

"Hey, there."

Joey wheeled around. Ian was on the far side of the pond. Dressed in waders, he was straddling the stream that fed the pond, digging into the water with a long pole.

Joey smiled and started toward him. "Hey! What are you doing?"

"Trying to clear this waterway. It's blocked with sticks and leaves."

The ground grew mushier as she approached him; she was glad she had worn her waterproof boots. She stopped a few feet away. She wanted nothing more than to throw herself into Ian's arms, but she resisted the impulse.

"How'd you know it was clogged?" she asked.

"I noticed it yesterday, when we were up here."

Joey nodded. "How'd that go?"

"Yesterday? Oh, fine."

"I was going to come by a little later, to talk to you before I call Massimo."

Ian smiled. "Do."

"What time?"

"You tell me. I work for you."

"No, you don't!" she protested. "We both work for — them!"

Ian smiled warmly. "Okay, if it makes you feel better to think of it that way."

"It's true!"

They were smiling now. They each took a moment to scan the other's eyes. "How are you?" Joey finally whispered.

Ian nodded, his expression open and trusting. "You?"

"Couldn't be better," she replied.

"Good."

"I'll drop Tink off and come over."

"Do that," Ian said.

Joey all but floated back to the apartment, and when she got there, there was a message on her BlackBerry. It turned out to be from Sarah, but Joey didn't want to call her back now. She fed Tink, ran a brush through her hair, dabbed on some lipstick and made her way over to the gatehouse. She tapped the door lightly then opened it.

"Hello? Ian?"

"In here!" came the response from the kitchen. Joey smelled toast, coffee and oranges. She crossed the space and stood in the kitchen doorway for a moment, suddenly nervous. It had felt natural to meet Ian outdoors on the grounds, especially when he was preoccupied with a care-taking task, but this was different. They were together in his house, alone for the first time since their glorious night in front of the fire. She felt inexplicably shy, which was crazy. Or perhaps it was simple nervousness: if Ian was harbouring second thoughts about becoming romantically involved, she would know this very soon.

He had been sitting at the kitchen table, but now he hopped up, poured Joey coffee and handed it to her.

"Thanks."

"Want some toast?"

"Sure."

He turned and cut two thick slices from a loaf on the cutting board. He put them in the toaster, then cut three oranges in half, squeezed them into juice with an elegant little press on the counter and handed Joey the glass.

"Hey! Fresh squeezed."

He nodded and sat back down.

Joey poured cream in her coffee and searched his expression for any sign of what he was feeling. She decided it might be better to talk first about work, and later about everything else.

"How'd it go with Massimo?"

"Good man. Knows what's what."

"Think you're going to like working with him?"

"I don't see why not."

"Were you able to get to everything?"

The toast popped up. Ian tossed it onto a plate and handed it to Joey. She was glad to have something to do, even if that only involved butter and marmalade. She found she was avoiding direct eye contact.

"We've got questions, but he seems to know lads who specialise in just about everything. He put in some calls, and they're all going to be trooping through in the next week or ten days."

"That's good. Isn't it?" Joey had a bite of her toast.

Ian nodded.

"So by the end of next week, it should be pretty clear what we're up against."

"I'd say so." There was a pause. Ian looked down then met her gaze. "When are you leaving?"

She put her toast down and sighed. "I don't know. Sometime in the next couple of weeks."

Ian nodded. 'So, then, it's probably a – pretty bad idea."

"What is?"

He pointed to Joey and then to himself.

"I like bad ideas," she said wryly.

Ian cleared his throat and shook his head. "I've spent enough time pining to be with someone who's not here."

"But I *am*!"

"For the time being, sure. Besides, for all I know, you've got somebody back home."

"I do not!"

"Ex?"

"Well, *everybody* has exes! Come on! There would really be something to worry about if someone my age – "

"And what age is that, Miss Rubin?"

"What do you think?" Joey smiled.

"Oh, no. Not a chance. I know better than to answer that question. Or to ask too many."

"You can ask me anything you want! What do you want to know?"

"Oh, a few things." He smiled.

It could have been the coffee, but Joey's heart was now thumping rapidly.

"Well, ask me. Go on. Ask me a few things."

"Five things?" A sly grin spread over Ian's face. "I ask, you answer?"

"We both ask, we both answer," Joey countered.

Ian sat back and appeared to be pondering his list of questions. Finally, he spoke.

"Do you live alone?"

"Yes. But that's not fair, because I already know your answer to *that!*"

"All right, you can ask me something else." Ian refilled his coffee cup and sipped it, black and strong.

"Do you have any brothers or sisters?"

"One. Sister. Lives in the Shetland Islands."

"What does she do *there?*" Joey asked.

"Is that your second question?"

Joey shrugged.

"They raise sheep. And children. Six, at last count."

"Wow! Okay, question number three: what's your favourite — song?"

Ian smiled. "You won't know it."

"Try me."

"It's an old Scottish tune: 'Kinrara'." And then he went on to recite the first verse of lyrics:

Red gleams the sun on yon hill-tap,
The dew sits on the gowan;
Deep murmurs through her glens the Spey,
Around Kinrara rowan.
Where art thou, fairest, kindest lass?
Alas! wert thou but near me,
Thy gentle soul, thy melting eye,
Would ever, ever cheer me.

A melancholy look washed over his features, and Joey wondered whether the words of the song had brought Cait to mind.

"You're not going to sing it for me?" Joey teased, hoping to jolly him out of impending gloom.

"I don't sing."

"Ever?"

"Ever. And if you heard me sing, you'd know why."

"Okay, so you're not big on — singing."

"Only my own."

Joey smiled and pressed on. "Then what's your favourite way to relax?"

Ian gave her a suggestive look.

"*Besides*, that!" she said.

"I like to ride, out in the woods. You?"

"Riding? No way. " Joey shook her head. "I'm a city girl."

"Ever tried it?" Ian pressed.

"Once when I was at summer camp. The horse took off. With me on him."

"You apparently survived."

"Yeah, but I had nightmares about horses for years!"

"About time you got over that, don't you think?"

"Is that an official question?

"I think it's more of an answer."

❋ ❋ ❋

Joey would never have agreed to it if the weather hadn't been so invitingly warm and sunny, or if anyone but Ian had been asking, but she found that she couldn't say no. So a little while later, almost trembling with anxiety, Joey was in the backyard, placing her left foot into Ian's clasped hands and throwing her right leg over the back of an enormous mare called Maggie.

"No! I'm not doing this. Let me down."

"She's not going anywhere," he said calmly, the horse's reins wrapped around his hand.

"There's no point to this," Joey argued, fighting the urge to jump off Maggie and back quietly away. "I live in a city. I'm never going to ride a horse again in my life."

"All the more reason to do it now."

"But I'm … too chicken."

"She's a nag, Joey. She's twenty-two years old. She isn't going anywhere fast."

Joey took a deep breath. "Don't let go! Hold onto the reins."

"It's okay. I've got you."

Joey's stomach muscles tightened up as the horse began to move. "Oh, my God!"

"You're doing fine." Ian led Maggie out of the yard. "We'll just walk down this road, okay?"

Joey didn't answer. She was hanging on for dear life.

"Okay?" Ian asked. "Joey?"

Joey nodded, holding the pommel of the saddle tightly. She drew a deep breath, willing herself to unclench her muscles. If Sarah's kids could do this, so could she.

"Good job," Ian said. "You're doing fine."

After several moments, Joey was surprised to discover

that she was — getting to be — a little more relaxed with this. Maggie was slow and sturdy beneath her, and as Joey swayed to the gentle movements of the animal's walk, she found herself able to glance up at the trees and fields bordering the country road. *Okay*, she thought. *I'm okay*.

The next step was for Ian to mount his own horse. He tried to hand Joey Maggie's reins.

"No! I'm too scared!"

"But I have to get Thunder."

"*Thunder?* Okay, I think I'm done now. This was great, but — "

"He's terrified of thunder. That's how he got the name. Look, I'll tie Maggie to the fence. She's not going anywhere."

"Are you sure?"

"I'm sure. She was always lazy and slow. She never moves more than she has to."

Ian tied Maggie's reins to a fence post then disappeared into the barn.

"Hi, Maggie," Joey whispered. Maggie ignored her. "You're a good girl. That's a good girl." Joey let go of the saddle, which she had been gripping fiercely, and laid her hand on Maggie's neck. The animal's warmth surprised her. She patted her gently, and Maggie turned her head in response. The sight of the horse's eyelashes and her enormous, limpid eyes somehow slowed Joey's racing thoughts. Maggie really *was* calm. She was gently submitting to carrying a complete stranger on her back, and Joey felt a rush of warmth and affection.

Ian came out of the barn on Thunder, a large chestnut with a regal bearing, and rode over to the fence. He untied the reins.

"I can hold them," Joey said tentatively. Inside, she was still nervous, but she was determined to be brave. She could see that Ian was pleased as he gave a surprised little nod and handed them to her. "Good lass," he said. "There you go."

They headed onto the road, past the churchyard with its ancient headstones covered in lichen, past the dense hedgerows, and the hills dotted with cottages built of the same yellow stone as Stanway House. Half a mile on, they turned off the main road and on to a gentle, winding path that headed through the fields and up to a clearing by the edge of the woods. Joey was riding more easily now, beginning to accept that Maggie had no intention of bolting for freedom.

The air was rich with earthy smells. Leaves blanketed the floor of the woods on either side of the road. For a time, so overcome with the sights, sounds and fragrances of the country in midwinter, Joey actually forgot that she was on the back of a horse. She now understood what Ian felt here, for she was feeling it herself. She would have said so, but their mutual silence felt so companionable that she didn't want to speak.

At the top of the hill, they turned their horses and gazed down at the countryside laid out before them, quiet and still, as though in a painting.

"Good for you," Ian finally said. "It was worth it, wasn't it?"

"Yes," Joey said softly.

The ride back to Stanway House was thrilling: part sheer terror, part joyous exhilaration. When they reached the bottom of the hill, Ian gave Joey a mischievous glance and kicked Thunder into a canter.

"Wait!" Joey called. "Ian!"

Maggie, perhaps sensing that Joey either didn't know how to instruct her to follow suit or didn't have a clue about what she wanted the horse to do, roused herself in pursuit.

Stunned and terrified at first, Joey soon discovered that the cantering horse was not really all that difficult to ride. She gripped Maggie's sides with her knees, holding onto the saddle at first and then gradually letting go, relaxing into the easy, rolling rhythms of the horse's motion. This was much easier than when Maggie had briefly trotted, earlier, bumping Joey up and down so that she hit the saddle awkwardly and hard.

She caught up with Ian at the corner of the road.

But they were no sooner there than he steered Thunder into a field and began to canter away.

"No!" she called after him. "Ian! Enough!"

But he was off. She had two choices: stay here until he returned, or go with him. What she definitely couldn't do was go back to the stables by herself. She didn't know how to get down from a horse.

Joey gave Maggie a little kick, and Maggie seemed to understand what to do. The horse started off slowly then began to trot. Joey bumped uncomfortably in the saddle, gritting her teeth. She gave another little nudge with her heels. And, just when Maggie's trotting had reached its most painful, she broke into a beautiful, flowing canter.

Joey's nervous smile gave way to a broad grin as the wind met her cheeks and she and Maggie fairly flew across the field, to catch up with Ian and Thunder.

Chapter 18

"Ian *McCormack?*" Sarah said.

Joey was surprised by the tone of her friend's voice on the phone. She was sitting in the empty kitchen of Stanway House, relishing the last warm rays of the afternoon sun pouring through the window.

"Yeah," Joey said quietly.

"Wow," Sarah replied.

Joey was taken aback and paused for a moment before responding. Sarah hadn't said "Wow" as in, "Wow, that's so fantastic!" She'd said "Wow!" the way one might pronounce the word while staring at an astronomically large credit card bill.

"You don't sound overjoyed," Joey said.

"I'm – surprised, that's all."

"Why? He's gorgeous and nice. And available."

"Is he?"

"He's not seeing anyone, as far as I know."

"But... is he ready to start dating?"

"I'm not sure I'd call it 'dating'. We haven't gone out anywhere."

"What *have* you done?" Sarah asked sharply. Joey could just imagine her friend's mouth, set in a prim, maternal pout of disapproval.

In response, Joey felt an impulse to be a little scandalous.

That was what Sarah deserved for being such a prig.

"What *haven't* we done is more like it," Joey whispered.

"Joey!!"

"*What?* I thought you'd be happy for me. Why are you acting like this? Do you know something I don't?"

'It's not that."

"Then what is it?" Joey's mood was darkening. She had been so excited to share her news with Sarah. She thought Sarah would be thrilled for her. She certainly hadn't expected this reaction.

"It's a small town," Sarah intoned.

"So?"

"Word gets around."

"He's not fifteen, Sarah. He's a grown man. If he didn't want to get involved with me, he wouldn't have. You'd think people would be happy for him. He's been alone for a while now."

"And he'll be alone again as soon as you leave!"

Joey sat back in her chair. She had moved past disappointment in Sarah's reaction and was headed toward righteous indignation.

"You're a New Yorker, Joey!" Sarah pressed on.

"So were you!"

"Yeah, but I was twent-three years old. I hadn't built a life and a career."

"Right, I see, so it was easier to for you to mould yourself into whatever Henry wanted you to be. Easier to slip into Henry's life that to create one of your own."

"Is that what you think I did?" Sarah asked coldly.

Though Joey was now angry enough to want to fling the word "yes" at her, something made her pull back.

"No," she said, summoning as much self-control as she could. "I think you fell in love with a wonderful man and decided that a life with him was worth some sacrifices." There was a tense pause. "I thought you'd be happy for me."

"I *am*," Sarah insisted.

"Well you have a pretty funny way of showing it."

"I just don't want you to get hurt," Sarah continued.

"No, you don't want *him* to get hurt. That came through loud and clear."

"I don't want *anyone* to get hurt," Sarah insisted defensively.

"To be alive is to get hurt," Joey replied. "There's no getting around that."

They were both silent for what felt like a long time. Joey, cupping her phone between ear and shoulder, stood and walked to the window; outside, the shadows were deepening and all was quiet.

"I'm sorry," Sarah finally whispered.

"Me, too," Joey added lamely, aware that she seemed to have spent most of her visit apologising to Sarah for things she had apparently done wrong, at least in Sarah's opinion.

"It's just that you're always down on me for being such a cynic, for not sharing your romantic view of life, and here I am telling you I think I'm really falling for someone – "

"It just caught me by surprise."

"Me, too!"

"And where can it possibly go, Joey? I mean, I can't see you moving here. Can you?"

"I have no idea. I just met him two weeks ago."

"And I can't see him moving to New York. What would he do there?"

"Search me."

"And there's Lily."

"I love Lily. We get along great. I took her to London last

week and we had a really fun time! I don't actually think she'd mind too much if Ian and I got together."

"You came to London? Why didn't you call me?"

"I was in meetings all morning and it was supposed to be kind of an outing, for her."

Sarah said nothing. *Great*, Joey thought. Now Sarah could add another item to her list of perceived slights.

"Look," Joey said. "We didn't leave things on the happiest of notes. What was I supposed to do, drag Lily over to your house so you and I could spend the afternoon figuring out why we seem to be fighting all the time?"

"We're not fighting," Sarah insisted.

"We're not? Then what are we doing?"

Sarah didn't seem to have an answer, so she changed the subject.

"Does Lily know? About you two?"

"Not unless he's said something to her. I certainly haven't."

"Don't! It's up to him to tell her if he wants to."

"I know. I'm not hanging around his house half-dressed all the time, if that's what you're worried about."

"I'm not worried about that."

"I'm here because of work, Sarah, not because I needed a romantic — escape."

"Interesting choice of words."

"Which words?" Joey asked.

"Escape. Methinks the lady doth protest too much."

"And what, exactly, do you think I want to escape?"

"New York?"

"I love New York!"

"Being alone? Because if that's what you're doing, Joey, it's just not fair. Lily and Ian have been through hell. The last thing they need is someone who's just after a romantic interlude.

Someone who will then disappear from their lives."

"I won't disappear."

"No?"

"Not from *them*."

"Meaning what? A life of emails and Skype? Great!"

Joey could feel her anger rising again and this time she just didn't feel like tamping it down. "Look, Sarah, you don't have to like the fact that Ian and I – "

"Ian and you!" Sarah said scornfully.

"Yes! Ian and I!" And now, Joey felt powerless to hold back. Her emotions rushed out in a torrent.

"I don't claim to know where this is going. I don't have any idea what the future will bring. I don't know what, if anything, I mean, or could mean, to Ian and I don't know for sure – though I have a pretty good idea – how Lily would feel about sharing her dad.

"But I do know that he feels *something* for me. And that he has been lonely for an awfully long time, and that this just might be the first time since his wife died that he's allowed another woman into his life. If that's all this ends up being, fine. I'm seriously okay with that. Even if I end up alone in New York."

"I don't want that to happen!" Sarah cried. "I want you to be with someone! I want you to be happy."

"But not with Ian. And not here."

"I'd love to have you here!"

"I don't really think you would, Sarah. I think you like being the happily married mother of four, all settled and blissful in England. As opposed to *me*, the lonely single dysfunctional woman who's given everything up for her career and who's the perfect foil for everything you have got right in your life: the poor friend who will never be happy. I think that arrangement suits you just fine."

Sarah gave a little gasp on the other end of the phone. When she spoke again, her voice was tearful. "If you really think that, you don't know me very well."

"I did, once. You were my sister."

"Before you stopped noticing when my children were born," Sarah shot back. "Before you couldn't make it to our wedding, before you started to think of me as the person you never wanted to be."

"I never thought of you that way!"

"No?"

"No!"

"You could have fooled me."

"Did you come to New York when my mother died? No. Did you even respond to the invitation to my father's wedding? I wanted you there. I *needed* you. Both times. The hurts go both ways, Sarah."

"I'm sorry," Sarah said, "I really am." She paused for a long while before speaking again. "So I guess we have two choices here. We can give up, just decide that our relationship has run its course. No hard feelings, part as friends."

"Or?" Joey asked.

"Forget who we used to be, way back when. Forget all the ways we've hurt each other since then. Forget what we *think* we know about each other and start over. From scratch. Turn the page."

Joey felt relieved by the clarity in Sarah's voice. She was being truthful. They could now stop pretending that they were close, that nothing could ever ruin their friendship.

"Too much time has gone by," Sarah whispered. "I hoped that we'd be able to pick things up where we left off, but too much has happened."

"I know. I want to try to — reconnect."

"I'd *like* to want to," Sarah said, "but to tell you the truth,

I'm not sure I do. Because I can't go halfway, Joey. I won't go halfway. If we're going to be in each other's lives, then we really have to be in each other's lives. That's the only kind of friendship I want."

"Okay," Joey said. "I guess we'll – think about it."

"Okay," Sarah replied. And with that, she put down the phone.

Chapter 19

Joey shifted on the pillow, and stretched her legs down into the warmth of the bed. Ian was dozing beside her, his arm gently resting on her stomach. A shaft of grey moonlight glowed on the windows. How had this happened? she wondered. Her tense phone conversation with Sarah seemed a lifetime ago. Ian had come to invite her for a glass of wine to run through the preliminary punch list provided by Massimo. One minute they had been sipping their drinks and talking shop, the next they'd been trading glances. Joey had imagined that their coming together would be tender and maybe even a little poignant, but in the last hour, Ian had conducted himself less like the cool, upstanding Scot he had purported to be, and more like a man in the grip of a fever.

Lily! Joey suddenly thought with alarm.

Ian opened his eyes when Joey leaned down for the duvet and covered him. "Where do you think you're going?" he whispered as she reached for her camisole and jeans.

"I can't stay."

"Yes, you can."

"I can't be here when Lily wakes up."

"I'll set the alarm. You can leave at six. We'll be fine."

"You sure?"

"Once she is asleep, she's dead to the world. I have to drag her out of bed in the morning."

"You sure?"

"I am. Come here."

He lifted the duvet and drew her toward him.

❋ ❋ ❋

"Dad?"

Joey opened her eyes. Lily was standing in the bedroom doorway.

"*Joey?*"

Ian flew to a sitting position and Joey reached for the covers. "What the – ?" Ian picked up the clock and shook it, as though the gesture might turn back time and undo the present awkwardness of his daughter standing in the doorway.

"It's seven thirty," Lily said calmly.

"It's not what you think, Lily," Ian said reflexively.

She cocked her head and gave him a wry stare. "No? Come on, Dad. Give me a little credit."

"I'm sorry!" Joey blurted out, putting an arm out and reaching for her jeans. "It's all my fault, I –"

"For what?" Lily asked. "Shagging my dad?"

"Lily!" Ian snapped.

"Oh, *excuse me*," Lily said, beginning to grin. "You were just – sleeping, right?"

"We'll talk about this later," Ian said, stepping into his trousers and pulling on his sweater.

"What's to talk about? I'm cool with it, Dad."

"I am so sorry," Joey repeated.

"I'm not," Lily replied, turning on her heels and heading down the hall. Ian raced after her and Joey buried her head in her hands. She *knew* she should have left! She should never have let Ian talk her into it. She would give them a few moments alone downstairs. Get dressed, wash her face and pull herself together, and then go down and say a calm, dignified goodbye.

She went into the bathroom, and on the spur of the moment decided to take a quick shower. She turned the water on as hot as she could stand and lathered up her arms, her face, her hair, then stepped into the cool bathroom air and towelled off and got dressed. She debated making the bed, then resolved it was probably better that she leave the house as soon as possible. Ian was no doubt furious with her. Lily would be deciding right now that no, come to think of it, she *wasn't* cool with it, she wasn't cool with it at *all*...

Maybe Sarah had been right, Joey thought. She *was* being selfish, putting her own needs and desires before those of two people she claimed to care about. She was being stupid and reckless.

As she began to descend the staircase, Joey heard the doorbell ringing. Lily padded across the space in her stocking feet and opened the front door just as Joey reached the halfway landing. There, in the doorway, stood Lilia.

"Grandma!" Lily said. She glanced at Joey in alarm as Lilia stepped inside, as yet oblivious to Joey's presence. Joey stood as still as she could. Perhaps, if she didn't breathe and didn't move a muscle, Lilia would somehow fail to see her. Lilia was fumbling with her handbag right now, and maybe, just maybe, Lily would lead her across the hall and into the kitchen, and Joey would be able to make her escape.

But Lily paused. She looked up and gave Joey a smile and nod: "Grandma, you know Joey Rubin, don't you?"

Lilia snapped to attention. Her eyes took in Joey's wet hair, the rumpled clothing that had clearly seen Joey through at least one day, the glow in her cheeks. She opened her mouth to speak, but only a little gasp came out.

"Good morning, Lilia," Joey said softly.

Suddenly, Ian was by his daughter's side. "Lilia," he said, looking alarmed. "Christ, how could I have forgotten?"

The old woman appeared to disintegrate. "Your own wife's birthday," she said, so quietly that they could barely hear her words. "Am I supposed to go to the churchyard on my own this year?"

"Of course not," Ian said kindly. "We'll go just like we always do. But come and sit down for a minute. Have a cup of tea."

He reached for the woman's arm, but she was shaking her head in disbelief, staring at Joey.

"What are you doing here?" Lilia asked.

"She's our guest," Ian said simply.

"But – but this is my daughter's house," Lilia said, emotion beginning to rise.

"It's *our* house, Grandma!" Lily said defiantly.

"You stay out of this!" Ian said to Lily.

"No! I won't. This is my house, too!" She glanced at Joey. "And I'm *glad* she's here!"

"Lily!" Ian said sternly. "Go upstairs! Now!"

"No!" She crossed her arms and came closer to Joey.

"Now!" Ian shouted.

Lily shot him a furious glare and raced past Joey and up the stairs.

"I'll go," Joey whispered. "I should go."

"You should never have *come*!" Lilia screeched. "On my daughter's birthday? You have the nerve to, no the *cruel*ty to – "

"Lilia," Ian said, "Come now, there's no need to – "

He tried to take her by the arm but she shook him off. "My daughter's house! My daughter's husband!" She turned to Joey, bitterness in her voice. "Who *are* you? Everywhere I turn, you're there – worming your way into places you don't belong, cosying up – "

"I'm sorry," Joey said. "I truly am. It was never my intention to be anywhere I wasn't welcome or do anything that might hurt someone."

"Well you did!" Lilia shot back.

"Then I'm really and truly sorry. I'll go now." She turned to Ian. "I'll talk to you later."

Ian nodded. Joey crossed the hall, eased herself around Lilia, who in her anger had begun to cry, and closed the gatehouse door behind her.

As she crossed the gravel, she thought she could hear Lily shouting. She was furious herself at this moment, but not because she had done anything she really considered to be wrong. Ian was a grown man and she was a grown woman, and neither one was attached. Why shouldn't they snatch at happiness? Didn't they have the same right as everyone else to try to wring a little joy from relationships with the people who happened to cross their path in life?

Of course they did, she consoled herself with thinking. It wasn't that. It was just – painful and awkward the way things had played out, and all because she had been too caught up in her own pleasure to do what she knew she should have done: if only she had got up and left in the middle of the night.

She usually dreaded early walks with Tink, wishing she didn't have to brave the streets – or here, the fields and woods – first thing. But today, she knew that a walk was just what she needed. She would take Tink way, way out, past where Thunder and Maggie were stabled, to the far corner of the estate, and maybe, just maybe, she would be able to figure out how to put all this to rights, with Ian, with Lily, with Sarah, even with Lilia. She was glad she didn't have any contractors coming by this morning. She wouldn't come back to Stanway House until she had a plan.

Chapter 20

Ian was just pulling his van into the spot beside the gate-house when Joey came out of the front door. She had tramped through the hills and woods with Tink for nearly two hours, had coffee and breakfast, and by all rights, she should have been feeling at least a little bit better by now. But nothing had worked. Not the brisk, fresh air, nor the scent of French Roast dripping through the coffee filter, which always filled her with a sense of optimism about the coming day. She kept replaying the scene at the foot of Ian's staircase, Lilia nearly breathless with shock and fury, Ian standing helplessly by, Lily filled with righteous anger at her own grandmother. And all of it, every bit of it, because of Joey.

That didn't even factor in the upsetting conversation with Sarah, which Joey had managed to put out of her mind during the time when she was with Ian. Years ago, she wouldn't have given a second thought to an argument like the one they'd had. Growing up, they'd *always* disagreed about things, easily, passionately and loudly. But they'd also been so close, their lives so intertwined, that a squabble would blow over like a sudden, dramatic cloudburst.

This felt different, very different. Their lives weren't intertwined any more, and Sarah had actually *said* that she just wasn't interested in having the kind of friendship they'd had for the past fifteen years. Joey wondered whether, deep down, Sarah was even interested in having the kind of relationship they'd had for the fifteen years before that. Joey had the distinct feeling that her oldest friend in the world just didn't really like her any more.

Ian glimpsed Joey on the steps and paused. Joey could tell that he wished they hadn't run into each other just now, which made *her* wish she could pretend not to have seen him and step behind one of the stone columns. But now he was coming toward her, his shoulders hunched, his face drained and pale.

"I'm so sorry," was all she could think to whisper.

Ian shook his head. "She was out of line."

Joey waited for Ian to go on, but he seemed withdrawn, preoccupied.

"And Lily," Joey said. "I feel terrible. I should have left."

"You tried," he said quietly. A smile flickered briefly then faded. Ian seemed very far away, so far that it was hard for Joey to imagine that just hours earlier, they had been blissfully entangled. Now, an awkward silence hung in the late morning air, and Joey was at a loss as to what to do to make anything better.

"Lily in school?" she finally asked, a little too cheerfully.

"She didn't want to go in late — "

"Why was she late?'

"We went to — Cait's — to the churchyard. We always do, just not first thing in the morning."

Joey sighed, now feeling a surprising flash of anger. She was doing everything she could to be sensitive to everyone else, but she had feelings, too. The morning's events had been embarrassing, if not downright humiliating. "Then why did Lilia come by this morning? Why did she just — show up like that?"

"Why does she do anything?" Ian said angrily. "It was what *she* wanted to do. She's so blinded by her own – I'm sorry." Ian struggled to keep his feelings in check. "I know the woman's to be pitied, but sometimes ... "

"You lost Cait, too," Joey said quietly. "So did Lily."

Ian set his jaw firmly. Joey reached out to comfort him, but instead of welcoming her touch, his arms seemed to tense and stiffen. He shook his head and pulled away, then hurried into the gatehouse.

Stunned, Joey stood for several moments, watching a few scattered snowflakes drift onto the gravel. The sky had clouded over in the last half hour and portended rain or snow. Slowly, she ascended the steps to the house and let herself in. She was grateful that she didn't have any appointments later in the day. Massimo, who'd been given a full set of keys, was now coming and going on his own, having assumed full responsibility for the first stage of renovations. She doubted that she'd be able to concentrate on paperwork. For a brief moment, she yearned for the comfortable routine of a busy office bubbling along around her. There was always *someone* to talk to at work, *someone* to entice out for a drink at the end of the day. In a way that she never did at home in New York, Joey felt totally and utterly alone.

What would help? she wondered, climbing the staircase to the apartment. She couldn't talk to Sarah. She didn't feel like a run, not after hiking for two hours this morning. She wasn't hungry, she wasn't thirsty, she was too keyed up to take a nap. For once in her adult life, she actually wished she had a *more* demanding work schedule, so she would have no choice but to buckle down and get focused. But there wasn't really much she could do until Massimo completed the first round of consultations and came back to her with all the specifics.

Tink perked up when Joey came in.

"Lousy," Joey said, "but thanks for asking."

Tink cocked her head, puzzled.

"Go back to sleep," Joey said.

Tink watched her warily for several moments, then laid her head on her paws with a contented sigh and closed her eyes.

Joey tidied up the room, folded the clothes she had thrown over chairs and made the bed. She browsed the bookcase for a title that might intrigue her: a PD James mystery? A biography of Nancy Mitford? A volume of Keats' poetry? Nothing seemed right, and she was pretty sure that she would have felt the same way even if she had at her fingertips every volume in the British Library. She flopped down on the bed, lay for a few moments staring at the ceiling. But it was no good. She longed for company – distraction. What she needed was someone – anyone! – to talk to. She would walk into the village, buy some groceries, sit in the Old Bake House and have a cup of tea. She might even walk over to the pond.

But what if Lilia were there? No, Lilia wouldn't be there, Joey reasoned, not swimming, not on the anniversary of Cait's death, and if by chance she *was*, then Joey would act as though nothing had happened. She would be pleasant and nice, not because she hoped to win Lilia over, but because it was the right thing to do. Forty years ago today, Lilia had given birth to a baby girl, now buried in St. Peter's Churchyard. If that didn't entitle a person to a little understanding and sympathy, then Joey didn't know what did.

❋ ❋ ❋

It was snowing steadily by the time she reached the pond. The path through the trees was carpeted with powdery fluff and the canopy formed by the leaves was dusted with white. Joey had found herself in tears in the tea shop, unable to shake the images of the morning: Lilia raging in the doorway, Ian turning away and hurrying into the gatehouse, leaving her speechless and alone in the cold morning air. Joey had reached for her purse and drawn out money for her tea and scone. She left the shop without finishing either and found herself on the road leading to the pond.

Her breathing relaxed as she walked to the edge of platform and stood looking at the water. Its serenity and beauty calmed her, as though its stillness were putting to rest all her anxious thoughts and fears.

"Joey? Is that you?"

Meg was swimming toward the shore, surrounded by Viv, Gala and Aggie. Joey scanned the surface of the water carefully; was Lilia with them? But she could see only four bathing caps, bobbing about like children's beach balls.

Relieved, Joey felt her spirits lifting. "You're all crazy!" she called. "Don't you know it's snowing?"

"The water's warmer than the air," called Aggie.

"Yeah, right," Joey shot back.

"It *is!*" screeched Gala. "Come see for yourself!"

"No way!"

"Chicken!"

"Yup!" Joey was smiling now, as the women ploughed through the pond like polar bears and then, one by one, clambered up the ladder. They quickly wrapped themselves in towels and blankets and hurried up the hill and into the hut. Joey trooped in behind them.

A large pan of milk had been left on low heat, and beside it, Joey saw a plate of chocolate bars and a bottle of vodka. Aggie opened the stove door and fed the fire three squat logs from the woodpile. The logs began to hiss and crackle immediately, and Aggie slammed the door. In the corners of the cabin, the women were peeling off their wet swimsuits and bundling up in heavy tights, socks, trousers, sweaters, scarves. Joey pulled a stool up to the woodstove, noticing how cheerful she was suddenly feeling, after the gloom of her morning and early afternoon.

Gala, the first to finish dressing, turned up the heat on the stove and stood over it watchfully until the milk began hissing.

"Can I help?" asked Viv, turning to wink at Joey, but not moving from the chair closest to the woodstove.

Gala looked over, grinning and shaking her head. "Viv can't boil water," Gala explained.

"Of course I can... I can make tea."

"She can make tea," Gala said. "And tea is all she can make."

"I can make toast," Viv added.

"And toast," Gala conceded.

"So, is that all you eat?" Joey asked. "Tea and toast."

"I could live very happily on tea and toast," Viv announced, "but Cook won't hear of it!"

Aggie, now dressed, had fetched five stoneware mugs from a shallow cupboard affixed to the wall. She placed them on the table.

"You're lucky, Joey," Aggie said. "Gala only makes her special cocoa, *White Hot Russian Cocoa*, when it snows, and we don't have much of that in the Cotswolds."

"But I'm always prepared," said Gala. She took a metal grater out of her bag and handed it to Meg with one of the chocolate bars. Meg balanced a dinner plate on her lap and began to grate the chocolate. When the bars had been reduced to a towering pile of shavings, Gala poured the steaming milk into the mugs, into each one of which Viv had already poured a generous stream of vodka. Meg handed Gala the plate of chocolate and Gala stirred it in. She handed each woman a steaming, fragrant mug of cocoa.

Joey took a sip. "Oh, my God! This is so great!"

"It packs a wallop, dearie," said Meg, "so sip it slowly."

"I will!"

"Did anyone talk to Lilia today?" Meg asked.

"I rang her this morning, but she wasn't at home."

Joey looked from Gala to Meg, then from Viv to Aggie. She wondered if she should say anything but quickly decided against it. She took a deep sip of her drink. Caution be damned; right now, she could use the 'wallop" of the cocoa!

"I stopped by her house at about ten," said Meg, "but she wasn't there."

"Was her car in the yard?" asked Aggie.

Meg shook her head.

"It's odd. A little worrying, don't you think?" Meg said. "She's such a creature of habit."

"She might not swim, not today, but she always stops by," Gala put in. "If she's holed up at home, now, all by herself, then she must be awfully upset."

"She is," Joey whispered, almost without thinking.

The ladies turned to look at her.

"She is?" Aggie asked.

"Even more than usual?" Meg prodded.

Joey nodded. She would have to tell them. Maybe that's why she had come in the first place, even though she hadn't been aware of it. She thought she had only wanted company, but maybe she had wanted – something more – to talk things out, try and make sense of burgeoning feelings.

"How do you know?" asked Gala. "Did you see her?"

Joey nodded miserably. "This morning. She came by early, to see Ian, and – "

The ladies stared at her intently.

"And – "Viv prodded.

202

"And — I was there." Joey took a sip of her cocoa. She looked around. Aggie looked puzzled, Meg looked amused, Gala looked shocked and Viv — did she look a little *afraid?* Yes, Joey concluded, Viv did look a little afraid.

"At Ian's." Gala said.

"Ian *McCormack's*," Aggie clarified.

"Early," Meg put in. Joey nodded guiltily.

"*How* early?" Viv asked.

"*Early* early," Joey responded quietly. As her words hung in the air and the ladies slowly began to grasp her meaning, she sprung to her feet and began to pace. The confession that followed surprised even Joey, but once her torrent of words had been unleashed, there was no turning back.

"I know. I live three thousand miles away and the whole thing is crazy, completely crazy. I know I can't replace Cait and I never *will* be able to replace her — and I don't *want* to. But I'm think I'm falling in love with him! And even if he can't let himself get really involved, if he's not ready for that but was just ready for — "

" — a little hoochie-koochie?" Meg suggested.

"*Hoochie-koochie?*" Gala shrieked in disbelief. "Hoochie-koochie? What is this, the forties?"

Viv howled with laughter. "Let the poor girl finish!"

Joey, having been stopped in her tracks, didn't know where to begin again. "I was just saying, that no matter where this goes, or doesn't, I'm glad it happened."

"So am I," said Meg. "It's about time!"

"He's a prince," added Aggie. "He's been alone long enough."

"You have excellent taste," giggled Viv. "If I were thirty years younger... "

"Thirty?" asked Gala. "How about *fifty?!*"

Joey sat back down on her stool. "You aren't shocked? You

don't all hate me?" The women shook their heads.

"Hate you? Because you have fallen in love?" asked Viv.

"Because – by falling in love with Ian, I may have hurt Lilia."

"Lilia's problems have nothing to do with you," added Aggie. "She's never been able to come to terms with Cait's death and I don't know if she ever will. But Ian's still a young man and Lily needs women in her life, happy women, strong women."

"Tell us," said Meg.

Joey nodded and over the next half hour, helped along by the fortifying brew of vodka, chocolate and hot milk, she told them everything: of Ian's initial distrust and suspicion, of their time spent with Massimo, their lunch with him, of her trip to London with Lily... She spared no details except the most intimate, knowing that she could trust these women not only to support and advise her, but to use what she told them, if that were possible, to help Lilia, who was so alone in her misery.

"When do you go back to New York?" Viv asked, when Joey came to the end of her story.

"Two weeks," she answered.

"What will happen then?" Meg pressed.

"How the hell does she know that?" snapped Gala. "How can anyone possibly know what's going to happen in the future? Give the girl a break!"

Meg looked chastened.

"It's okay," said Joey. "I've been asking myself the same question. I know I don't want it to end. I'd like to at least *try...*"

"Does he want that, too?" Viv asked.

"If you had asked me last night, I would have said – well, would have *guessed* – that the answer was yes. But after this

204

morning, I really don't know. He seemed pretty upset. Anyway, thank you for listening."

"Of course!" Viv said.

"Darling!" Gala cried.

"You poor baby! It will all work out. It always does," Meg pronounced.

Joey had to fight back tears. She had nearly forgotten what it felt like to be on the receiving end of this sort of support. And when was the last time *she* had offered anything like this to any of *her* old friends? She was ashamed, once again, to realise how much time had gone by since she'd even picked up the phone to call them. She had meant to send flowers when she heard that Martina's mother had died, but she had never got around to it. She had heard through friends that Susan and Nick, her long-time boyfriend, were going through a rocky patch, but again... How had she got so adrift? It was as if she had cut the moorings of her own life.

Slowly, the conversation moved onto other topics — a knitting problem Viv was having with the sweater she was working on, the price of a crown roast of lamb at the local butcher's, the dilemma of whether to join Facebook, which was presenting itself to Meg and Aggie, the only real computer users in the group.

"Are you on Facebook, Joey?" Meg asked.

Joey shook her head.

"I'm thinking of joining," Meg announced.

"I prefer the phone, or at least I thought I did. Truth is, I'm very bad at actually picking it up," Joey said. "And I like to think I'm good at writing letters. There's a beautiful paper store in my neighbourhood, and I bought all this gorgeous stationery. But I don't have anyone to write to!"

"Now you do!" Viv announced.

Joey helped the women clean up, then said her goodbyes, hugged the ladies each in turn and headed out into the cold. She had just started up the path, when she heard Aggie's voice.

"Joey?"

She paused and turned, then waited for Aggie to catch up to her.

"Are you in a hurry?" Aggie asked.

"No. Why?"

"Would you like to come back for a bite to eat?"

"Back where?"

"To my house."

"Why, sure, but – "

Aggie seemed to sense Joey's question. "I spoke with Sarah this morning," Aggie explained. "I gather you two had – "

"A fight?" Joey nodded.

Aggie smiled warmly. "You don't have to talk about it if you don't want to, I just thought you might – "

"I would," Joey replied, interrupting.

Chapter 21

They were seated before a blazing fire in the drawing room, waiting for Anna to bring in the light supper Aggie had requested. Joey had longed to be offered a full tour of the house, which seemed like the sort of place a person might buy a ticket to snoop around in, but Aggie had led her straight in here. A cheerful, ruddy-faced man named Simon, who was apparently a sort of butler, had moved a card table nearer to the fire, so that Joey and Aggie could eat there.

Anna appeared at the door.

"Sorry to interrupt, but Mrs Williamson is on the phone. Shall I ask her to ring you back?"

Aggie sighed. "No, no, thank you. I'll take care of this now, if you'll excuse me for a moment, Joey."

"Of course."

As Aggie followed Anna out into the hall, Joey rose to her feet and gazed around the room. The walls were upholstered in what looked like aged silk taffeta, in a shade of dark maroon, and above the fireplace was an elaborately carved mahogany mantelpiece. Gilded standing screens painted with bird and floral motifs enclosed the area by the fire.

Joey crossed the room to have a closer look at some of the prints on the far wall, etchings of classical Roman buildings displayed in gold frames. She strained to read the artist's signature: Giovanni Piranesi. *The* Piranesi? Joey thought. Probably, she concluded.

She drifted around the room, admiring the hanging tapestries, the highly waxed tables bearing silver frames displaying family photos. Some of the people she recognised: Henry and Sarah at their wedding, Christopher and Matilda in riding outfits, Meg and Viv in elegant dresses. And there, in the centre, was a formal portrait of a handsome man who had to be Aggie's late husband, Richard.

Joey returned to her seat by the fire. She didn't want Aggie to find her nosing around when she came back in. But in truth she felt a bit stunned. She knew plenty of rich people in New York, people who had made pots of money or whose parents had. She'd been to her share of flashy homes and apartments, had even designed a few, but not one of them sent the message communicated by this room: that the people who had passed through it over the centuries were not just wealthy but from a long family line of privilege and power.

Joey suddenly felt a little sheepish about how chummy she had let herself become with Aggie. Had she been crossing social lines she shouldn't have crossed? Had she been clueless and gauche, like the worst sort of stereotypical American, tone deaf to social cues that any European would have understood intuitively? Maybe inherited wealth and social class really *did* matter, and only a young American, even one raised in sophisticated New York, would be naïve enough to believe otherwise.

Aggie reappeared at the door followed by Simon, who asked what they would like to drink.

"How about some Sancerre?" Aggie asked Joey. "You do like fish?"

"Love it."

Moments later Simon returned with the wine, and then withdrew and reappeared again, this time bearing two steaming plates – filets of Dover sole, buttery asparagus and wild rice. It smelled wonderful.

"We should start," Aggie said, unfurling her napkin and setting it on her lap.

Joey smiled and picked up her fork. "It's delicious," she said, after savouring a bite of the delicate, lemony fish.

Aggie lifted her glass, signalling Joey to raise hers. They clinked them gently.

"To friendship," Aggie said.

"To friendship," Joey echoed.

"Which is why I asked you here," Aggie added.

Joey was sipping the cool crisp wine. She swallowed, set her glass down and looked up. "Really?"

Aggie nodded.

"Friendship in general?" Joey asked. "Or one in particular?"

"One in particular…" Aggie continued. "Sarah told me about your conversation."

"I feel terrible," Joey confided.

"So does she," Aggie replied, then waited for Joey to go on.

"We were like sisters."

"I know. She's always talked about you like that. My question is, what happened?"

"Yesterday?"

"No. What happened between you two, to bring you to this point?"

"Nothing, really. We've just sort of drifted apart. Living so far away."

"It's not so far any more. And it doesn't sound to me as though physical distance is what this is about."

Joey sighed. "Our lives are so different. I don't think they could *be* much more different."

"Oh yes they could. But I didn't invite you here to lecture you, Joey. I just thought that maybe I could provide a little perspective."

"What kind of perspective?"

"On my son. And, indirectly, I suppose, on Sarah."

Joey nodded and sat back, curious.

"I'm very close to Henry now," Aggie began, "and to Martin and Lucinda, his brother and sister. But when they were young, I'm not sure I was a very good mother."

"I find that hard to believe."

"It's true. It was how Henry's father and I were raised: children in the nursery with Nanny, brought in to kiss the parents good-night, sent away to school at a very young age, all of us. Our parents would be away for weeks at a time, even months, leaving us with governesses and the household staff. It was just how things were done, and how *we* were taught to do things. I realise now how much our children missed us, how much they suffered. They were packed off with their trunks by the age of seven, all three of them."

Aggie had a sip of her wine.

"I'm not saying there weren't many lovely things about their lives. But their childhood – "Aggie broke off and shook her head. "I'm telling you this because, well, Henry came to parenthood with certain very strong ideas."

"What sort of ideas?"

"Put simply, to give his children the exact opposite of the childhood he and his brother and sister had."

"Ouch," Joey said softly.

"Oh, it's all right. We did the best we could, Richard and I. But Henry wanted to be a different kind of father."

"And for Sarah to be a different kind of mother," Joey

added, suddenly understanding where this was going.

'Yes. So this *distance* you speak of, between you and Sarah, some of it is my fault."

"You can't blame yourself!"

"I don't, not really. But Sarah's a smart girl, ambitious, a great businesswoman, very savvy. And if I had been a better mother to Henry when he was small, it might not have been so important to him to have the mother of *his* children dedicate herself so completely to their little darlings' every need. But she's done it, Sarah has, in spades, and as a result, they have four of the happiest children I've ever seen. But Sarah is the one who's paid the price."

Joey suddenly felt sad and ashamed of herself for having been so judgmental. She had never thought of Sarah like this.

"What I'm trying to say, dear," Aggie continued, "is that, if you're patient, I think you'll have your old friend back one of these days. The children aren't going to be small for ever. And Henry understands what she's done for him, for them all. The day is going to come when she has a good measure of her time and freedom back. And I think she'll want to spend some of it with you."

Joey was about to respond when they heard a tap at the door.

"Yes?" Aggie called.

The door opened to reveal Anna, looking flustered. "Madam, there's someone here to see you."

She stepped aside to reveal Lily, her face tear-stained and her clothing all askew.

"Lily! Darling!" Aggie said, pushing back her chair. "What are you doing here?"

"I hate Granny!" Lily sobbed, rushing forward, kneeling beside Aggie's chair and throwing her head on to Aggie's lap.

"Thank you, Anna," Aggie said. "We'll be fine."

The housekeeper nodded and withdrew.

"And my father!" the girl continued. She looked up just long enough to greet Joey.

"Hi," she said miserably.

"Hi, honey," Joey responded.

Joey got up and fetched another armchair, carrying it to the table. Lily flopped down.

"Now, now," Aggie said warmly, stroking Lily's hair as the girl commenced with a dramatic display of tears. Joey had no doubt that Lily truly did feel miserable, wretched, betrayed by the world. But there was also a little hint in Lily's melodrama of the budding actress executing a passionate and persuasive performance. Finally she sniffed and sat back in her chair.

"Have you eaten, darling?" Aggie asked.

Lily glanced at their plates. "I'm not hungry," she said glumly, eyeing the fish.

"Are you sure? A cup of cocoa, perhaps? A piece of cake?"

Lily brightened slightly at these prospects, so Aggie rang the hand bell.

"Does your father know you're here, Lily?" Aggie asked.

Lily's expression grew hard. "No. And I don't care. Let him worry."

"You don't mean that," Aggie said softly, taking the lead.

"Yes, I do! They're horrid! Both of them! Granny's always mean and angry, and Daddy goes along with whatever she says! They act like they're the only ones who lost Mummy! I lost her, too, and I'm not going around making life miserable for everybody!"

"No," Aggie said calmly. "You're not. You're the only one behaving like a grown-up!"

Surprised and vindicated, Lily smiled for the first time. Then her face grew serious again. "Can't you talk to her,

Aggie? I know you're her best friend. Can't you make her understand?"

"Is that why you came here?" Aggie asked.

Lily nodded, suddenly looking vulnerable and very young.

"I've tried, dear. We've all tried. But I will try again. For you."

"Thank you." Lily turned to Joey. "Granny was so mean to you! I wanted to slap her!"

"I'm glad you didn't," Joey said, eliciting another tiny smile from Lily.

"Daddy needs you, Joey! We need you!" Lily was suddenly fighting back the tears. "The house is so depressing. *He's* so depressing. I can't stand it any more. Ever since you came here, he's been different, happier! I thought maybe – we had so much fun when you came over, and when we went to London, I – I – "

Lily began to sob again. Aggie's eyes found Joey's and indicated distress at Lily's state.

"Let me get you a handkerchief, darling," said Aggie, going out into the hall.

Lily now turned to Joey. "Take me back to New York with you, please?"

"Honey! You have to go to school! You're not ready to – "

"I want to go to Juilliard. I have my own money. My mother left me an inheritance, and I can have it any time I want. I can sleep on your couch. I'll pay rent."

"Oh Lily, when you finish school, if you still want to come to New York, I will put you up anytime – "

"But I want to come now! When you go back!"

Joey shook her head. "That's not possible, sweetie."

"Why not? I can take care of myself! You won't have to look after me. I can pay for everything."

"Juilliard's like college, honey. You have to audition and

get in, and the competition's fierce. You can't just show up."

"Even if I can pay?" Lily asked miserably.

"It wouldn't be such a fantastic school if everybody who wanted to go could just write a cheque and get in. You have to prepare for the audition and learn to analyse plays. You have to really want it … "

"But I do!"

"I know. But you're not ready. I can try to help you get ready, if you're willing, and then if they take you, my couch is your couch."

"Really?"

"Really." Joey smiled.

Lily was on her second piece of cake when Joey heard the front doorbell ring.

"Would you see to that?" Aggie asked Joey, shooting her a significant glance.

"Uh, sure," Joey said, getting up and going into the front hall.

Simon had beaten her to it. He opened the door to reveal Ian standing in the porch, hands in his pockets, his brow furrowed. He stepped inside.

"Thank you," Joey said to Simon. "Hello Ian."

"What are you doing here?" Ian asked.

"Aggie invited me for supper. I guess she called you."

"She did. And just wait until I get my hands on that little – "

"Ian!"

"Where is she?"

"Please, wait."

Ian glanced around, as though hoping to catch a glimpse of Lily.

"I can't believe she came here! What would possess the child – "

"She wanted Aggie to talk to Lilia. She knows what good friends they are. That's not so unreasonable."

"Talk to her about what?"

Joey hesitated. She longed to speak directly to Ian but wondered if she had the right. They hadn't known each other very long, and what she wanted to say was the sort of thing only old friends dared to say to one another. And she wasn't doing so well with her old friends.

"I don't know if I should say this," Joey admitted.

"Say what?"

She looked him directly in the eyes, eyes that yesterday had affectionately sought hers. Tonight, they looked hard and cold. Joey shook her head. "Never mind."

"Say what?" he demanded.

"It's none of my business," she responded.

"*Say* what you were going to say!" Ian said flintily

Joey folded her arms. She looked away, then back. "All right," she said softly.

She took a deep breath, as Ian waited.

"I've never been a mother," she began, "so I don't know much about raising kids. But I do know something about teenage girls, because I used to be one. And Lily's at the end of her rope."

She paused.

"Meaning," Ian prodded.

"She's unhappy, Ian. And she wants to be happy. And for you to be happy."

"That's easier said than done."

"But you've got to try!" Joey snapped. "If not for yourself, then for her. You're going to lose her, Ian. Because she can't take much more."

"Of what?"

"Of living with a ghost! Of living with the shadow of the

man her father once was. It's tough enough that she lost her mother. She feels she's lost you, too."

"I'm doing the best I can!" Ian flashed. "You have no idea."

"I know I don't."

Ian seemed visibly to shrink before her eyes. He hung his head.

"I shouldn't have – let anything happen between us."

"This has nothing to do with you and me," Joey said.

"Yes, it does. Everything's all tangled up together. I made a promise to Cait, Joey."

"With all due respect, Ian, I think the words are: 'Till death us do part.'"

He looked up quickly and Joey could tell that she had struck a nerve. There would be no more talking now.

"She's in there," Joey whispered, motioning in the direction of the drawing room.

Ian looked as though he were about to say something, then decided against it. He swept past her and disappeared from sight.

Chapter 22

Saturday dawned clear and slightly warmer. Over coffee and toast at quarter to eight, Joey made a list of all the things she was going to do before the sun went down. Most of the items were fairly unimportant, tasks she could accomplish any time in the next few days, but the purpose of this exercise wasn't really the organisation of her time. It was to get herself moving and keep herself distracted. She'd spent half the night tossing and turning, obsessing about all the things that had gone wrong in the past couple of days.

First, she was going to clean the apartment: wash the sheets and towels, throw open the windows to air the whole place out. She'd been living there for two weeks now, her stuff was all over the place and the bathroom was getting a little grungy. Next, she'd sort all her paperwork and notes, make a list of the questions she had for Massimo, and then download and print hard copies of all the contracts they were going to be giving to the subcontractors. All this would probably take until about noon, bearing in mind that she would also have to get Tink out for a walk.

There wasn't much food left, either, so she would go into the village in the afternoon. Maybe stop by the pond. Even have a swim. In any case, she'd have to get some food before the shops shut, just enough to see her through until Monday or Tuesday. And she most definitely had to get some wine.

Joey poured another half cup of coffee. She wondered what Ian and Lily were doing right now. Lily was probably still sleeping, but Ian was an early riser. She imagined him seated at his own kitchen table, drinking his coffee, alone. She wondered if he and Lily had argued last night, and whether Joey had made things better or worse by the things she said.

Now, in the cold light of morning, she could hardly believe what she had uttered – "until death us do part"? What a thing to say to a person! What right did *she* have to suggest that Ian's promise to his wife had been fulfilled upon Cait's death? Joey could think whatever she wanted, privately, but to say it out loud? Besides, what did *she* know about losing a spouse? No man had ever loved her enough to ask her to marry him.

Joey stood up abruptly. There was no point in going over this again. It wouldn't do any good, and she had spent hours in last night's darkness travelling just these avenues of thought, only to find herself at dead ends. The fact was, she *had* said these things, the damage was done. Of one thing she felt pretty sure: she wasn't likely to be seeing Ian over this weekend, unless they ran into each other. She seriously doubted that he'd be knocking on her door, and she wouldn't dare knock on his.

By one thirty, Joey had cleaned the apartment, got all her documents organised, and walked Tink. She'd made the list for Massimo and left a message on his mobile, asking him to be in touch with her first thing Monday morning. She'd also called Sarah, hoping the call would go to voicemail, then feeling guilty that she had wished for that outcome.

"Sorry to miss you," she lied into her BlackBerry, secretly relieved. "I'll try you later today."

She managed to scrape together a light lunch from pitiful left-overs, an egg scrambled with tomato, made into a toast sandwich with the ends of the loaf. And a handful of soft grapes, mouldy-tasting at the stem ends. None of it was really worth eating, and she wished she had waited – the meal seemed the perfect indicator of her wretched state.

She was crossing the gravel drive a little later when the door to the gatehouse opened.

"Hi," Lily called, stepping out of the interior darkness.

"Hi." Joey glanced around, noting with relief that Ian's van was nowhere to be seen.

"Where are you going?" Lily asked. "Can I come?"

Joey hesitated. "Sure, but I'm not doing anything exciting. Just getting some food."

"That's okay." Lily looked chastened, subdued. Joey wondered again if she and her father had argued last night.

Joey shrugged. Lily stepped out and closed the door.

"You'd better get a jacket."

"I'm not cold," Lily said. "I don't need it."

"You might. I know it feels like spring now, but it's supposed to get colder."

Lily sighed and went back into the house. She returned a moment later in a navy pea coat, unbuttoned. Together, they walked through the arch and out onto the drivve.

"So, how are you?" Joey finally asked.

"Daddy and I had a massive row. He was really cross that I went over to Aggie's."

"Why *did* you?"

"Because she's always been really nice to me. And Granny likes her better than the others."

"What others? The ladies at the pond?"

"No. At church, like Mrs Norton. And Mrs *Furth*." Lily gave a dramatic shiver.

Joey made a conscious effort not to speak. She wanted Lily to go on. But Lily turned toward her, obviously hoping that Joey would pick up the thread.

"So you're still mad?" Joey prompted.

"Kind of. Not *as* mad. I just wish Granny would listen to me. But she won't."

"Have you ever tried to talk to her about how you feel?" Joey asked. "When you're not mad, I mean."

"That's what Dad said I should do. I tried calling her a little while ago, but she's not home."

"Maybe she's at the pond," Joey said, without thinking.

"Maybe," Lily said. "Do you know where it is? I used to know exactly where the path was, but I tried to find it last summer and it's all overgrown."

Joey regretted bringing up the subject of the pond. She wasn't sure she wanted to go there herself, and she definitely wasn't sure that bringing Lily there was a good idea.

"Granny used to take me there in the summertime, when I was little," Lily continued. "But I haven't been in a long time. It's not that much fun. It's all old ladies. And who wants to swim in the freezing cold? They're bonkers, all of them!"

"I love it," Joey said.

"The pond?"

"The swimming."

"You went in? When?"

"I've gone in a few times. I thought I'd hate how cold the water is, but it's amazing!"

"Isn't it like ice?"

"At first, yeah, but then you feel so – alive! I can't describe it. But I totally get why they love it."

Lily suddenly stopped in her tracks. "Can we go there?"

"To the pond? Now?"

Lily nodded. "I actually think it might make Granny happy. She was always after me to come with her, and I turned her down so many times that finally she stopped asking."

"I have no idea if she's there," Joey said.

"Well, somebody will be," Lily replied. "They're always hanging around that hut. And at least they can tell her I came by."

Joey hesitated. Maybe Lily was right. Maybe Lilia would be touched by the gesture. Maybe it would even give Lilia pause, make her think a little differently about Joey, as a peacemaker rather than a person who sowed discord and pain.

"Are you sure she'd want that?" Joey asked.

"I told you, she was always trying to get me to come," Lily replied, smiling.

Joey still felt uncertain; she dearly hoped that she wasn't about to make another mistake. But Lily seemed sure, and she certainly knew her grandmother better than Joey did. She seemed to *want* to see Lilia now, which had to be a step in the right direction.

"Okey-doke," Joey said. "You're on."

❊   ❊   ❊

Viv was sitting in her big chair, knitting away, with a mug of tea at her side. Without dropping a stitch, she looked up, startled, "Lily McCormack!" she cried out. "As I live and breathe! Come give Auntie Viv a hug!"

Lily kissed and hugged Viv, then stood up and glanced around. "Is my granny here?" she asked.

Viv nodded toward the pond. "Out there, doing her laps." They all gazed off at the water as Lilia and Aggie, oblivious to Joey and Lily's arrival, swam back and forth. Meg came out of the hut and, seeing Joey and Lily, hurried down to greet them.

"Lily! You brought spring with you! Hello, darling!" Meg swept Lily into a hug, then hugged Joey as well. "The winds are blowing in from the south, apparently. It is the warmest winter day since 1916, according to the BBC. But I didn't need the radio to tell me that.

Joey walked to the edge of the pond, where early snow-drops were poking out their tiny white buds.

"I thought you were going in," Viv said to Meg.

"I am," Meg responded.

"Well, you'd better do it before you lose your nerve!"

"Me?" Meg shrieked. "When was the last time *you* went in?"

"I want to finish my sweater!"

"That's an excuse."

"For the record, I went swimming the day before yesterday."

Meg shook her head, grinning, and strode off toward the water. "Want to come in, Lily?"

"No, thanks," replied Lily.

"Joey?" Meg urged.

"Maybe later."

"How about a nice cup of tea and some cookies?" Viv asked. "They're homemade. Butterscotch."

"Yes, thank you," answered Lily politely.

Viv led Joey and Lily into the hut. A moment later, Gala appeared.

"Gala, Lily's here!" called Viv. "She came with Joey."

Gala paused, slightly breathless, and locked eyes with Joey. "Consider yourself forewarned, ladies," she said curtly. "Lilia is *not* in the best of moods."

"I was hoping I might cheer her up," said Lily.

"Well, here's hoping." Gala said.

Lily burst into a wide grin, obviously relieved to know that other people noticed and had to endure her grandmoth-er's moods.

"Bring that chair over, Lily," said Viv. "Sit right down next to me. You *have* learned how to knit, haven't you?"

Lily dragged over an old wooden chair. "Mrs Christie at

school tried to teach me once, but I wasn't very good at it. I kept dropping stitches."

"Do you still have that jumper I knitted you?"

"It's on Lucius, my teddy bear!" Lily turned to Joey, who was helping herself to a piece of butterscotch shortbread. "It's so cute, Joey. Turquoise and lavender stripes, with a bright yellow daisy on the tummy."

Joey poured two cups of tea from the pot on the hob and handed one mug to Lily. Together, they all settled into their chairs.

"That's so pretty, Viv," said Lily, studying Viv's rectangle of knitting.

"Thank you!" replied Viv. "It's the back of a sweater for Meg's granddaughter." Viv held up the garment, which was knitted in a complicated Aran pattern of twisted cables, stockinette and seed stitches. "I got ten skeins of this fabulous wool at a street market in Devon. I guess it was the end of the dye lot."

"What's a dye lot?" Joey asked.

"It's wool that's been dyed using the same vat of colour," Viv explained. "There can be slight colour variations from batch to batch, of the dye, I mean. That's why they tell you to buy all the wool you need for a project at the same time, so it's from the same lot. Otherwise, you might end up with a few different shades."

Joey nodded.

"Do you knit, Joey?" Viv asked.

"Not me."

"It's very meditative."

"If you're good at it," Gala put in. "I suppose it's like cooking that way. People who are good at it find it relaxing, but people who don't know what they're doing turn into nervous wrecks when they have to roast a chicken."

Between the crackling woodstove and the hot tea, Joey was suddenly sweltering. Lily seemed happy in the company of Viv and Gala, and Joey began to think about going in for a swim. She wasn't going to be in England much longer, and after the dispiriting events of the past couple of days, she found herself longing for the joyful exhilaration she had experienced in the freezing water.

"I might go in for a dip," she announced, when the conversation had reached a lull.

"Be my guest," said Lily, in a tone that communicated that she had no interest whatsoever in joining Joey in the water. "We'll cheer you on from the sidelines."

"You don't know what you're missing," Joey teased.

"I know exactly what I'm missing," Lily shot back. "Double pneumonia!"

Aggie, Lilia and Meg were still a fair distance away when Joey slipped off the dock and into the pond. Perhaps because she was prepared to be shocked by the temperature, or perhaps because of the unaccustomed warm weather they had been experiencing, her first few moments in the water were less shocking than in the past. She felt the familiar tightening of her arm and back muscles as she launched into an easy crawl, her spine lengthening and stretching out, her legs propelling her across the expanse of grey-blue. She wished she had made more time for swimming in the past two weeks and wondered whether she might join the health club with a pool when she got back to New York. It wouldn't be the same, of course; nothing could match the thrill and joy of swimming like this. But all the pounding of running was beginning to take a toll on her knees. Swimming was an exercise you could do for life.

Joey dived under the surface and burst into a fierce underwater breaststroke, propelling herself forward, holding her breath for as long as she could: eight frog kicks, nine, ten. Reeds moved around her in slow motion as the sun lit the water from above. She glimpsed the tiny webbed feet of a passing duck and wondered if she could do twenty kicks and arm circles without coming up for air. But on the sixteenth kick, she had to break the surface, gasping for oxygen. Turning to swim back, she saw Lily standing on the dock, smiling and waving.

And now Lilia, Meg and Aggie were approaching the ladder, finished with their laps. Joey dived under the water again, and when she resurfaced, she saw Lilia and Aggie on the dock with Lily. Meg was just climbing up the ladder. All the joy was gone from Lily's expression. Lilia had grabbed her granddaughter by the forearm.

Joey mustered all her energy and swam back to the dock as fast as she could. Lilia turned to glare at her as Joey approached the ladder.

"I'm leaving right now!" Joey heard Lily shout.

"You stay right where you are, young lady," Lilia snapped.

"I came to be nice! I came to make you happy. But nothing makes you happy!" Lily sputtered. Joey had reached the ladder by now, and she hauled herself out of the water. Meg, having apparently decided to opt out of the inevitable fireworks, was making her way back to the hut. Gala and Viv had come out and now stood behind Lily on the dock.

"Lily just wanted to see you," Gala said.

"This is none of your business, Gala!" Lilia snapped. "Just stay out of it!"

She turned her fury on Joey.

"Why don't *you* just leave us all alone," she yelled at Joey. "No one asked you to come here."

"I asked her, Lilia," Aggie said calmly. "Now let's not ruin this beautiful afternoon."

"What about ruining my family?" Lilia shouted. "That's what she's doing, poking her nose in where it doesn't belong, waltzing right in like – like a typical American, helping herself to whatever she pleases: Stanway House, my daughter's *husband*, my own granddaughter!"

"*I* asked to her to bring me here, Granny! I thought you'd be happy to see me!"

"With *her?* You thought I'd be happy to see you in the company of that – that *tart?*"

Joey, stunned into silence, glanced at Aggie, who looked dumbfounded, and then at Viv, who looked terrified.

Gala turned and headed purposefully back to the hut.

"Lilia." Aggie's voice was steady. "Calm down now. Please."

"Let's all go inside and have a nice cup of tea," Viv suggested nervously. "Or get Gala to make us her special cocoa."

Lilia tightly grabbed her granddaughter. "We're leaving. Right now."

"No," Joey said, finding her voice at last. "*I'll* leave. I made a mistake by bringing Lily here, obviously, and I'm very sorry – "

"You should be!" Lilia shouted. "You are a foolish, selfish woman and I, for one, shall be very glad to see the back of you!"

"Well *I* won't!" Lily shouted. "She's been really nice to me! Much nicer than you!"

Lily tried to pull away from her grandmother's grip. Lilia, forearms strong from her years of swimming, held on tight, forcing Lily to use the weight of her full body to try to break away from her grandmother's grasp. Lily bent her knees slightly, attempting to anchor her weight, not realising that she had placed her right foot on a partially thawed patch of ice at the edge of the dock. When Lilia let go, Lily flew off balance, then tried to right herself, slipping on the ice, and toppling into the water, cracking her head on the edge of the iron ladder as she fell.

"Lily!" screamed Lilia, as Lily seemed to arch her back against the cold and then suddenly go limp in the water.

Adrenaline kicked in and spread like wildfire through Joey's body. She dived into the pond, and Aggie was right behind her.

"Call an ambulance, Viv! Hurry! She's unconscious," instructed Aggie, as soon as her head cleared the surface.

"Lily!" wailed Lilia. "Lily!" The woman seemed paralysed, unable to do anything but speak the name. Hearing the noise, Gala appeared at the door of the hut and then raced to the edge of the water.

"Get a board!" Aggie yelled. "Bring us a board."

Lily was breathing, but still hadn't come to.

"We have to stabilise her, she may have broken her neck," Aggie whispered. "The wrong movement could paralyse her."

"Oh my God!" said Joey. "Lily? Lily, can you hear me?" Joey and Aggie slipped their arms under her torso and head and gently held her at the surface of the water, so she could breathe.

"You're okay, Lily," Aggie said calmly. "You'll be fine, darling. We'll have you out of this water in a minute."

Viv and Gala had located a board, and they ran to the dock, placed the board on the surface of the water, and slid into the water themselves. Lilia watched from the dock, seemingly unable to move.

"Slip it under her spine," Aggie instructed them. They were all treading water, which made everything awkward and difficult, but soon they were able to slide the board under the water so that it supported Lily's spine, neck and head. She still hadn't opened her eyes.

"Hang in there, honey," Joey kept whispering. "You're doing great. You're doing fine."

"We have to get her out," Aggie said. "We can't wait for the ambulance to get here, the water's just too cold. Joey, you get up on the dock and hold her head steady while Gala and I lift her on the board. Viv, you go help Joey."

Viv and Joey scrambled up the ladder as fast as they could.

Joey saw Meg rushing from the hut, mobile phone in hand.

"They're on their way," Meg shouted. "They'll be here in a minute or two."

"Lilia!" Viv screamed. "We need you! Help us!"

This seemed to snap Lilia out of her state of shock. She hurried over and knelt down between Joey and Viv on the dock.

"You and I will lift her, Lilia," Viv instructed. "Joey will keep her head stabilised."

Lilia didn't speak, but she nodded. Meg knelt down, ready to help.

Aggie and Gala floated the board so that it was right next to the dock. Joey leaned down and placed her hands on either side of Lily's head, so it wouldn't move from side to side when she was lifted.

"Ready?" Aggie called, placing Lily's arms across her chest.

"Ready," Joey and Viv replied.

"Okay, on three, Gala. One, two, three!" Aggie and Gala lifted the dripping board out of the water with difficulty and Lilia, Meg and Viv took it from them, as Joey held Lily's head stable. As they were lying the board gently on the dock, they heard the sound of an approaching siren.

"Thank God," Viv whispered.

"I'll get blankets," Gala cried, hurrying up the ladder and stumbling off toward the hut.

Joey reached for a towel that was on the dock, and used it to apply a little pressure to the gaping wound in Lily's scalp. She didn't want to press too hard, but now that Lily was out of the water, the cold temperature of which had temporarily staunched the flow of blood, Lily was bleeding profusely. After what felt like hours, Joey looked up to see paramedics hurrying toward them, carrying a back-board on top of a stretcher.

Joey must have been in shock herself, because she resisted turning Lily over to the paramedics. They had to pull her hands gently away from Lily's head wound.

"No," Joey said. She didn't want anyone but her and Lilia and the other ladies to hold Lily's fate in their hands.

"It's okay, Ma'am," said the paramedic. "We'll take good care of her."

They carefully placed Lily's head in a brace, cupped an oxygen mask over her mouth and nose and applied a gauze bandage to her head. Then they lifted Lily and the board straight onto the stretcher. Because the terrain was rocky and uneven, they carried rather than wheeled the stretcher up along the path into the woods and out of sight.

Lilia, ashen-faced and with Viv's woollen coat draped over her shoulders, went with them, to ride with Lily in the back of the ambulance. The others would follow as soon as they were dressed.

"Where are they taking her?" Joey asked, as the women hurried up the path to the hut to dress.

"Broadway General," Viv replied.

"How far away is it?"

"Ten, fifteen minutes."

"Call Andrew, Meg," Gala said.

"I've already called him. He's in the hospital, he's going downstairs to meet the ambulance."

"Meg's son is head of surgery," Aggie explained.

"Do you think she'll need surgery?" Joey asked. "Oh my God." Joey was peeling off her suit now, and struggling to pull dry clothes onto her damp limbs.

"They'll have to watch for a brain bleed," Meg said solemnly.

"What's that?" Joey said.

"It's when the brain hits against the inside of the skull. The blow can tear blood vessels, and then you bleed right into the brain." Meg shook her head, imagining the worst.

Joey suddenly felt light-headed. Lily's skin had felt so warm between her hands. Her eyelids were creased with tiny blue veins, like an infant's. *Please let her be okay.*

"Let's not jump to conclusions, now," said Gala.

"No one's jumping to conclusions," countered Viv sourly.

"It could be nothing worse than a knock on the head," Gala continued.

"It's all my fault," Joey said, "If I hadn't brought her – "

"It was an *accident*," Gala snapped. "She slipped on a patch of ice. It could happen to anyone, any time."

"We should call Ian," Joey said. "Somebody has to call Ian."

"I'm sure they have," Aggie said gently.

"Lilia's in a state of shock," Joey said, reaching into her jacket pocket for her phone. As she dialled Ian's number, she found herself praying that he was home.

"*Pick up, pick up*," she intoned, as the phone rang, three, four, five times.

"Hello?" she finally heard him say.

"Ian, it's Joey."

She hadn't rehearsed what she was going to say next, but

there was silence on the other end of the line.

"Ian," she whispered. "There's been an accident. Lily's being taken to the hospital, Broadway General."

There was a little cry of anguish on the other end of the line. "What kind of accident?"

"She slipped and fell into the lake — banged her head. She's in good hands, gone in an ambulance with Lilia."

"I'm on my way," Ian said, and then the line went dead.

Chapter 23

By the time they reached the hospital, Ian had arrived and had been taken into the emergency ward, where a doctor was already evaluating Lily. Upon receiving his mother's frantic phone call, Meg's son Andrew had briefed A&E, and the trauma team had met the ambulance. As horrible as the situation was, at least they had done all the right things at the pond, and within half an hour of being injured, Lily was being tended to by the best doctors in the hospital.

Aggie and Joey approached the charge nurse with the pile of Lilia's clothing.

"What are these?" the distracted nurse inquired.

The term "battleaxe" bubbled up into Joey's consciousness. In the woman's defense, Joey thought, one probably needed a stern constitution to deal with what came through the emergency ward doors.

"Dry clothes," Aggie replied. "For the grandmother of the girl who was just brought in, Lily McCormack."

"What does she need with dry clothes?"

'We were swimming," Joey answered. "She's only got a bathing suit on under that coat."

"Swimming?"

"At the pond behind Gordon Robinson's farm," Aggie explained.

"In January?" the nurse exclaimed, taking the pile of

clothes gingerly, as though she suspected that they might infect her with the sort of madness that would lead otherwise sane people to go swimming outdoors in the middle of winter. Joey didn't mean to be unkind, but it occurred to her that the ruddy, heavyset charge nurse could do with a little swimming herself.

Joey and Aggie joined Meg and Gala in the waiting room. It was just like every other hospital waiting room Joey had ever spent time in, except that there was no television mounted up by the ceiling. The tables were piled with well-thumbed, out of date magazines: *Golf Weekly*, *Woman's Own*, *Hello*. The chairs were bolted together in groups of three and the stale, overheated air smelled of rubbing alcohol and disinfectant. Gala, Meg and Viv sat down in a row. Joey felt Aggie's hand in hers, leading her over to another group of chairs along the far wall. They sat down.

"Just so we're crystal clear here," said Aggie firmly, "none of this is your fault."

"I shouldn't have brought Lily to the pond."

"Bringing her to the pond isn't what made this happen. An impulsive teenager slightly prone to melodrama slipped on a patch of ice. That's what made this happen." Joey shook her head, desolate. Just then, a tall, sandy-haired man in scrubs pushed through the doors marked "No Entry".

"Andrew!" Meg flew to her feet and the man walked over and put his arm around her.

"Hello, Mum," he said.

"How is she?" Gala blurted out.

Andrew walked over to where Gala, Meg and Viv had been sitting. Joey and Aggie stood nearby.

Andrew took a deep breath and eyed them warily. Joey and Aggie exchanged nervous glances.

"She's in good hands," Andrew began. Looking around

at all of them, his gaze stopped at Joey; he was obviously wondering who she was.

"This is Joey Rubin," Aggie explained. "She's a new friend of ours. She's overseeing the restoration at Stanway House."

"Pleasure," Andrew said, nodding.

"Nice to meet you," Joey replied.

"Normally I wouldn't be allowed to tell you anything, but Ian gave me permission," Andrew said. "Lily took quite a hit. There are rough waters ahead."

"Dear Lord," Viv whispered.

Andrew's words seemed very far away. Joey suddenly felt as though she were watching the whole scene from outside of herself, her breathing slow, her ears filled with cotton. She wondered if she were going to faint, so she sat down and took a few deep breaths, hugging her knees.

"She's a ten on the Glasgow Coma Scale," Andrew continued.

Joey's stomach lurched at the mention of the word *coma*.

"What does that mean, darling?" Meg asked.

"Under eight indicates a very severe injury, with the possibility of lasting brain damage, or – worse. Ten is in the middle of the moderate range. The higher the score, the better. Points are assigned according to how long a person stays unconscious, and then, when they wake, whether they can speak, answer questions, whether they withdraw from pain, obey commands for movement. How dilated their pupils are."

"Does she have a concussion?" Gala asked.

"Most definitely. But many concussions aren't all that serious. The real question is whether the impact caused any tearing of the veins that supply the brain with blood, and how much, if any, bruising occurred to the brain tissue itself."

"How can you tell?" Joey asked.

"It plays out over time, usually about seventy-two hours.

The first twenty-four are the most critical, though. If the brain has been injured, it swells, just like an ankle will swell if you hurt it. But since there's so little room inside the skull, swelling can cut off the brain's blood supply by compressing the veins. We don't want that to happen. Also, we have to watch for signs of intracranial bleeding. If she bleeds and clots, we'll have to get in there and remove the clot. Fortunately, we're well equipped here to monitor Lily for all these things."

"The poor thing!" Meg cried.

"She's young," Andrew said. "She hasn't any underlying conditions. Both these factors are in her favour, but head injuries are tricky. Things can go downhill very fast."

"What's happening now?" Aggie asked.

"They're shaving her head, then they'll suture the wound."

Tears filled Joey's eyes. Lily's beautiful hair! She knew, rationally, that hair didn't even deserve to be on the list of the things they were presently worrying about, but the image of Lily without her beautiful blonde waves brought home just how serious the situation was.

"We'll need to attach electrical sensors directly to her scalp," Andrew continued. "And, of course, if there's a sudden need for emergency surgery, every minute matters."

"Of course," Meg said.

Andrew made to go. "I should get back in there," he said.

"Thank you, dear," Meg said. "Tell Lilia we're all out here, if she needs anything."

"Shall do," Andrew replied, and then he was off.

Afternoon turned to evening, and no one emerged with any news. They took turns visiting the small cafeteria on the first floor, drinking watery tea and eating sandwiches that tasted of clingfilm. At eight o'clock, Lilia and Ian emerged from the emergency ward, looking pale and drained. The women stood up almost in unison, and offered Ian and Lilia seats. No one dared to utter a question.

"She opened her eyes," Ian said.

"And smiled," said Lilia, fighting back tears.

"She's heavily sedated and they've transferred her to intensive care. The first twenty-four hours are the most risky. Lilia needs to go home, but I'm staying here."

"I'll drive her," Aggie volunteered. "In fact, I'll take her back to my house. I think she should stay with me. All right, Lilia?"

Lilia seemed too worn out to argue. She nodded weakly.

Ian, preoccupied, rose to go back inside. As the women crowded around Lilia, Joey followed him several steps toward the doors.

"Ian."

He stopped and turned. His eyes were weary and empty. He was clearly impatient to get back to Lily's side.

"I'm so sorry."

"Thanks."

"I shouldn't have taken her to the – "

I don't want to talk about this now."

"All right. Is there anything I can do?"

"No."

"Can I get you some food? Something to drink?"

He shook his head. He turned to go, and then wheeled round. "Actually, there is something. I ran out the door so fast that I left my wallet and phone at home. Could you possibly go and get them?"

"Of course. Is your van here?"

Ian dug the keys out of his pocket and handed them to her. "In the back car park."

"Anything else?"

"No, thanks."

"I'll wait for you here. Come out whenever you can."

"Okay."

"The wallet's on my bedside table, I think. But if it's not there, it would be in the kitchen somewhere. The phone is on the table."

"I'll find them."

Ian nodded soberly and pushed through the doors.

"Better get back in there."

❋ ❋ ❋

It was strange to be back in the gatehouse. It was dark now, so Joey turned on the overhead light as she climbed the stairs to Ian's bedroom. She paused briefly to gaze at the photographs in standing frames on the upstairs hall table. She picked up a frame containing a picture of a smiling woman on a horse. It had to be Cait.

Joey flipped on the table lamp and brought the picture close. Cait had been so beautiful, so obviously happy and full of high spirits. In these last few weeks, it had been all too easy to dismiss her as less than a real person, as simply an obstacle to be overcome, an irritating source of pain and regret.

"I'm sorry," Joey found herself whispering to the photograph, though she hardly knew what she was apologising for. For not taking better care of Lily? Or for falling in love with Ian? It was so unfair, she thought, staring at the image as tears came to her eyes. For the first time, she experienced a little of the sadness that had all but swamped Ian and Lilia.

She put the frame down and went into the bedroom. What she really longed to do was to go into Ian's closet and inhale the fragrance of his shirts and sweaters. She wanted to pore over the contents of all his drawers, peruse all the titles of the books in his bookcases, lie down on his bed and take in his private world. But she couldn't allow herself to do any of this. Even being here in the house made her feel like a voyeur. Now that she had felt a faint connection with Cait, the real person who had lost her life so early and so tragically, Joey felt almost as though Cait was watching her drift about the room, taking her own time doing the one and only thing that Ian had asked her to do.

The wallet was on the bedside table. She picked it up, resisting the impulse to open it. She grabbed an extra sweater from the back of the chair, then went into the bathroom to collect Ian's toothbrush. As she turned on the light, she caught her breath at the sight of Ian and Lily's toiletries commingled on the sink and table: Lily's hairbrush, with thick strands wound around the bristles; Ian's bottle of aftershave; dental floss; a bottle of plum frosted nail polish in which sparkles hung suspended; an old-fashioned shaving brush in a lather cup. The objects said everything about their intimate life together, as father and daughter.

Please let her be okay, Joey found herself whispering.

She grabbed the toothbrush and headed downstairs. Maybe this was stupid, she thought. They certainly had toothbrushes in the hospital. Nevertheless, she found a plastic bag in the kitchen and folded the sweater neatly on the bottom. She wrapped the toothbrush in paper towels and grabbed a couple of apples, a can of mixed nuts and a bottle of orange juice. Picking up his phone, she glanced around, wondering if there was anything else he might want or need, then put out the lights, locked the doors, and nervously, carefully drove Ian's van back to the hospital.

It was almost nine o'clock when she came back out to the waiting room. Ian was sitting in one of the chairs, resting, with his eyes closed. She sat down beside him and he roused himself. She handed him the bag.

"Thank you."

"How is she?"

"Holding steady. She's talking, and everything she says makes sense."

"That's good."

"So they say. She can follow the movement of a light with her eyes, and she pulls away when they poke her with something sharp."

"That's mean!"

Ian smiled for the first time. He sat back and sighed.

"What can I do?"

"Nothing."

"I'm so sorry, Ian. She really wanted to come with me into the village."

"I know. Lilia told me everything."

"I shouldn't have let her!"

"What? Walk into the village with you?"

"Go to the pond."

Ian look confused. "You weren't anywhere near her when this happened."

"I was right there. I had just got out."

"Lilia said that she and Lily were arguing and Lily slipped on a patch of ice. Isn't that what happened?"

"Yes, but…"

"But what?"

"But if I hadn't taken her to the pond, she wouldn't have *been there* to slip on the ice. And they were arguing, in part, about me."

Ian shook his head. "Look, it's best if we don't talk about this right now."

"I know. I'll head off. If there's anything I can do, just let me know."

"How are you getting home?"

Joey shrugged. "I'll get a taxi."

"Take the van." He handed her back the keys.

"What if you want to leave?"

"I'm not going anywhere. If I need it, I'll call you."

"You sure?"

Ian nodded.

"Is there anything else I can do?"

"Could you perhaps call Angus for me? He should know. I'm just not sure I can face explaining the situation to him at the moment." Ian pulled a scrap of paper out of his wallet, grabbed a pen from the counter and scribbled a number on the paper. He handed it to Joey.

"What about your sister?"

"Let's hold off on that. Wait till we know what we're dealing with."

"Any idea when that will be?"

"Some time tomorrow," Ian said.

"Okay. I'll bring you some coffee and breakfast."

"No need to do that."

"I'll go crazy if I don't have something to do."

"See you in the morning," Ian said.

For an instant, Joey wondered if she should kiss him goodbye, but almost immediately thought better of it. She took his hand, squeezed it gently and headed out into the night air.

❋ ❋ ❋

She called Angus from Ian's van, before making the drive back to Stanway House. His first impulse, upon hearing of Lily's accident, was to head straight for the hospital. Joey tried to dissuade him.

"Ian doesn't want to leave Lily's side," she explained, "and they won't let you in there. We were here for eight hours today, and we only saw him once, for about two minutes."

"But he shouldn't be alone. Did you call his sister?"

"He wants to wait until tomorrow."

"*God…* Okay."

Angus sounded distraught. It might not be of any help to Ian to have his friend sit by himself in the waiting room, but maybe it would be of help to Angus. He'd known Lily since she was a baby, after all. They were his only family.

"Look," Joey said, "you're his best friend. It's not *my* place to tell you what to do. If you feel you need to be here, by all means, come on over.

"Are you there now?"

"Yes, but I'm just leaving. My poor dog's been locked up all day. Everyone's gone home."

"So Ian thinks I should wait until morning?" Angus asked, his voice now surprisingly vulnerable.

"I told him I'd bring him over some breakfast. We could go over together in the morning."

"All right," Angus replied. "Let's meet for breakfast in the café in town. I've been wanting to talk to you."

"What time?"

"Seven-thirty? We'll get them to pack up some food."

"All right," Joey said. "I'll see you then."

❋ ❋ ❋

Joey turned on her BlackBerry when she got back to Stanway House. Sarah had left her four messages.

"I've been trying to call you for hours!" Sarah cried, as soon as she picked up.

"I turned it off in the hospital — there was a sign saying you had to — and I forgot to turn it back on."

"How is she? Aggie called Henry a little while ago. Do you want me to come down there? I'll get in the car right now."

"Yes," Joey said, then immediately erupted into sobs. "Please! Sarah, I need you."

Two and a half hours later, Joey threw herself into her friend's arms.

"I'm so sorry," she cried, between sobs. "I've been such a bitch! I'm just a horrible, horrible person! I don't blame you for hating me."

"I don't hate you," Sarah cried. "Who said I hated you?"

"You *should!*"

Sarah patted her back, holding her close until the sobs began to subside. Then she marched Joey over to the sofa, fetched two glasses from the cupboard, and pulled a bottle of Macallan out of her bag. She poured them both two fingers of Scotch.

"Drink up," she commanded. Joey threw hers back. Sarah watched, her eyes a little wide, but she didn't say anything. She poured her another two fingers.

"Tell me everything, sweetie," she said.

That was when the first good thing happened. As Joey poured out the story of the sorrowful day's events, and as Sarah listened with total concentration and compassion, all the distance that had grown up between them began to fall away. Looking back later, Joey would wonder just what it was that had caused them to shed like worn overcoats their competitiveness, their petty resentments, and all the things they had found to dislike about each other, from the distance of a continent away.

Perhaps it was the raw nature of the emotion Joey revealed, and the vulnerability with which she spoke with her friend, vulnerability Sarah hadn't glimpsed in nearly twenty years. Perhaps it was the nearness of tragedy, the keen awareness of how fragile life was, and how in a few seconds it could be taken away.

Sarah reassured Joey as no one else had been able to do. "Look, honey," she said. "You didn't grab Lily's arm and you didn't scream at her. You didn't place her foot on that ice and you didn't pull her or let go. There is no way in the world you can hold yourself responsible for what happened."

"I should never have slept with him. I shouldn't have gotten involved with them, when I was only going to be here for a couple of weeks. You were right. It was totally selfish of me."

"I wasn't right, I was being a prig."

"No you weren't!"

"Yes I was! It's just that — sometimes I'm — I'm — jealous of you!"

"And I'm jealous of you," Joey surprised herself by saying.

"You still look gorgeous! You waltz into town and Ian McCormack just falls for you! You don't understand: every woman in a twenty-five mile radius, single or not, is in love with that man! And who does he fall for? You!"

"But you have a husband who adores you!"

"And you have a career, and a life of your own!"

"You have so many people who love you."

"Who love what I *do* for them, I sometimes think."

"Who love *you*," Joey insisted.

They were silent for several moments, each startled by the unfiltered admissions that had suddenly burst forth, as though an emotional dam had burst.

"I wish we could go back," Joey finally whispered. "You and me."

"We can't."

"Then I wish we could start over. Just turn the page and move on."

"Henry and I do that sometimes."

"You do?"

"Yeah. For me, it was like a light bulb switching on. We had this big row one Friday morning. It was one of our typical fights, and I thought to myself, you know, we could spend the whole weekend deconstructing everything he said and everything I said and where I was wrong and where he was wrong. But I just don't want to do it! I mean, we're not going to get divorced! It was just a stupid fight over something silly, the kind of fight married people just can't keep from having."

"So what did you do?"

"I called him up at work. I said, 'Henry, we could carry on with this all weekend long, and nobody's going to win, and we'll just end up being miserable and exhausted on Monday. *Or* we could just admit that we we're both stupid, pigheaded idiots and we're doing the best we can. And we can turn the page and forget about it and have a nice weekend. What do you say?' He was all for it, and he came home with tulips and a bottle of wine and by nine o'clock Friday night, the whole thing was forgotten. I really learned something."

"Let's start over," Joey said.

"Let's," replied Sarah.

Chapter 24

Joey was seated in a booth by the window when Angus came through the door. Sarah had left to drive back to London at the crack of dawn, hoping to beat some of the commuter traffic and Joey had arrived at the café early, not knowing what else to do with herself. Angus looked tired.

"Morning."

"Any word?"

"No, but I wasn't expecting any."

The waitress came over, and set a place in front of Angus.

"Morning, Sally," Angus said

"Angus," the waitress replied. "Awful about Lily. Have you had word?"

Angus shook his head. "We're heading over there now. Put together something for Ian, would you?"

"Sure thing," she replied. "What'll you two have?"

"Porridge, please, and some toast. Joey?"

"Sounds fine."

While they waited for their breakfasts to arrive, Joey filled Angus in on everything that had happened the previous day. When they had exhausted everything that could be said on that subject, there was only one place for the conversation to go: to whatever Angus had wanted to speak with Joey about.

Joey took a deep breath and dived in. "I'll spare you having to say it," she began.

"Say what?"

"That I have no business getting involved with Ian. That I'm a — a clueless, pushy American who doesn't understand — "

Angus cut her off. "So you *are* involved with him."

Joey sunk down a little in the booth. "Uh — yeah. A little. Though now, I'm not sure."

"And you'd think I'd disapprove of that?"

"Uh-huh."

"Why would you think that?"

"Because everyone else does. Well, not everyone. Not Lily. Not Aggie —"

"Not Ian, presumably." Angus smiled, revealing charmingly craggy teeth.

Joey shook her head.

"I wasn't going to say any of these things."

"Oh."

"I was actually going to give you a bit of a heads-up."

"About what?"

"You know he lost his wife."

"I do know. I've made some friends while I've been here, and Sarah Howard and I grew up together. I've heard the story."

"So you *do* know that the lad hasn't given a lass the time of day since Cait passed away."

"I do."

"All right, you've had fair warning. There's a lot of heart-break built up, and this is a first."

"What is?

"His falling for someone. It was pretty obvious that first night, Joey. The fellow lit up like a firecracker."

"He *did?*"

"Well, for Ian, that is. We Scots tend to keep these things to ourselves. You might not actually have noticed, but *I* could tell."

Joey smiled and tried to keep the tears that had suddenly welled up from spilling over. It was such a relief not to face disapproval. A couple of tears trickled down her cheeks.

"Oh, good God," said Angus. "See, this is why *I'm* not married! This is what I do best – make women fall all to pieces."

Joey dabbed at her eyes with a succession of thin paper napkins. "I just don't know what to do. I'm leaving soon, and, I mean, I will be going back and forth, for a while, at least until we open Stanway House, but it's not as though I live here."

"Could you? Would you ever want to?"

"I don't know. I've never lived anywhere but New York. And I can't see them coming there." Joey had been aware of these obstacles from the very beginning and had always known that she would have to deal with them at some point. But now, her return to New York was looming. The moment she had been dreading was upon her.

"So, let it play out," Angus said. "Don't do anything at all. See where the damn thing means to go. And above all, give it time. Don't play the short game here, Joey. Because that's a game you're not going to win."

Joey sat in silence for several moments. The waitress came over with a bag containing rolls and coffee for Ian. Angus insisted on paying the bill. As he laid a note on the table, Joey covered his hand with hers. Angus looked up.

Her words spilled out before she had time to second-guess herself. "You're his oldest friend, Angus. Do *you* think I could make him happy?"

"I'm not a fortune teller, Joey. But you certainly seemed to make him happy the other night."

❋　❋　❋

Joey was relieved to discover a different charge nurse on duty – a tiny wiry-haired woman with a sweet, solicitous smile.

"We brought some breakfast for Ian McCormack. He's in there with his daughter, Lily," said Joey.

"Lily, yes … now let me see." The nurse scrutinised the clipboard in front of her. "She's been transferred upstairs."

"She has?"

The nurse nodded. "You can go on up, if you like."

"Is she still in intensive care?" Joey asked.

"She is. But there's a waiting room up there – Third West."

Joey and Angus went up in the lift in silence and marched grimly to the intensive care nurses' station. Moments later, Ian appeared in the waiting room. Joey and Angus studied his expression, hoping for clues as to Lily's condition. But they couldn't really tell much. He looked rumpled and careworn, much as he had the previous night.

"Come sit down," Joey said. "We brought you something to eat."

Angus put his arm around Ian's shoulders and steered him to a chair. Joey prised the lid off the cup of coffee and handed it to him.

'Thanks," he said, taking a sip. "Thanks very much."

"How is she?" Joey asked.

"She's downstairs having an MRI. She had a quiet night, which is good, but she's heavily sedated. They're checking her for bleeding on the brain."

"Jaysus in heaven," Angus exhaled.

Ian nodded solemnly, then glanced at his watch. "They took her down at six o'clock. They said it would take – "

A doctor in full scrubs was now striding toward them. Joey and Angus noticed him before Ian did, and Angus instinctively stood up. Ian looked up, and they all braced themselves for the worst.

"I have some good news," said the doctor. "No sign of bleeding."

"Thank God," Ian cried, as his breathing quickened. "So she's — she's — "

"She's got a hell of a headache. And she's got a five-inch gash that's going to take a bit of healing. But everything inside looks fine. We'll keep her here for a day or two, to keep an eye on things — you never say 'never' with head injuries — but I am very optimistic. If all goes well, and I think it will, you should have Lily home by the end of the week."

"Oh my God," whispered Ian. "Thank you. I can't thank you enough." It seemed to take every ounce of strength he possessed to keep himself from breaking down.

❀　❀　❀

Lily came home on Thursday. Her head was wrapped like a turban in gauze, and her walk was anything but spritely, but she was alive and she was on the mend. Joey made an executive decision to put all the contractors on hold for two weeks. There was no way she was going to allow building work to begin while Lily was trying to rest and recuperate. She would be back in school in a couple of weeks, her doctors had predicted, but in the meantime, she needed peace and quiet.

The truth was that Joey was finding it hard to focus on the house renovation at all. New York — Dave, Alex, Preston Kay, all her colleagues at the Apex Group — felt suddenly very remote, like the characters from a book she had read and was fast forgetting. She drifted through her days, concentrating as best she could on what she had to complete before she left, aware all the time of the real story filling her heart — hoping each morning that Ian would appear at her door, invite her to come over and visit Lily, ask her to join him for a cup of coffee, a glass of wine.

He never came. On a couple of occasions, Joey saw Lilia coming and going, and another woman she took to be Ian's sister. She delivered pastries and fruit, and magazines she thought would amuse Lily, and she slipped notes under the door offering to stay with Lily if Ian needed a break, or to read to her if she needed diversion other than television. But the message was loud and clear. Ian wasn't ready to have her back in his life, or Lily's.

Joey had avoided the pond since the accident, and she hadn't seen any of the women. Every time she thought of the pond now, terrifying images surfaced in her mind. The whole idea of going there again made her uneasy. She dreaded having to face Lilia. But the pond had been such a wonderful, magical place, right up until that near-tragic last visit and she didn't want to remember it as the place of Lily's accident, she wanted to remember all the pleasure and the happiness she had experienced there – the exhilaration of swimming, the fun of being knocked on her ass by Gala's *White Hot Russian Cocoa*, the tender camaraderie of Meg's birthday party, the knitting and the tea drinking and the arguments and laughter.

She had to go back. And she had to do it without Lily.

❋   ❋   ❋

Joey arrived just as two burly deliverymen were carrying a huge crate along the path that led to the pond. She followed them into the clearing, where Aggie, Gala, Meg, Viv and Lilia were waiting. Lilia looked puzzled. The others looked about to burst, like children waiting to yell "Surprise!" at a birthday party.

The men set the crate down.

"Where do you want it?" one of the men asked.

"Just here," said Gala, indicating a patch of flat land that faced the water.

"You can't just put this on the ground," the other man said bossily. "It has to be properly mounted."

"We know that," said Meg. "That's Phase II."

"You don't want us to take it out of the box?" the first man asked.

"No!" the ladies shouted in unison.

"But thanks," Viv mollified.

The men placed the box where specified. Aggie signed a piece of paper and the men trooped off through the woods.

"What on earth is going on?" asked Lilia. She had carefully avoided making eye contact with Joey, but at least she hadn't been on the offensive.

"Meg's going to make a speech," Viv announced.

"So, what else is new?" quipped Gala.

The sun was dropping in the sky, bathing the water in soft, coral tones.

"Lilia," Meg began, "we have a little something for you. It's something we've wanted to do for a very long time."

Lilia looked around, confused, nervous. Joey caught her eye and smiled tentatively. Lilia held Joey's gaze for a moment, nodded gently then peered intently at the box.

Meg consulted a piece of paper, on which she had written some notes for her speech. She cleared her throat and began, dramatically, and in earnest.

"Once upon a time, we called ourselves 'the lost girls'."

She paused and turned to Joey. "It was when I was writing my book on J.M. Barrie and the Llewelyn Davies boys. How they might have been the inspiration for the 'lost boys' of *Peter Pan*. Well, we all had a little too much wine one night, and Gala – I think it was Gala – "

"It was me," Viv called, interrupting.

"It was," Gala confirmed.

Meg continued. "And *Viv* said, 'Why are you mucking around with all that, Meg? You should write a book about *us*! You could call it 'The Lost *Girls*'!"

Joey glanced around at the women, who were all nodding and smiling at the memory.

"You might find this hard to believe, Joey, but each one of us has been lost. Some for months. Some – for years."

The women had grown quiet and sombre.

"Gala was lost first. In Auschwitz," said Meg. She paused, and gathered herself. "Aggie was utterly lost without Richard. Viv got lost a couple of times in the – cancer forest – and I've been lost so many times that it's a wonder I'm here at all. I wouldn't be, I daresay, without all of you." Meg's voice cracked, and when Joey looked around at the faces of the ladies, there were tears on everyone's cheeks. "I know that in my bones. I'm surer of that one fact than I am about anything else."

Meg paused to recover her composure. Aggie stepped forward and rubbed her friend's back. Meg took a deep breath and attempted to continue.

"And you, our dear, dear Lilia, have also been lost, for what feels to us, as I'm sure it does to you, like a very long time. But you have never, ever – ever! – been alone. You're not alone now, and as long as we all shall live, we shall be by your side. Longing for the Lilia that we know and love to return to us. For we 'lost girls' have our own never-never-land, and it is here."

Everyone looked up and around, gazing at the slashes of light above the pond. Meg's eyes found her paper again and she continued:

"'If you shut your eyes and are a lucky one,' wrote our beloved Mr. Barrie, 'you may see at times a shapeless pool of lovely pale colours suspended in the darkness; then if you squeeze your eyes tighter, the pool begins to take shape, and the colours become so vivid that with another squeeze they must go on fire.' I'm sure he was writing about our pond. Because we *are* the lucky ones. We have each other."

Meg nodded to Gala and Viv. They stepped forward and lifted the lid off the box, then unfastened the cords that held the container together. They lifted away the wooden sides to reveal a magnificent hand carved wooden bench.

"Oh, my dear sweet friends... this is... it's beautiful!" exclaimed Lilia.

"It's in honour of Cait," Aggie explained quietly.

A sob escaped from Lilia's lips as she slowly walked toward it and ran her hand over the back.

"It's inscribed," Meg said.

Joey walked over slowly and peered at the long bronze plaque. She read:

"God gave us memory so that we might have roses in December."
J.M. Barrie
In memory of
Catherine Margaret McCormack ~ 1972–2002

Lilia was speechless.

"It's meant to give you strength, Lil," Meg said. "It's meant to be a place where you can sit and be with all your *happy* memories."

"They're all happy," Lilia said softly. "Even the ones that hurt."

"Well, we'll leave *those* somewhere else, dearie," Gala said kindly. "In the churchyard, say." She popped the cork on a bottle of champagne, which bubbled over. Gala held the bottle aloft. "I hereby christen thee the official 'remember the roses' bench of the J.M. Barrie Ladies' Swimming Society."

"Hear, hear!" cried Aggie.

"Bravo!" called Viv.

"Of course," Joey smiled to herself, remembering the dedication in Meg's book.

"We couldn't very well go around calling ourselves the 'lost girls' now, could we?" said Gala. 'They would have locked us all up!"

"Time for pictures,"Viv said, brandishing a camera. "We're losing the light already. Just let me set up my tripod."

"I can take it," Joey offered. "I've got a pretty steady hand. Why don't some of you sit on the bench and the others stand behind it."

Joey framed the shot as the women settled themselves on and behind the bench. "You'll have to email me a copy," Joey said. "I'm going to frame it and put it right on my desk."

She lowered the camera as the women settled in. "I don't want to leave you all," she said, trying to smile. "I don't know if you realise what you – how much I – I needed someone to – take my hand, to let me belong. Even for a little while." Tears were gathering now in her eyes. She had better get the picture, before she really fell apart. She might never see them again. They were old, one never knew. She might come back in a month or two to find that one of these precious, irreplaceable women had been swept away by a sudden stroke or a heart attack. How could that be possible? How could they be so alive and beautiful, and yet so insanely vulnerable to what life threw in the path of people their age.

Looking through the viewfinder, she saw Lilia getting up.

"What are you doing, Lil? Come on!"Viv said.

"I'm setting up the tripod," Lilia said firmly.

"But why? Joey said she – "

"Just help me, Viv, would you?" Lilia said quietly. "Joey needs to be in the picture."

Joey felt her heart give a little flutter, and then Viv was taking the camera away and mounting it quickly on the tripod. She felt Lilia's thin, frail hand in hers, leading her to the bench, where she settled Joey in beside her. They were still holding hands when the flash of light immortalised them all for ever, together.

Chapter 25

Lily was sitting up in bed, pale and thin, her head encircled in colourful silk.

"I like the scarf," Joey said quietly. She kissed Lily on the cheek and sat down in the chair beside the bed.

"It's Granny's. It's Hermès."

"Wow."

"She says it'll be mine one day. I think it's hideous, actually. I'm only wearing it because it's so soft. Everything else is too scratchy. But I'm really not the horse-and-bridle type."

"No. All the same, you're rocking it pretty well."

"Thanks."

"Speaking of which, I have a present for you."

"You've been leaving me presents for a week! Thanks, by the way. The strawberries were heaven."

"This one's even better."

Lily looked at her suspiciously, as though she'd had quite enough surprises in recent days. Joey reached into the large shopping bag on the floor and pulled out her Fendi boots. She set them on top of the quilt covering Lily's legs.

"No!" Lily said, a real smile spreading across her face for the first time. She sat up a little straighter.

"They look way better on you that they do on me."

"You are joking?" Lily was grinning as she pulled herself up to a full sitting position. She picked up one of the boots and ran her hand across the buttery suede. Joey shook her head. "I don't want you to forget me, kiddo."

"Not much chance of that," Lily returned, entranced by the feel of the boots in her hands.

Lily raised her gaze to meet Joey's. "You really mean it? You're really giving them to me?"

"I am. And I want you to think of me every time you put them on. Promise? Cross you heart and hope to – sorry! Scratch that last part." Joey ran her hand jokingly across her forehead, as though wiping away sweat.

Lily laughed and leaned forward and Joey embraced her.

"Cross my heart," Lily whispered. She sat back and took Joey's hand. "I wish you didn't have to go."

"I think I've caused enough trouble for now, don't you?"

"What do you *mean?* You haven't caused any trouble! You've been – the best thing that happened in – in this house for a very long time!"

Joey shook her head, determined not to get emotional. "I'm not sure everyone would agree with that."

"You *have!*" Lily said dramatically. "The two of them, God!"

"Who?"

"Dad and Granny. They're driving me absolutely mad!"

"Yeah, well, you've got to cut them some slack. They've been worried sick about you. What happened to you was – not nothing."

"I know, but geez, it's *me* that it happened to and *I'm* dealing with it. If they don't let me go back to school next week, I swear I'm going to – can't you take me back to New York in your suitcase? Please? I'll be good! I promise!"

"My couch is your couch, I told you. You say the word and I'll be waiting at the airport."

"You mean it?" Lily now looked fifteen again. A blush of colour had risen to her cheeks.

"I'm counting the days." Joey glanced at her watch. "But my ride's going to be here soon. I ought to go."

"Okay." Lily made a glum face. Joey couldn't be sure, but it seemed that tears were glistening in the corners of her eyes.

"I am not saying goodbye," Joey said firmly as she stood up, "because I'll be back before you know it."

Lily seemed to take the cue. She wasn't going to allow herself to get weepy either.

"My hair will be really short next time you see me. And I'm going to dye it black."

"Oh yeah? What'll your dad have to say about that?"

"He said yes!" Lily crowed, beaming.

❀ ❀ ❀

Ian was sitting in the kitchen, pretending to read the newspaper. He looked up when he heard Joey's footsteps and smiled when she appeared in the doorway.

"Cup of coffee?"

"I wish I had time."

"When's your flight?"

"My car's coming in five minutes. I have to be there two hours ahead of time."

Ian nodded. He opened his mouth as though he were going to say something, but then thought better of it. There was so much that Joey wanted to say: how sorry she still felt for whatever part she had played in the crisis that had rocked his family, how much she wished them all nothing but health and happiness, how desperately she longed to be his again, in his bed, breathing in the scent of his hair. She wanted to kiss the side of his neck. She wanted to feel his weight upon her again and to hear his laugh, which had seemed to bubble up from a secret cavern of good humour and joy — only to be sealed up once again by the desperate events of the past two weeks.

Ian looked pensive and drawn. She wanted to wrap her arms around him and cook him massive meals, make him drowsy with wine, and watch over him while he slept, watch over Ian and Lily until spring came and welcomed them back, with her help, into the world of the living.

"Another time?" Joey whispered. "Another place?"

"We don't have either of those things," Ian said sadly.

"We might."

Ian shook his head. "All anyone has, Joey, is what's here, right now. I learned that the hard way, once. And I learned it again last week."

Joey knew he was right, of course, at least for him, at least for now.

"But thank you," he said kindly. "I'm not sad that — you and I —"

"Me neither." She didn't want to cry. She was *not* going to cry. She took a deep breath and said, "I should go."

Ian nodded sadly. "This time of day, the traffic can be a nightmare."

He stood up and came around the table. Wordlessly, they came together. There was a moment when their closeness threatened to overturn all they had just said, but neither one of them let it happen. Ian pulled back, took Joey's face tenderly between the palms of his hands and kissed her gently, softly.

With a catch in her throat and tears beginning to gather at the back of her eyes, Joey gave him one last squeeze, turned and fled.

Chapter 26

The rocker was even more beautiful than it had looked in the antique store. It had a rich, golden walnut frame and pale green damask upholstery, reminiscent of the drapery fabric in Lady Margaret's apartment. As soon as the deliverymen left, Joey carried it across the room and placed it between the windows in front of the blank rear wall.

The wall wouldn't be blank for long. She had used the first big cheque she'd received following her promotion to order a gas fireplace and this, too, was due to be installed in the next few weeks. It was sort of silly, putting in a fireplace now that spring was right around the corner, but Joey didn't care. Just the idea of it had filled her with happiness, and now the thought of sitting before a fire in this beautiful old rocker brought a smile to her lips. She would get a cosy rug, maybe an antique oriental, and a table, and another comfortable chair or two. And on the mantel she planned to have built, she would place the framed photograph of herself with Aggie, Viv, Gala, Meg and Lilia.

Today's project was to frame a dozen other pictures she had chosen to put up on the wall leading to her kitchen: various photographs of her parents, of her and Sarah at twelve and thirteen, of her grandmother and grandfather at Coney Island, of family gatherings enlivened by cousins she rarely saw any more. She'd bought the frames weeks ago but had been so busy at work that she hadn't had time to frame them. She could have been working today – she probably should have been working today – but the delivery of the chair had required her to be home between ten and four. So she was allowing herself the first proper day off she'd had in a while, a whole day to potter around doing house things she hadn't had time for, washing the blue Spode teacups and saucers she'd bought at a street fair in Chelsea, polishing her mother's old silver, which she had put in storage, thinking she wanted more modern flatware. And, of course, getting those photographs up on the wall.

She tried not to think of all the things she given away in her zeal to modernise the flat and make it her own. Now, she could barely believe what she had taken to the charity store, not realising that the objects that made her sad were the very objects that had made this place feel like home. Joey was sure her mother would have appreciated the irony of Joey's recent compulsion to "nest". For every time she had contemplated putting yet another item in yet another charity box, she had heard in her head her mother's voice saying "You not getting rid of *that*, are you?"

Joey washed the kitchen table and dried it thoroughly, and then spread the photographs out over the surface. She loved mindless tasks like this, jobs which required just a little concentration yet allowed one's thoughts to wander. She found herself thinking of how many things had changed since her weeks in the Cotswolds.

She'd taken one week off when she first got back to New York and followed through on her promise to herself to get back in touch with old friends, especially Martina, Susan and Eva. It had been almost unbearably hard to pick up the phone and make those initial calls, but if she'd learned anything from the women at the pond, she'd learned how vital it was to love and be loved by friends. There was nothing saccharine about the bond these women had: they fought, they harboured simmering resentments, they competed with each other, but they were absolutely devoted and loyal, decade after decade. As Aggie had explained it, they decided to *be* friends and then they continually decided to *stay* friends, through hell and high water.

Joey had never thought of friendship that way. She had seen it as something dispensable, something to be enjoyed as long as everyone was getting along, something to let go of when difficulties in the relationships arose. She remembered her mother saying something once when Joey was young, something that had puzzled her at the time. Leah had argued with one of her oldest friends, Sylvia Webster, and they didn't speak for weeks. Then, out of the blue, she was back in all their lives.

"I thought you didn't like her any more," Joey had commented, bewildered.

"You're not really friends," Leah had explained, "until you've had a big fight and come through it."

Now, for the first time in her life, she really understood and believed this.

Joey had been in touch with Martina first, despite having a sense that of the three women, Martina was the likeliest to be chilly. And she was. Her tone was clipped, as she begged off on getting together, claiming to be too busy for the next few weeks, claiming she was travelling for work, which might well have been true. She promised to be back in touch with Joey when things calmed down, but Joey wondered if she would.

Susan and Eva, on the other hand, had seemed really happy to hear from her. In the past couple of weeks, they had gradually begun to spend time together the way they had in college.

They were meeting for drinks after work, catching movies on weekends and hanging out at each other's apartments like old times. Susan had sworn herself off men for a while, having just broken up with a guy she'd been seeing for a year. And Eva had wandered into the waters of Match.com. They spent hours picking out people for her to "wink" at, arguing over whether she should be more or less specific in filling out her preferences for the sort of people she wanted to date, and helping her to write and rewrite her online profile.

Joey told them all about Ian, of course. Eva had tried to talk Joey into creating her own profile on Match.com, arguing that there was safety in numbers. They could meet new guys on double dates. But Joey had no interest in meeting anyone, not yet. The memories of Ian were too fresh and too precious. There might come a time when she would be ready to dip her toe into the dating pool again, but she most certainly wasn't there yet.

She and Sarah were getting along well, thanks to a weekly Skype session. They hadn't missed one Sunday. Sometimes they talked for ten or fifteen minutes, but once they talked for two hours. Joey had avoided the subjects of Ian and Lily, but Sarah managed to drop a few details. Lily was back in school.

"I know," Joey had said. "Ian told me."

"So you guys are in touch?" Sarah asked.

"Quite a bit actually."

"Joey!" exclaimed Sarah, coming a little closer to the computer camera. "Do tell."

"Oh, it's only about work. We never talk about — us — but I do ask him about Lily. How does she look?"

"I don't know," said Sarah. "I haven't seen her."

Joey always asked about the ladies, and Sarah always said that they sent their love. Whether or not this was true, Joey didn't know, but it could well have been. Aggie and Sarah spoke often. And Sarah had sprung another surprise on Joey during their last phone call.

"I'm thinking of coming to New York," she said tentatively.

"You *are?* When?"

"Whenever you can take some time off to hang out with me."

"That would be *so* great! Will you bring the kids?" Joey had struggled to keep smiling. It was important to appear to be excited, not to display any reservations whatsoever about having four rambunctious children staying in her apartment.

"Lord, no! I'm leaving them all with Henry. We had one of those *turn the page* battle royals last weekend. And when we *turned the page* I said, 'Oh, and one more thing, darling – *I'm* going to New York to see Joey.'"

"What did he say to that?"

"He said 'Splendid!' and then I added 'by *myself!*' I thought I detected a little panic on his face."

"Will he be able to handle the kids?"

"Well, if he can't, that's his problem," Sarah had said.

Joey set the glass of the frames down on the photographs.

An hour later, they were on the wall, arranged in a casual pattern just above eye level. Joey stepped back, pleased – barely pausing as her eye fixed on a rogue piece of fluff caught between one of the photographs and its glass. Too bad, she said to herself. And realised that something in her... yes, something had definitely changed.

She glanced around the room at all the objects that were beginning to make this place feel like home: her mother's water pitcher filled with the season's first tulips, the rocker that would soon be her favourite place to sit, at her very own hearthside. She didn't want a ton of clutter. This was a modern apartment, after all. She'd chosen a sleek granite fireplace that couldn't have been more modern and understated. But still. It would be a hearth. It would signify home.

✳   ✳   ✳

Joey looked up from her drafting table, lost in reverie.

Tink was fast asleep by the rocker. She had jumped up onto the seat before Joey could stop her, but then had been so freaked out by the fact that the chair rocked that she jumped right down again. *Good*, Joey had thought. Maybe that would keep her down. But as though Tink could already envision the fire that would soon be burning in the fireplace, she had lain right down in the middle of the area to be covered by a rug.

Joey had been working on a rendering for one of the Barrie rooms, the "Wendy Room", a place specially dedicated — in Joey's mind, at least — to mothers, given that Wendy had been the mother figure for all the "lost boys" in *Peter Pan*.

Joey got up, went into the kitchen and poured herself a glass of wine. The name Wendy had supposedly come from Barrie's interaction with the daughter of his friend, a small child named Margaret Henley. Like so many of the children in his life, Margaret had adored Barrie and had called him "my friendy". But because she had a lisp, she pronounced it "my fwendy" or just "fwendy".

Did Barrie feel like a parent, a "Wendy" to Margaret? Did he grieve when she died at the age of six, as he grieved for the rest of his life for his other lost children, George Llewelyn Davies, killed in World War I, and his younger brother Michael, drowned while at Oxford. There had been so much sadness in Barrie's life, so many missed connections, so few intimate relationships that came to anything and lasted.

Would Joey live a life like Barrie's, she now wondered?

What if she never found anyone to share her life with? She didn't care about getting married, had never been one to dream of the white dress and the first dance. But to be alone for one's whole life? She didn't want that! Yet, it happened to a lot of people. The mere thought filled her with dread. She took a sip of wine and a deep breath. She would *not* go down this road. Being alone was not the worst thing in the world. It was far better than spending one's entire life with a selfish narcissist like Alex.

She went over and sat down in her new chair. She loved the way it felt, the way it rocked. She thought back to her time in England, as she often did when she wanted to feel a sense of belonging and of joy. No longer did images of the darker chapters of her time there flash before her eyes, as they had when she'd first returned to New York: of Lily's accident, the hospital, Lilia having her meltdown at the bottom of Ian's stairs. She thought of the rolling fields now, of drinking Gala's cocoa, of the night Ian made them haggis and the afternoon he took her riding. She thought of Lily trying on her Fendi boots, of sitting in Aggie's library, of drifting around the kitchen at Stanway House, not able quite to believe that its future was partially in her hands.

Now she thought of the English sky at night, the pinpricks of stars that had made the silent countryside feel like her own private Neverland, full of mysteries and secrets, invisible and sacred, and yet alive with promise and purpose. She could go back of course, but she would never be able to return to those precious weeks in midwinter when everything changed.

Suddenly Tink looked up and glanced at Joey.

"What?" Joey asked.

Tink was now on her feet, alert and expectant.

"What? Do you have to go out?"

Tink began to bark as Joey heard several knocks on her

door, and then flew towards it, yelping wildly. Joey crossed the room and peered through her spyhole. She gasped. Her hand began to shake as she slid the chain and turned the two bolts on her locks. She slowly opened the door.

He was wearing her favourite sweater, the grey Aran with the ravelled sleeves, and holding a bottle – some kind of wine or champagne. He looked at once hopeful and fearful.

Tears of happiness sprang to Joey's eyes as she struggled to find words.

"What are you doing here?" she finally whispered.

He smiled, his eyes as kind and warm as they always were in her dreams, his windswept cheeks flushed with emotion.

"What do you think?" Ian said.

Acknowledgments

James M. Barrie donated the first trophy called the Peter Pan Cup over a hundred years ago to the winner of the outdoor Christmas Day swimming race held every year in the Serpentine in Hyde Park. Six years ago my London friend Stella Kane took me to the Ladies Swimming Pond in Hampstead Heath and told me the history of it. It was the day of my mother's funeral in New York City and I was stuck across the ocean. I was sad, I cried and then I was given a bathing suit and invited to swim by one of several very elderly women who were there that day. I met May Allen, and her friends, who had been swimming every day for over fifty years in the outdoor pond. My swim on that heartbreaking but beautiful October afternoon was spiritually uplifting and unforgettable. When I decided to write about the Cotswolds it was because I remembered many years ago when I was taken there by Linda and Michelle Grant. I drove with them on a cold, foggy morning, sitting in the front seat of their car, listening to Gregorian chants on the CD player and occasionally I would see a sheep on the road or a lone rider galloping across a field. I returned to the Cotswolds over twenty years later to discover why I kept thinking about the trip all those years before. Chris Peake, a local tour guide, took me on an all day adventure and brought me to Stanway House, the magnificent estate where J. M. Barrie had been inspired to write *Peter Pan*. He regaled me with stories, local history and laughter and took me to Snowshill, Moreton-in Marsh, Chipping Campden, Stanton, Winchcombe, Naunton, Temple Guiting, Guiting Power, Broadway, Buckland, Laverton, and Upper and Lower Slaughter. After spending two days wandering around the Cotswolds, I re-discovered the magic and beauty of the place and every village, building and monument that still stands there today.

This book took over five long years to write and there were many people who supported me, encouraged me and urged me to keep going during difficult times and when I thought I should just burn the pages and never think about this book again. I am indebted for ever to my international agents who simply do not let me give up; they are Anoukh Foerg in Germany, Maru du Montserrat in Spain, Gabriella Ambrosioni in Italy, Donatella D'Ormesson in France, Marianne Schonbach in Holland, Ana Milenkovic and Tamara Vukicevic in Serbia, Flavia Sala and Cristina Purchio in Brazil and Georgina Capel in the United Kingdom. A dream can appear on paper but until a book is edited and published a writer can never really come to life. David Isaacs first discovered me and Aurea Carpenter edited me and Short Books turned me into the writer that I am today. They gave me my voice and my own name, literally. Esther Escoviar of Planeta gave me the entire Spanish speaking audience for my book and I am very thankful to my foreign publishers; Stefanie Heinen of Bastei Lubbe in Germany, Frederic Thibaud of City Editions in France, Elena Vinogradova of Azbooka-Atticus Publishers Group in Russia, Miranda Van Asch of Allen & Unwin in Australia, Sabrina Annona of Fabbri Editore in Italy and Sander Knol of Xander Uitegevers in Holland.

I am so grateful to "my own ladies of the pond", my girlfriends in New York City who listened endlessly, always with interest and generosity, to my story for years and years and read each draft and offered critical evaluations that always made sense. Thank you for ever to Doris McGonigle, Bonnie Ruben, Toni Rigopolous, Ana-Lisa Gertner, Toby Sternlieb, Lisa Sternlieb, Anita Mandl, Cathy Grey, Marietta Bottero, Anastasia Portnoy and Eileen Johnson. Thank you so much to my friend, Marie Therese Wenger, who took time to photograph my official portrait even though we were on vacation in Barcelona and to Linda Henrich for managing my business so I can write.

I am so lucky to have undeniably the most fantastic sister in the world, Mary Millman, who gives me never-ending support, encouragement and love and is like an entire JM Barrie Ladies Swimming Society in and of herself. And her son and my one and only nephew, Robert Millman, who is my best friend and my knight in shining armor.

I am often awestruck by the courage of my sister, Michelle Zitwer, who starts every day with such energy and verve no matter what. She is a force of nature that inspires me.

And last but never least, my deepest gratitude to my husband and life partner, Gil Alicea, who has an amazing ear and the truest compass for literature and life. His love and the home he has made for me allow me to wander to the farthest destinations on the globe and to those in my mind, to experiment, to create, to be free and to disappear sometimes, because he is always there waiting for me to return.

Barbara J. Zitwer is an international literary agent. She graduated from Columbia Film School and, prior to working in publishing, she produced films including *Vampire's Kiss* with Nicolas Cage. Zitwer co-wrote the play *Paper Doll* about Jacqueline Susann. She lives in New York City with her husband and their two dogs. This is her first novel.